# ROAD RAGE

## LINDA A. FOLEY

Road Rage

ANDERSON
HOUSE

To sons and daughters: Tim and Monique, Reen and Richard

I would like to thank my dear friend and honest critic, Dick Bizot, who has taught me so much. Thank you to my friends and supporters: Afesa Adams, Jim and Laura Crooks, Kathleen McKenzie, David Lafitte, Joyce Bizot, Shirley Stetson, Bryant Rollins and Sandy Hansford. Thank you also to Holly Bebernitz and Kathy Combass, for their helpful comments and suggestions. Thanks to my sisters, Betty and Judy Anderson, for their unwavering support. Special thanks to Richard Hecht, my wonderful and talented son-in-law, for designing the cover. And of course, Roger, the wind beneath my wings

*Also by Linda A. Foley*

Fiction

*A Taste of Vengeance*

Non-fiction

*A Psychological View of the Legal System*

*The YoCoShe Experiment: An evaluation of a Model Program for Delinquent Youth.*

*Female offenders in Duval County (with C. Rasche and L Finely)*

# CHAPTER ONE

The gray-haired woman limped past houses reminiscent of a scene from a Magritte painting, windows lit against the predawn dark with sun lighting the sky above the treetops. "Hail Mary, full of grace, the Lord is with thee, blessed art thou amongst women…" she prayed, massaging the rosary beads in her pocket. The woman took no notice of her surroundings or of the approaching vehicle. "…blessed is the fruit of thy womb…"

The truck screeched across the road. "Mother of God!" The impact hurled her into the air. She slammed onto the hood of the truck clinging to her rosary beads. Unconscious, she could not hear the truck driver laugh as he backed over her body. The pick-up truck careened away, squealing loudly. The woman's straw hat floated to rest on the grass beside her. Blood oozed across her tee shirt, blurring the red "I love New York" heart.

A loud scream shattered the peaceful dawn. A blue bath-robed woman ran toward the victim, leaving one fluffy slipper on the driveway next to the newspaper she had been retrieving. The sight of the blood-covered body momentarily silenced her. She threw her hands over her eyes. Her renewed screams aroused other residents. Neighbors mostly in nightwear rushed to the scene as the woman sobbed and gasped for breath, hugging herself. An elderly man in khaki shorts took control. He directed two younger men to take care of the whimpering woman. They moved her away from the scene while the older man called 911 on his cell phone.

1

"Who is she?" whispered a young man, motioning towards the victim with his head. His neighbor shrugged as he gently guided the distraught woman away from the body. Her keening resumed with the arrival of the first police cars.

By the time Detective Herb Morrison of the Gainesville Police Department lifted the crime scene tape for Dr. Victoria Vincent an hour later, the neighborhood was ablaze with blue lights pulsating on half a dozen black and whites. The lithe woman, wearing a jacket over black yoga pants, glided beneath the tape before standing to survey the scene. The sun spread a peach-colored tint over groups of neighbors relaying their observations to police officers entering the information into notebooks.

Morrison was a big man, a former football player going soft with age. He was in his Sunday gardening clothes, as yet unsullied by yard work. The detective grunted at Tori Vincent to follow him as he lumbered over to show her the woman's crumpled body. He warned, "Not pretty, Doc." The forensic psychologist recoiled at the sight of the mangled body still clutching her rosary beads. The impact had torn open the victim's navy warm-up jacket, showing her blood-saturated tee shirt. Her body had suffered most of the trauma, leaving her unscarred face peaceful in death, her rimless glasses askew on one ear.

"Poor old soul," Tori said before turning to Morrison to ask, "Who is she?"

"Margaret Curry O'Neal, retired school teacher," Sgt. Dottie Epstein, Morrison's sidekick, responded as she joined them. The tall black woman patted Tori's shoulder in greeting.

Tori turned to Morrison, "What are you doing at a hit-and-run, Morrison? I thought detectives investigated robberies and murders."

"Yeah, here's the thing," Morrison said. "Mrs. O'Neal's a burglary suspect." He guided Tori away from the body. "Let the techs do their job."

Tori stood watching the police officers interviewing the neighbors for a moment. "My question still stands, Morrison. More to the point, why did you call me? How can a psychological autopsy help in a hit-and-run?"

Morrison looked into the early morning sky. "Not a hit-and-run. Mrs. O'Neal was murdered." Morrison ran his fingers through thinning hair. "Something strange's going on. You know, something crazy. You have to get in the killer's head. Why'd he kill her? Get in O'Neal's head. Why'd she burglarize a house?"

Tori turned to Dottie. "Any witnesses?" she asked.

"Mrs. Collins from across the street was getting her newspaper when she heard tires squealing," Dottie said, indicating the brick house on the other side of the road. "She saw the victim thrown into the air and bouncing off the truck's hood before hitting the pavement. Then the creep backed over her."

"Oh, Yuck." The image of the broken body flashed across Tori's mind. She shook her head, her strawberry blond ponytail swaying.

Dottie scowled. "We haven't got much else from Mrs. Collins. She was still upset when I got here. All she could tell us was the truck was old and a dark color, maybe red or green. Didn't see the driver, but was sure it was a man."

"Why's that?" Tori asked.

"She heard the bastard laugh."

"Anyone else see anything?" Tori asked.

"Nah, no one else saw or heard a thing until the truck screeched away and Mrs. Collins started screaming. You can see the rubber in the road where the truck peeled out," Dottie said, pointing to the skid marks.

"What do you think, Doc?" Morrison asked. "Murder?"

"Probably, Morrison," Tori said. "If, as Mrs. Collins said, the driver backed over Mrs. O'Neal, it was murder."

"What can you tell us about the murderer?"

"It's too soon to tell much. It sounds like the man enjoyed killing Mrs. O'Neal. Either he hated her, or he likes to kill, likes to watch his victim die. If the murderer likes to kill, I'd wager he's killed before and will probably kill again."

"He?" Morrison asked.

"Yes, odds are the murderer's a man. Almost all serial murderers are men."

"A sociopath?" Dottie asked.

"Most likely. And a sadist," Tori said. "He probably saw Mrs. McNeal's face when she bounced off the hood of the truck. He

3

knew she was dead or soon would be. Yet he drove back over her. Then he laughed—like he enjoyed hearing her bones cracking under the truck." Tori thought, *I'm going to have nightmares tonight.*

"Think he'll kill again?" Morrison asked.

"Probably," Tori said. "His behavior suggests he's a serial murderer."

"Organized or disorganized type?" Dottie asked.

"Those are Hollywood classifications, only used in movies or on TV," Tori said. "I'd guess he's a Compulsive type. His laughter says he got a thrill out of killing Mrs. O'Neal. He's like a cocaine addict; he gets a high when he kills, then it wears off and he looks for another high."

"How long before he wants another high?" Dottie asked.

Tori scratched her head. "It could be days, weeks, a year. Depends on the person and the tensions in his life."

# CHAPTER TWO

"Don't get me wrong," Morrison said. "I know it's my job."

"But???" Tori asked.

"People get mad, you know, when I…you know, tell them."

"You want me with you when you tell Mrs. O'Neal's sister."

"Yeah." Morrison looked down. "Why do they take it out on me?" Morrison asked.

"Displaced anger," Tori said. "It's like when a boss chews out his employee and the man goes home and kicks his dog."

"I'm the dog," Morrison said.

"You're the dog."

Tori strapped on her seat belt in Morrison's car. "Okay, let me get this straight," she said. "You have a home surveillance video showing Margaret O'Neal burglarizing a house, right?"

"Yeah, yeah. Right." Morrison looked over his shoulder and pulled out of the parking space. "You say, go with your gut feelings, right? My gut says Margaret O'Neal's no burglar." He stopped at the corner, checked the cross street and made a right turn. "She's a retired school teacher, for God's sake—not a crook. Why'd she burglarize a house? It doesn't make sense." Herb slapped the steering wheel.

Tori said. "You think someone wanted you to stop investigating the burglary, so they killed her."

"Yeah, right."

"How did Mrs. O'Neal react when you showed her the video of the burglary?"

"Upset—beside herself." Morrison stopped at the traffic signal and pulled his earlobe as he waited for the green light.

"Someone caught in the act would be upset," Tori said.

"Yeah, but she denied it. Said she wouldn't take anything that didn't belong to her."

"That's an interesting way to put it," Tori said. "Did she think the stolen items were hers?"

He rubbed his chin. A horn blasting behind them brought him to the present. "All right. All right. Hold your horses."

"Well?"

"Nah. The stolen stuff—Rolex watches and fancy rings—not her thing."

"Maybe she thought the owners used her money to buy them."

"Farfetched," Morrison said.

"Did she have an alibi?" Tori asked.

"Nah, had an appointment with her shrink. Didn't show up. When Epstein read her her rights," Morrison said, "she demanded an attorney."

"End of questioning?"

"Yeah." Morrison sighed. "Bob Frances got her out like that." He snapped his fingers.

"Bob Frances? How does a retired school teacher know a high-powered criminal defense attorney?"

Morrison said, "On a board together for some kids' thing. She's a Guardian ad Litem, too. Frances said I was crazy. She'd never rob anyone."

Morrison turned into a neighborhood of winding streets canopied by live oaks. "That's it," he said pulling into the driveway of a neat white house with blue shutters. He parked in the driveway and they walked on steppingstones to the front porch, where two white wicker rockers sat. Matching pots of red geraniums flanked the front door.

"Those ceramic pots are beautiful—Tuscan Majolica," Tori said. "They cost hundreds, close to a thousand."

"Yeah, Margaret's husband left her a bundle." Morrison leaned down to pick a couple of dead blossoms off the plants before ringing the bell.

"What can I do for you?" asked an attractive middle-aged woman, pushing her honey blond hair behind her ears. Morrison stuffed the dead flowers in his pocket and introduced himself and Tori. "You Mrs. Curry?"

"I'm Miss Curry," she said with a husky voice suggestive of Marilyn Monroe.

"Can we come in?"

Annie Curry looked from Morrison to Tori, nodded and led them into a pristine living room with a flowered couch and pastel chairs.

Tori thought, *Annie resembles her sister, but Margaret was a dowdy, old-looking 67. Annie is youthful and elegant. I saw that sweater set she's wearing in a Bloomingdale's catalog. Expensive taste for a retired nurse.*

Sitting erect on one of the Queen Anne chairs, Annie Curry asked, "What is this about, Detective?"

Morrison clenched his hands together as if in prayer, resting his forearms on his thighs and looked at her. "You're Margaret O'Neal's sister, right?"

"Yes, I am. I told the other police officers my sister would never rob anyone."

Morrison put his hands in the air, "I...I..."

"Miss Curry, this is not about the robbery," Tori said.

Annie Curry cocked her head.

"Miss Curry, I'm sorry. I have bad news," Morrison said. "Your sister was run over." He paused. "A hit-and-run."

Curry looked at Morrison. Her mouth dropped open. She looked at Tori. "Where is she? How's she doing?" She half stood, and then sat back down, her hand to her heart.

"I'm very sorry, Miss Curry," Tori said. "Your sister is dead."

Curry's face crumpled. She put her fist to her mouth, tears streamed down her face. "No. No. It's not possible. She's just late for church." She sobbed and searched the pockets in her slacks. When she came up empty-handed, she turned to Tori. "Do you have a tissue?"

Tori handed the weeping woman some tissues. When the sobs abated, Tori said, "This must be difficult for you. I hate to impose, but I need to know about your sister."

"Why?" Annie wiped at the tears seeping from her eyes.

"We're trying to determine whether a crime was committed," Tori said.

Annie frowned. "It was a hit-and-run. Isn't that a crime? And what good does it do to look at her life? How would that find the driver?" Her voice was taut as if her throat were strangling the words.

"Detective Morrison thinks your sister might have been murdered."

Annie opened her eyes wide and jumped up. "Blessed Mary." She rushed through the arch to the Florida room and out the French doors. Tori motioned Morrison with her head and followed Annie outside. Annie walked along a path in the garden.

"Are you all right, Miss Curry?" Tori asked as she caught up with Annie.

"No, I'm not all right."

Morrison stood in the doorway watching the women. *Leaving me to deal with the emotional issues,* Tori thought.

Annie asked, "The detective thinks someone killed Margaret on purpose? Why? Why would someone do that? Margaret didn't have an enemy in the world."

Movement in the house next door caught Tori's eye. She looked up to see someone pulling the drapes aside.

Following Tori's eyes, Annie said through gritted teeth, "It's nothing that concerns you, you nosy old fart." She forced a smile in the window's direction and the drapes closed. "Mr. Harrison, our neighborhood gossip."

Annie sat on a wrought iron bench. Morrison left the doorway and sat next to her. He said, "Miss Curry, the police asked you about your sister and this burglary."

"Yes, I told them Margaret would never take anything that didn't belong to her."

Tori noted Annie used the same words that her sister had. *Was there something in the house that belonged to Margaret O'Neal?*

Morrison said, "I interviewed your sister. She was no burglar."

8

A squirrel jumped from a branch above their heads to a trellis, showering leaves on them. Annie looked at the spot where the squirrel had been. "I can't get used to leaves falling in the spring. That's supposed to happen in autumn—the fall."

Morrison nodded. Annie picked up a few leaves, crumpled them, and let them cascade through her fingers.

"Miss Curry, I think the guy that did the burglary might've killed Margaret, you know, so we'd stop asking questions," Morrison said.

Annie stood up and walked to a waterless fountain—the stone woman tipped an empty pitcher into the leaf-filled basin. Annie crossed her arms, her back to Tori and Morrison. She said, "I'll help in any way I can. What do you want to know?"

"Tell me what Margaret was like," Tori said.

Annie sat on the bench. "Margaret was kind and selfless. Her religion wasn't that phony holier-than-thou stuff. She loved God." Annie picked up a dry leaf and examined it. "I resented her when we were kids." She looked at Tori. "I mean I thought her goodness was an act to get my parents to like her better than me, and to impress the nuns at school. It wasn't until we moved to Florida that I realized it was real.

She looked at the leaf in her hand. "Sometimes she drove me nuts—she saw the good in everyone." Annie crumpled the leaf. "I worried some scam artist would put one over on her. But if I told her someone was trying to get her money, she'd say they probably needed it more than she did. How can you reason with someone like that?" Annie shook her head. "She never saw evil in people."

"Did your sister have close friends?" asked Tori.

"Her best friend was Ellie Frances."

"Bob Frances' wife?" asked Morrison.

Annie nodded. "Recently Margaret spent time with Karen, another client of Dr. Rothstein's." She looked at Tori. "That's her psychologist. Karen couldn't drive. Sometimes Karen was waiting for her daughter to pick her up when Margaret got there. They became friends. Margaret took Karen with her to Curves."

"To what?" Morrison asked.

"Curves. It's a gym for women," Annie said.

"Do you have Karen's last name and address?" Tori asked, reaching for a notebook in her purse.

9

"No. Sorry, I can't remember. She lives somewhere over on the Eastside, I think. You can get her name from Dr. Rothstein."

"No, he'd be violating confidentiality if he gave us a client's name. But, if you hear from her, please let me know. I'd like to talk to her." Tori wrote her home number on the back of her business card and handed it to Annie.

"Miss Currie, why was your sister seeing Dr. Rothstein?" Tori asked.

"She wanted to lose weight. She thought he was the best thing since Dr. Phil."

# CHAPTER THREE

Morrison sat at his desk in the incident room while Detective Dottie Epstein leaned against the wall downing a Coke and Tori fidgeted in a hard vinyl chair, attempting to get comfortable. None of the three was overjoyed that a homicide had interfered with their Sunday activities. The call for the hit-and-run came before Morrison began to prune his beloved roses, before Dottie and her sometimes live-in lover Bruce had their blueberry pancakes, and before Tori Vincent began a session of stretches and ballet exercises.

"Coffee, Doc?" Morrison asked. His New Jersey accent pronounced coffee "cawfee."

"That gunk you're drinking? No thanks." Tori pulled a bottle of water from her Coach purse.

Morrison poured coffee into his New York Knicks mug. "How're you going to get your head in gear with no caffeine?"

"I'll manage."

Morrison's knees creaked and he groaned as he pulled himself out of his chair. "Damn, getting old ain't for sissies." He walked to the whiteboard and rubbed his lower back as he bent backwards.

"What was Mrs. O'Neal seeing a psychologist for?" asked Dottie.

"To lose weight," Tori said. "What did the psychologist tell you about Mrs. O'Neal?"

"Nothing," Morrison said. "Said it's confidential. What do you know about this Rothstein character?"

11

"My partner Kevin's wife swears by him," Tori said. "She's going to him to quit smoking."

"How come the wife of a shrink goes to another shrink?" he asked.

"It's not ethical to counsel family members," Tori said.

Dottie asked, "You know Rothstein?"

"I've met him once or twice at FPA."

"FPA?" Morrison asked.

"Florida Psychological Association."

Morrison said, "Talk to him, Doc. See what he knows about Mrs. O'Neal."

Tori pulled her iPad out of her purse and made a note.

Morrison put a photo of Mrs. O'Neal on the whiteboard. He wrote: "People who knew her. Rothstein, Ellie Frances, Bob Frances, Annie Curry and Karen something or other from Rothstein's office." He took a gulp of coffee. "Anyone else?"

"What about the man from Guardian ad Litem?" Tori asked.

"What man?" Dottie asked.

"When Morrison and I interviewed Ellie Frances," Tori said, "she said Margaret O'Neal had a judge take a man's children away from him."

"Yeah, bastard beat his wife," Morrison said. "His kid, get this, seven years-old, tries to stop his old man. Bastard broke the kid's arm."

Morrison added GAL man to the list on the whiteboard and went to the window where he rested his haunches on the sill.

"Don't forget the man with a dream," Tori said.

"The who?" Dottie asked.

"Ellie Frances said she talked to Margaret O'Neal yesterday morning," Tori said. "Margaret told her about some man who had a recurring dream. He saw a TV program that brought it back. Margaret said it was important and wanted to tell Bob Frances about it."

"What'd she tell Bob Frances?" Dottie asked.

Morrison said, "Nothing. He's out of town."

A loud knock interrupted. As the door opened Morrison shouted, "Did I say come in?"

Chief Connie Murray in full uniform strode into the room.

Morrison stood. "Sorry, Chief."

She nodded at Morrison and turned to the others. "Dr. Vincent, Detective Epstein." Before either of the women could respond, she said, "What've you got, Detective?"

Morrison walked to the whiteboard and summarized the case.

The chief stood in front of the whiteboard. Her icy blue eyes took in every detail of his report. "Why do you need Dr. Vincent? It's not suicide."

"Dr. Vincent's a forensic psychologist, you know. She can help us identify the murderer."

"Profiling?"

"Yeah."

"That only works for serial murders," the chief said.

Tori said, "There's a strong possibility this is a serial murderer."

The chief raised her eyebrows at Tori. She turned to Morrison. "She better be worth her fee. The press'll be all over us on this."

"Yeah." Morrison said.

"Get on with it, Detective."

"Yes sir, Ma'am." Morrison saluted.

"Cut the crap, Morrison," the chief said. "You might get away with sexism with Detective Epstein, don't try it with me." Her heels clicked as she went to the door and closed it loudly behind her.

Tori said, "She's even tougher than I'd heard."

"Fourth generation cop," Morrison said. "Three older brothers all in law enforcement."

"Used to playing hard ball with the boys," Tori said. "No wonder she's tough."

Dottie said, "She's worked her way up the ranks. Doesn't like to fail."

"You heard her," Morrison said. "We got to get something."

"We don't have a motive for Mrs. O'Neal's murder," Dottie said, "unless it's connected to the burglary."

Dottie took a gulp of Coke and went to the whiteboard. She started a new column—Motive. Under that she wrote "Burglary" and "Hit-and-Run."

Morrison said, "Put that Guardian ad Litem guy under motive—she took his kids."

"Both Mrs. O'Neal and her sister said she would never take anything that didn't belong to her." Tori scrunched her forehead. "Maybe her motive for burglarizing the house wasn't financial. Maybe she was getting even for something—some wrong." She refocused on Morrison, "Have you found any connection between Mrs. O'Neal and the home owner?"

"None. Owners never heard of her."

Tori folded her arms, stretched out her legs and stared at the floor. A moment later, she looked up. "What about the watches? They were Rolexes, weren't they? Did you find them?"

"Yes, they were Rolexes and no, we didn't find them." Dottie half sat against Morrison's desk drinking her soda. She answered the ringing phone, "Incident Room." After a moment she said, "I'll get him. Morrison, it's Ruth."

Morrison walked to the desk and took the phone. "Sorry, honey, it's a murder." There was a pause. "Yeah, yeah, I know. I promised. Be home in an hour. Promise" He sat behind his desk. "I told Jennifer I'd take her to the butterfly museum this afternoon."

Dottie said, "We tore Mrs. O'Neal's house apart. No watches, no tennis bracelet, no rings, and nothing from the other burglaries, either."

"Other burglaries?" Tori asked. "You didn't tell me there were other burglaries."

Morrison made a church of his hands, resting his elbows on the desk. "This case's been a pain in the arse for years—burglaries of wealthy homes—like the one Mrs. O'Neal supposedly burgled."

"All the houses had alarm systems." CLANG! Dottie tossed her empty drink can into the metal pail by the whiteboard. "In each case the alarm went off, but the burglar was long gone by the time we got there. Now we know it wasn't our response time. The burglar set off the alarm after lifting the jewelry. The video of Mrs. O'Neal showed us that."

"Clever," said Tori. "I've read about the burglaries."

Dottie said, "No one saw anyone out of the ordinary in the neighborhood."

"If Mrs. O'Neal was seen in the neighborhood," Tori said, "no one would think she was a burglar."

"Yeah, yeah, right," Morrison said. "All the burgled people are out of town. Don't know what was stolen 'til they get back."

"You think Mrs. O'Neal burglarized the other houses?" Tori asked.

"None of the other homeowners recognized her photo or ever heard of her," Dottie said. "Besides, she had alibis for half the other burglaries."

Morrison jumped up. He paced back and forth, counting off alibis on his fingers. "Accepting award from Guardian ad Litem— dozen witnesses; on vacation with sister—receipts from hotel in Barbados; having tests in hospital; it goes on and on."

"You said the burglar had keys to the house?" Tori asked. "How did Mrs. O'Neal get the key to the house? And the alarm code?"

"If I knew that, I wouldn't need you." Morrison grumbled.

"That so?" Tori said.

Morrison put both his hands out, palms forward. "Hey, sorry. Case is getting to me."

# CHAPTER FOUR

"Mom, can you drive me to school?"

Tori looked at her son over her newspaper where she had been reading about Margaret O'Neal's hit-and-run.

"Where's your bike?"

"I don't have it. C'mon. I'll be late."

"What do you mean you don't have it? Did you leave it somewhere?"

"No."

"That's an expensive bike."

"I know," he said.

"It's the most expensive present your father ever gave you. Where is it?"

"Someone took it."

"If it was stolen, we need to report it."

"No, we can't report it. I can handle it."

"What do you mean you can handle it? Sean, you're only 13. What's going on?"

"Nothing, Mom. Randy will help me get the bike. Can you drive me to school?"

"I'll drive you to school when you answer some questions, young man. Who took your bike? And when?"

Sean stormed out of the kitchen. "Never mind. I'll walk," he shouted over his shoulder.

"Sean Arroyo, you come back here this minute," Tori said in her mother-in-charge voice. The front door slammed. "Darn!" She picked up her purse and headed to the garage at the same rate her blood pressure was going up. She backed her car out of the garage and sped to the corner where her son was turning right. She took a deep breath and pulled to the curb next to him. She rolled down the passenger window.

"Sean, please get in the car. I'll drive you to school."

Sean climbed into the car. He looked down, depression weighing on his stooped shoulders.

"Let's stop this foolish fighting. Tell me what happened," Tori said in a softer voice. She parked the car on the side of the road, put her arm around her son's shoulders. "Sean, what's the matter?"

"You wouldn't understand," he mumbled.

"Give me a try."

Sean's shoulders trembled. His voice was barely audible. "This kid...Barry... the big kid I told you about. He beats up on everyone. He was at the park yesterday when Randy and I went for a ride. He and his friend Frank. They knocked me off my bike and took it."

"We need to tell the police."

"I can't, Mom. He said if I told anyone his gang would beat up me and Randy. Like they beat up Tony."

"Okay. Let me think about this. I'll take you to school and we'll talk about it tonight."

"I wish Dad were here. He'd know what to do," Sean said.

"Maybe." Sean's words cut into her heart like a hot knife into ice. *Gerry, damn you,* she thought. She turned to her son, "But, I don't want you to confront Barry, do you understand?"

"What do I do? Just let him steal my bike?"

Tori picked up her Starbuck's café latte and turned to find a seat. A deep voice greeted her, "Dr. Vincent, I'm Seth Rothstein."

Tori looked at the man—square jawed and tan. His graying hair and beard were Freudian, but his clothes looked like he stepped out of GQ. *Better looking than I remember*, Tori thought.

"Call me Tori." She switched her latte to her left hand extending her right. "We've met before."

"Yes. FPA. I took a CE class with you." He took her hand in both of his. "I never forget a lovely face," he said.

17

"Thank you for meeting with me." Tori looked at her hand and he released it.

"Happy to do so. Let's sit outside." He reached for her cup, "I'll carry that for you."

"I can get it. Don't you want something?"

"I'll get a cappuccino and be right out." He got in line at the counter while Tori found a table.

A few minutes later, Rothstein put his cappuccino on the table, his navy blue linen blazer on the back of the chair, and sat adjacent to Tori.

Tori said, "I want to talk about Margaret O'Neal."

"Margaret…" He shook his head. "I just heard about her accident. I was away on a hunting trip."

"Hunting? That's an unusual activity for a psychologist."

"Yes." He looked at her with sad eyes. "My interest is the result of a personal trauma." He paused. "What do you want to know about Margaret?"

*A personal trauma? I'll have to ask him about that sometime,* Tori thought. She explained about the psychological autopsy.

Rothstein laughed. "Never done one—can't remember what it is—too long since grad school."

"I'll reconstruct Mrs. O'Neal's life. Find out what she was thinking, what was happening in her life, determine whether the death was accidental, a suicide, or homicide."

He tilted his head to one side. "But, but…I thought she was the victim of a hit-and-run?"

The waitress brought Rothstein an egg sandwich. He smiled and thanked her. "I didn't get a chance to eat this morning," he said to Tori, taking a bite of the sandwich.

Tori said, "Mrs. O'Neal was the victim of a hit-and-run. But people sometimes commit suicide by causing someone else to kill them."

"Of course, but you mentioned homicide. Surely, no one thinks she was murdered?"

"Right now, I'm just gathering information. I've no preconceived ideas."

"Sorry, I spoke out of turn. I don't know anything except what I read in the papers and we both know how inaccurate those stories can be." He stood and adjusted the umbrella so it shaded Tori's face.

"Thanks," she said.

He sat down and took another bite of the sandwich. "How I can help."

"Tell me about Margaret."

"Sure. Confidentiality dies with the patient, so I'll tell you whatever you want to know.'

Tori wasn't positive confidentiality died with the patient— professionals still debate that issue, but she wasn't going to argue with him as long as his view suited her purposes.

"She was a delightful old gal," he said, "bright and informed about current events. She was fun to talk with."

"If she was so together, why was she seeing you?"

"Good question." He chuckled. "She was trying to lose weight. She'd actually lost most of what she wanted to lose, but we were working on the last ten pounds and keeping the weight off." He adjusted the umbrella again, this time blocking the sun from his eyes. "She'd hit a plateau and was having trouble with the last few pounds."

"What procedures were you using to help her lose weight?"

"Primarily, Cognitive Behavioral Therapy. She was conscientious about her therapy. That's why I was surprised when she didn't show the day of the burglary."

"So you think she burglarized the house?"

Rothstein held his hands up, "Wait a minute. All I know is what the police told me. The detective said they had a video of Margaret burglarizing the house."

"Let's say the video was wrong. If I asked you about Margaret, would you say she was someone who would burglarize a house?"

Rothstein stood again, fiddling with the umbrella. "I hate to have the sun in my eyes." He sat. "Margaret is the last person in the world who would do anything illegal. I didn't believe the detective when she told me about the video. I'm glad to hear it wasn't accurate."

"Tell me about the day of the robbery. You told the police Margaret was a no show. Was that unusual?"

"Completely out of character. She never missed an appointment. I was surprised she didn't call to say she wasn't coming."

"What did she say when she came for her next appointment? Did she explain what happened? Did she say anything about the burglary?"

"She never came again. Her next appointment was set for this coming Thursday."

"Did you call her when she missed the appointment?"

"Yes, but I didn't talk to her. Her sister took the message. She said Margaret was fine, so I decided to let it pass."

"Did Margaret tell you anything about being threatened by a man she worked with in the GAL program?"

"The what?"

"Sorry. The Guardian ad Litem Program. Margaret volunteered for it. The father of one of the children threatened her."

Rothstein ate the last bite of his sandwich. He looked pensive while he chewed. "I remember her saying she was concerned about someone. She seemed frightened."

"Did she tell you his name?"

"Not that I remember, no," he said. "Anything else I can help you with?"

"Nothing about Mrs. O'Neal," Tori said. "Tell me about this 'personal trauma' and how it caused you to take up hunting."

Rothstein looked at his watch and stood. "Unfortunately, I've to get back to the office. I have a client coming. Let me walk you to your car."

As they approached her car, he said, "I knew that was your car. It's cute and sexy."

"Really?"

"The car is cute and sexy, but I knew it was yours because a client told me what you drive."

"Of course, Edi." She got in the car and opened the window. "Are you avoiding telling me about your trauma?'

"No. I really don't have time. Are you going to the CE session for FPA this week?" He rested his arm against the roof of her car, leaning down to look at her.

"Yes."

"Why don't we go to dinner before the meeting and I'll tell you the whole story."

"I can't go to dinner. I'm meeting my partner, Edi's husband."

"Perhaps another time," he said. He tapped the roof of her car and stepped away.

"Thanks for your help," she said, closing the window. *He is good-looking. And interesting,* she thought.

# CHAPTER FIVE

"So this is the women's domestic violence shelter?" Tori asked as Dottie pulled to the curb in front of a dark brown Victorian house. "There's no sign." The house was indistinguishable from the others on the residential street. "How'd you know where it is?"

"I volunteer here on my days off."

"I'm impressed."

Dottie got out of the car and rested her arms on the roof looking across at Tori. "Morrison suggested I volunteer here. He tried to volunteer, but they don't need male volunteers. Most victims of domestic violence would be terrified by a man Morrison's size with his gruff manners. I'm not sure why he's interested."

"I know," Tori said. "One night after a few beers, Morrison told me his father abused him. He beat his mother and brothers, too."

"What happened?" Dottie asked.

"His brother joined him and they gave his father a once over. The father never hit any of them again."

"No wonder Morrison is concerned about domestic violence."

Dottie and Tori proceeded to the door. Dottie said, "According to the file Jennifer Delgado is 29 and her husband's 38. She's a stay-at-home mom and he's a banker. The children were placed with the father's older sister. Jennifer doesn't have any family or friends to speak of."

"Of course, he's isolating her."

Dottie stooped to pick up a candy wrapper on the walkway. She continued to the door and rang the bell. "You'll need to show them your license." When the buzzer sounded she pushed open the door. She showed her ID through the window to the woman on duty and said, "Hi, Janet."

"Hey, Dottie, who do you want to see?" Janet asked.

"Jennifer Delgado," Dottie said as Tori showed her ID to Janet.

"I'll have her go to the visiting area," Janet said.

"I know where it is." Dottie led Tori down a hall to a reception area. She tossed the candy wrapper in a basket by the hall table.

A couple of minutes later an emaciated woman entered the room. Her hair was limp, her eyes sunken, and bruises lined the side of her face. *She looks older than 29, closer to mid-forties*, Tori thought. The woman's eyes darted back and forth across the room.

Dottie introduced herself and Tori. "Mrs. Delgado, please sit down."

Delgado sat. She clutched the arms of her chair as if afraid someone would take it from her.

"We aren't from DCF or GAL," Dottie said. "We're trying to get information about Margaret O'Neal, the Guardian ad Litem woman assigned to your children."

Delgado fidgeted in her chair and looked over her shoulder.

"Mrs. Delgado, do you remember Mrs. O'Neal?" Tori asked.

"Where are my children?" Delgado asked.

Dottie said, "They're with your husband's sister, Marcia."

"I want to see them." Delgado clenched the arms of the chair and tears formed in her eyes.

"Mrs. Delgado, your children are being well taken care of," Dottie said. "I'll contact GAL and ask them to assign another volunteer to work with them. We have no control over your seeing your children."

"Why should I talk to you?" Delgado asked in a loud voice. "You people never help."

At the sound of raised voices a counselor came running.

"It's all right, JoAnne," Dottie said to the counselor.

The counselor put her hand on Delgado's shoulder. "Dottie's a volunteer here, Jennifer. She'll help you. I'll stay with you." She sat on the arm of Delgado's chair.

"Mrs. Delgado, did Mrs. O'Neal say you would be able to see your children?" Dottie asked.

"She promised I could see them Sunday." Delgado said. She picked up a magazine from the coffee table and started thumbing through it.

Tori said, "Mrs. Delgado, Mrs. O'Neal was the victim of a hit-and-run on Sunday morning."

Delgado looked up, eyes flitting back and forth between Tori and Dottie. "Is she okay?" She tossed the magazine onto the table.

"I'm afraid not," Dottie said. "She's dead."

"Oh no." Delgado buried her head in her hands. Through her fingers she said, "She was such a nice lady."

"Jennifer, is this too hard for you to discuss?" asked JoAnne.

"I'm all right." Jennifer sat up and wrung her hands. "Did my husband kill her?"

Dottie asked, "You think your husband might have harmed her?"

"He threatened her. She told me. He hates women with power. Talk to my neighbor, Doris Maass. He threatened her."

"Mrs. Delgado, how did your children come under the care of DCF?" Tori asked.

JoAnne asked, "Do you want to talk about it?"

"Yeah, I'm okay." Delgado looked down at her hands. "My husband was beating on me. My boy tried to stop him. Little Eddie's only seven. He grabbed his father's arm and said, 'don't hit her.' My husband tried to shake him off and sent him flying into the kitchen cabinet. He broke his arm." Delgado wrung her hands. "We took him to the ER. My husband warned Eddie to say he fell down the stairs when the doctor asked what happened. But the doctor looked at my face. I was bleeding and he knew my husband was lying. He called DCF."

"Did your husband beat you often?" Tori asked.

"It's a long story."

"We have time."

"Would you like some coffee?" asked JoAnne.

Jennifer shook her head, as did Tori and Dottie.

"I met my husband at Santa Fe Community College. I took a class he taught."

Dottie said, "I thought your husband was a banker."

"He is. He taught at SFCC when he was getting his masters at UF." She let out a mirthless laugh. "I thought he was brilliant and charming." She sighed. "He was controlling. He made me quit college when we got married."

"When did he start beating you?" Dottie asked.

"He didn't hit me 'til I was pregnant with Nicole. I was sick all the time. One night I didn't fix him dinner. He went berserk. He slapped me across the face. Knocked me down. I think he broke my nose, but he wouldn't take me to the doctor."

"What happened?" Tori asked.

"The next day he brought me flowers and begged me to forgive him. He promised it'd never happen again. I was stupid enough to believe him."

"Did he stop?" asked Dottie.

"For awhile. Then he got furious when Nicole was born. He'd wanted a son. He wouldn't even come see me in the hospital. After that he got mad a lot." She stopped and frowned. "I think that's when those nasty guys from Miami started hanging around." She shuddered.

"Tell us about the nasty guys," Dottie said.

"Big guys in expensive suits—they gave me the creeps."

"Did your husband say who they were?"

"Said they were friends from Miami. I didn't like them around the children."

"What did they do when they came?" asked Tori.

"Sometimes they played cards. They went to his office. One time I went in and he got really mad. He shouted at me never to go in his office. His friends laughed and said something in Spanish. I left. The next day he brought me flowers."

Dottie asked, "What happened this time?"

"Last fall Doris Maass moved in next door. We became friends. Edward told me to stay away from her. I pretended I did."

"But you didn't," Tori said.

"No. We talked. She was nice. I told her I wanted to be a teacher. She helped me apply to UF. I thought Edward would be proud of me. Instead he beat me. This time Eddie tried to stop him…And you know what happened."

Tori said, "Mrs. Delgado, what are you planning to do now?"

"What do you mean?"

"Where will you live when you leave the shelter?"

"I'll go back home."

"To your parents?" Dottie asked.

"No. I don't want my children living in a trailer. We'll go back to our house. Edward will be good to us, now."

"That's not very smart," Tori said. "Besides, the judge won't let the children live with Edward until he goes through anger management and parenting classes."

Mrs. Delgado looked at Tori. "I…I…"

Tori asked, "Have you filed charges against your husband?"

"No. I'm not sure what I should do."

"It's important for you to file charges," Tori said. "Living with your husband is dangerous for…"

JoAnne stood up. "Hey! You can't advise our clients," she said.

Dottie said, "Tori, you are overstepping your…"

"I know what I'm talking about," Tori snapped.

Dottie stood and took Tori by the arm. "We are leaving *now*."

# CHAPTER SIX

"What the hell were you doing?" Dottie stomped out of the shelter pulling Tori by the arm. "You can't tell someone in a domestic violence shelter to file charges. Counseling staff help clients make those decisions."

"She'll be in danger…"

"Tori, you're interfering with the treatment of a client."

Tori looked down, "I'm sorry. I wasn't thinking straight."

Dottie glared. "I can't believe you did that."

"My sister was in an abusive marriage. When she finally left she went into denial. She won't get a divorce. I don't know what to say. I guess I was reacting to her situation."

Tori got into the passenger side of the car. Dottie sat in the driver's seat and slammed the door. "That's too bad about your sister, but it doesn't excuse your behavior. You need to watch what you say to people we're interviewing."

Tori looked down. The pair drove in silence to meet Morrison at the Medical Examiner's office at the University of Florida.

After a few moments Tori crossed her arms. "I said, I'm sorry."

"You don't have a clue how much harm you did." Dottie's voice could have cut stone. "You're a professional. You should know better."

"I didn't think…"

"That's for sure."

Dottie stopped at a STOP sign and looked both ways before turning. She took a deep breath. "Let's drop it."

"Thanks. I'll be more careful in the future."

"Did you notice Jennifer Delgado's nose?" Dottie asked.

"Yes. It was off-center or something."

"A boxer's nose. Typical unset broken nose."

"Those bruises on her face were horrible. Her husband's a monster."

Dottie said, "Let's interview this Edward Delgado after lunch."

"Shouldn't Morrison go with us?" Tori asked.

"Do you feel safer with Morrison than with me?"

"Oops. That was sexist," Tori said. "Sorry, I can't say anything right today."

"No problem. I'm used to it."

"But I pride myself on not being sexist or racist."

"It's not easy. I catch Jason saying something every once in awhile."

"How is Jason?'

Dottie stopped the car at the red light and fiddled with the steering wheel. "Okay." She picked a speck of lint off her sleeve.

"Okay? Okay? What aren't you telling me?"

"Jason and I are back to being friends."

Tori looked inquiringly.

Dottie took a deep breath. "He's back with Kitty. They'd been together since high school. His mother likes Kitty." She looked at Tori. "Kitty's white."

Tori reached across and put her hand on her friend's arm. "I'm sorry."

"Me, too."

Tori said, "At least Morrison won't be on your case for fraternizing with a fellow officer."

"No. But if he finds out whom I'm dating he'll kill me. Instead of fraternizing with a friend, I'm fraternizing with the enemy."

Tori opened her eyes wide. "You're dating a criminal?"

Dottie smiled. "Worse than that. I'm dating a civil rights attorney."

"Is that bad?"

"It is when he's about to sue the police department for abuse of suspects."

Music blared over the speakers. "What kind of music's that?" Morrison asked.

Dr. Nguyen looked over his glasses at the detective and said, "It's Vivaldi. It's opera."

"Couldn't you play Frank Sinatra or something?"

"I like classical music."

"You don't think Sinatra's classic?"

"You want to do the cutting, you can pick the music."

"Okay, okay. Why so loud?" Morrison sniffed the cold odor of death.

"It's distracting. I don't think about the person she used to be when music plays."

Morrison understood. As a young cop Morrison had been queasy watching autopsies. Gradually he had learned to keep thoughts of the live person out of his consciousness while observing. He hated to see the body on the steel table and cringed when the pathologist made the initial incisions and pulled back the skin to expose the internal organs, but he could tolerate it now. He watched as the medical examiner conducted the post-mortem examination of Margaret O'Neal.

"What about the vehicle that hit her?" Morrison asked.

"It was red. I can't give you anything more until the flecks of paint are tested."

Morrison looked over his shoulder as Dottie, dressed in a white gown and latex gloves, entered the room. "Where's Tori?" he asked.

"She isn't into watching autopsies. Something's bothering her. She's not herself." Dottie moved closer to the steel table where she could see the medical examiner working. "Good morning, Dr. Nguyen."

"Morning, Detective." Nguyen waved her over. Dottie was an interested observer of autopsies and she asked questions. The ME explained to her what he was doing and why he did it.

As Nguyen was finishing the autopsy, Morrison asked, "What'll your report say?"

"Probably homicide. I found the damage you would expect from being run over—twice. She died of severe head trauma. Dead by the time he ran over her the second time. Ribs were crushed. The woman was in pretty good health. A sixty-seven-year-old's problems: arthritis of the left knee, damage to the heart, gallbladder surgery, and appendix removed. She would have lived many more years."

"Thanks, Doc." Morrison looked at the clock. "When'll I get your report?"

Dr. Nguyen pulled off his gloves and turned to Morrison. "In a day, maybe two."

Morrison and Dottie found Tori staring out the window in the lobby, fidgeting with something in her pocket. Tori turned around as Morrison sat.

Morrison said, "Thought you'd planned to watch the autopsy. What happened? Weak stomach?"

"Yes, I couldn't handle it today," Tori said. "I can't get the image of Mrs. O'Neal's body out of my mind. I had nightmares all night."

"What'd you find out from the Delgado woman?" he asked.

Dottie and Tori brought Morrison up to speed, carefully avoiding any mention of Tori's unprofessional comments.

Morrison said, "You need to pay Mr. Delgado a visit."

"Don't you want to go with us?" Tori asked.

Dottie sighed.

Morrison grinned. "Dottie can handle any man in the state. She'll piss that abuser off. Wife said he hates women in power, right? No one wields power like Dottie."

"You say the nicest things," Dottie said.

Morrison stared at Tori. "What's wrong, Doc?"

Tori started. "What do you mean?"

Dottie said, "I noticed it, too. You're not yourself. You worried about something?"

Tori told them about Sean's stolen bike. "To make matters worse, Sean said if his father were here, he'd know what to do."

"Ouch," Dottie said. "Damn, I hate bullies. Don't we have a program in the schools to stop them?"

Morrison said, "Yeah, yeah, right. I'm on the task force. Work with principals to stop bullying." He turned to Tori, "Who's Sean's principal?"

"Mr. Eccles."

"Fred?"

"Yes. You know him?"

"Yeah, yeah. Good guy." Then he asked, "What time Sean get out of school?"

"Why?"

"I'll pick him up."

"You won't frighten him, will you?"

"No, but I'll put the fear of God into that bully. Make sure he leaves Sean and the other kids alone."

# CHAPTER SEVEN

Tori looked around the bank lobby. "Pretty dinky lobby."

Dottie nodded her agreement. They walked to the receptionist's desk. Dottie said, "Please tell Mr. Delgado we're here to see him."

"I'm sorry. Mr. Delgado is with a client. Maybe Miss Porter can help you."

Dottie flashed her badge. "We need to speak to Mr. Delgado."

Tori watched the receptionist's eyes dart to the glass enclosed office across from her. Tori followed the receptionist's gaze. The man behind the desk had his suit jacket draped across the back of his chair, revealing muscular shoulders in a white dress shirt.

The receptionist smiled. "Of course, detective. I'll tell him you're here." She stepped into the office and whispered to the man behind the desk. He frowned as he looked out at Tori and Dottie. His frown disappeared when he realized they were watching him.

Edward Delgado put on his jacket. He emerged from his office wearing a wide smile with white, even teeth against an olive complexion. "Please come into my office, ladies," he said shaking Dottie's hand. He was a couple of inches shorter than Dottie, about 5'11." He apologized to the client sitting in his office as the receptionist escorted the man into another office. Delgado said, "Ladies, please have a seat." He indicated the two chairs facing his desk.

Dottie sat. "Where were you Sunday morning?"

Delgado furrowed his brows and asked, "Why? What happened Sunday morning?"

"Margaret O'Neal was hit by a truck," Dottie said.

"Who's Margaret O'Neal?"

"The Guardian ad Litem for your children."

"Oh, Mrs. O'Neal, of course. I didn't know she was hit by a car, poor woman."

"Where were you 6:30 Sunday morning?" Dottie asked.

He narrowed his eyes. "Surely, you don't think I had anything to do with Mrs. O'Neal's death."

"Answer the question."

"I was at a lodge in Ocala. I went hunting with friends."

"When did you leave Gainesville?" Dottie asked.

"Sometime after work on Friday," he said. "I got back late Sunday night."

"Anyone with you?"

He gripped the edge of the desk. "I told you a group of friends."

Dottie said, "I'll need their names and numbers."

"Of course."

"Did you get along with Mrs. O'Neal?" Tori asked.

"Are you a detective?"

"No. I'm a forensic psychologist."

He smiled at her. "I knew you were too pretty to be a cop." Tori glanced at Dottie who crossed her arms at the not so subtle dig.

"How well did you get along with Mrs. O'Neal?" Tori asked.

"Quite well. She was very helpful."

"You threatened her. Didn't you?" Dottie asked.

"Why would I threaten her?" Delgado picked up a pencil and tapped the eraser on his desk.

"People reported you threatened her."

"They meant I threatened to get an attorney to challenge her recommendation. I had breakfast with my attorney this morning."

"What recommendation?" Dottie asked.

"Her recommendation that my sister take the children." He grasped the pencil and squeezed it. "I'm their father and I can care for them."

"What about your wife?" Tori asked.

"What about her?"

"Can't she take care of the children?"

"Poor Jennifer is out of touch with reality," Delgado said. "She hallucinates and is incoherent. DCF did the right thing taking the children away from her. But I should have custody of them."

Tori said, "I'm a psychologist, Mr. Delgado. I spoke with your wife this morning. She was completely coherent."

"You spoke to her? Why?"

"To find out more about Mrs. O'Neil."

Delgado sighed. "My wife can put on a good act for a short time. But she can't maintain it." He tapped the pencil on his desk. "She's been fired from every job she's ever had."

"She claims you don't want her to work," Dottie said.

"She doesn't know what she's talking about. She's unbalanced." He put the pencil down, sat back in his chair, and made a steeple of his hands. "I'm the one stable factor in her life. My sister warned me not to marry her."

Dottie asked, "Why was that?"

"My sister said Jennifer was trailer trash." He shrugged. "I was in love and wouldn't hear it. Marcia was right." He shook his head. He picked up the pencil and tapped it on the desk.

"The only problem I could see with your wife was she's been abused and is afraid of you," Tori said.

"I didn't abuse my wife."

"I saw the bruises and scars."

"Who are you going to believe—an unfit mother who's unbalanced or a successful banker?" He clenched the pencil so hard it snapped in two. He looked at the broken pencil. He tossed the pencil pieces in the trash can under his desk.

"She's the one in a domestic violence shelter," Tori said. She stood up and leaned on his desk knocking over a cup of cold coffee, spilling it across the papers on his desk. He jumped up and snatched up the papers. "Look what you did."

Tori said, "Sorry." She picked up the papers still on the desk, but he plucked them out of her hands.

"I don't need your help."

Tori sat down.

He took a deep breath and said, "Jennifer's an awful mother and horrible housekeeper. I've done nothing but protect her and our children." Delgado clutched the arms of his chair so tightly his knuckles whitened. A vein began to pulse at his temple. "She got what she asked for."

"She asked you to break her nose?" Tori asked, glaring at the banker.

Delgado stood with his hands on his desk, his nose flared, his face morphed into a gargoyle. "How dare you speak to me like that? Do you know who I am?"

"Yes," Tori said. "You're a wife beater who got caught because you broke your son's arm."

"You listened to that O'Neal woman, didn't you?"

"What would she have told us?" Dottie asked.

He looked from Tori to Dottie and said, "Get out of my office before I call security."

Dottie stood, leaned across his desk to look directly into his eyes and said, "I am the police, Delgado. I'll leave when I'm good and ready."

"I want my attorney."

Dottie picked up the receiver and held it out to him. "Call him."

# CHAPTER EIGHT

Tori rubbed her eyes, yawned and picked up the next paper in the pile of exams from her psychopathology class. Even grading good exams was tedious, especially when trying to be fair. The exam she was grading had the same wrong answers as a previous one. She groaned. *I hope no one cheated.* She looked through the previously graded exams and was relieved to see who had turned in the similar paper. She knew the two students. They studied together but did not sit near enough to copy from one another on the exam.

The ringing phone was a welcome reprieve.

"Tori Vincent," she said.

"Hungry?"

"Who is this?"

"The man of your dreams. Want pizza?"

She chuckled. "Hi, Herb. Thanks, but I need to get home to fix supper for Sean."

"Sean's here—with me. So's his pal Randy. Big Lou's Pizza on SE 2nd Ave. Kids say you know it."

Ten minutes later Tori walked into Big Lou's where she spotted Morrison sitting at a table with Sean and Randy. The threesome was downing the largest pizza she had ever seen. It had so many toppings the two boys were struggling to get their mouths around slices of pizza. An empty liter bottle of coke and three glasses holding various amounts of soda sat on the table.

"Wow!" Tori said. "Can I sit with you or are only gluttons allowed?"

"Want pizza?" Morrison asked.

"She'll order a salad. Pizza has too many calories," Sean said after he swallowed the food in his mouth.

"Knows his Mom," Morrison said. "It's fun eating pizza with people who enjoy it."

"That would be teenage boys." Tori turned to the waitress, "I'll have the raspberry walnut salad with grilled chicken." She turned back to Sean. "I take it everything went well after school."

"Both bikes're in my car trunk," Morrison said. He swiped a napkin across his mouth, removing pizza sauce and cheese.

"Both?"

"They took my bike, too," Randy said.

"Mom, you should've seen Barry and Frank. They came into the principal's office like they were kings of the hill and stopped dead."

Randy said, "They looked like they'd seen vampires when they spotted their fathers."

"Barry's dad's a correctional officer at the jail," Morrison said. "We go back years. He was ready to kill when he found out his kid stole bikes."

"What about his son being a bully?" Tori asked.

"Doesn't care if Barry's a bully, but stealing bikes is a no no. Barry won't try something like that again. Mom's a nurse—works nights. Barry's supposed to stay home when his dad's on night duty. He won't—roams  the streets with Frank getting in trouble."

"What's going to happen?" Tori asked.

"Got them in an afterschool program for bullies."

"Dr. Tori," Randy said, "Frank was so scared when his father pointed his finger at him, he wet his pants."

Boys' laughter filled the restaurant as they high fived each other.

"I can't wait to tell Dad," Sean said. "I wish he could've been there."

Tori felt the familiar stab at Sean's mention of his father, but kept the smile on her face. Morrison caught her eye and frowned his empathy.

Morrison said, "Remember, you guys promised not to tell anyone."

"You told Mom," Sean said.

"Yeah, yeah, tell your folks. You can't tell the kids at school."

"That's half the fun," Randy argued.

"Yeah, yeah, sure," Morrison said. "But we got to stop bullying through the Stop Bullying Program."

"They'll stop bullying if the kids find out what happened to them." Sean stuck his chin out. "They told everybody when they took our bikes."

"Yeah, but we got to stop the cycle, not increase hostility," Morrison said. "You tell the other kids, Frank and Barry'll get mad. Go after kids that tease them."

"Detective Morrison is right. You can get enough enjoyment by talking to each other and your parents. You don't need to rub their noses in it." Tori was impressed with Morrison's understanding of bullying.

Morrison said, "I worry Frank's dad beats him. Might abuse his wife, too."

"What makes you say that?" Tori asked.

"Frank was terrified of his father—you heard Randy. Father was furious. Kept clenching his fists like he couldn't wait to hit his kid. Let out a stream of curses at Frank. Ranted about it being the kid's mother's fault. She should control the kid."

"It serves Frank right if his father beats him," Randy said.

"Yeah. And I've met his mother," Sean said. "She's a witch. She yells and calls Frank's dad awful names. She asks for it."

Tori seized Sean's wrist. She narrowed her eyes. "No one asks to be abused, Sean. Don't say that." She squeezed Sean's wrist.

Morrison's huge paw latched onto Tori's arm, immobilizing it. She tried to shake off Morrison's hold. It was hopeless. She took a deep breath and loosened her hold on Sean. When she regained her composure she looked at Sean. His eyes were enormous. "Mom…"

"You're done," Morrison said to the boys. "Get your bikes out of the car. It's light enough to ride home. Go do your homework. Maybe you'll finish in time to catch the Knicks."

The boys moaned, but did as they were told. Sean left with Randy, but kept looking back at his mother.

Morrison pulled Tori's arm toward him and took her hand. "All right. Tell me what's going on here. I've never seen you lash out."

Tori sighed. "I've never hit Sean. I lost it." She buried her face in the crook of her arm and wept.

Morrison patted her shoulder. "Tori, what's going on?"

"This case is too close to my reality. My sister's husband abuses her. He says the same thing—she deserves it. She's beginning to believe him. I don't think she's going to go through with the divorce. I can't get through to her. My mother's in denial. She refuses to believe there was any abuse and is pestering Cindy to drop the divorce."

"Tori, you can't make someone do something they don't want to."

"Don't I know it?" She sat up. "I thought I raised Sean to be more sensitive."

"Sean's 13. He wants to be macho. Don't blame yourself for what he says."

"I know that intellectually, but I still feel responsible. My mother was psychologically abusive. I worry I'm going to be like her."

"Tori, as long as you worry about being a good mom, you will be one. I know boys and I know abuse," Morrison said, looking into his glass. "I'm the second oldest of five boys. Dad was 6'5" and over 300 lbs.—a cop in Paterson. A tyrant. When he drank he listened to no one but his inner devils. He blamed my brothers and me for everything. Smacked us around. If Mom tried to stop him, he'd swat her across the room. My mom was tiny—no match for Dad. Of course, Dad was sorry the next day. He'd bring Mom flowers and take us kids to a Knicks game."

"Herb, that's horrible."

Morrison continued to examine the bottom of his glass as if he were reading tea leaves. "One time—I was 15. I heard dad smack mom. I saw red and twisted Dad's arm behind him. My older brother, Mike, joined in. We gave Dad a once over."

"That took courage. What happened?"

"Never hit us again. Forgot us. Hung out at a bar with other cops. Come home drunk in the wee hours, and collapse. Get up for role call and do the same next day. We avoided him."

"Herb, I'm sorry."

# CHAPTER NINE

Herb Morrison hunched over his small bowl of Special K, muttering about his unappealing breakfast as he checked the previous day's basketball scores. The Knicks played the night before. He spotted the score and pumped his fist in the air. Crash! Splash! "Damned cat," screamed Morrison, swatting at the offending animal as it jumped off the table and darted out of the kitchen.

"Herb, watch your language," said his wife Ruth.

"I'll watch my language when Jennifer keeps that animal out of the kitchen and off the table." Morrison stood, wiped the water from the overturned vase off his slacks and picked up the pink roses scattered on the table.

"Here, let me do that. At least the vase didn't break."

"Where's that lousy cereal?" Morrison asked. "The cat spilt water in my bowl."

"You already ate most of it."

"I save the milk till last. I'm not asking for a banana split. I just want a bowl of Special K with milk."

"You're on a diet. You gained two pounds yesterday. You're supposed to lose weight, not gain it."

"I told you I had a slice of pizza with Tori's kid and his pal."

"You don't expect me to believe you gained two pounds from eating one slice of pizza."

"It wasn't two pounds. It was a pound and a half."

40

"A pound in a half, two pounds—who cares? How could you gain weight from eating one slice of pizza? You must've eaten half of it."

Morrison avoided her eyes.

"Why were you eating pizza anyway?"

"Kids wanted pizza. They'd had a bad time—Tori said it was traumatic. They chose where to eat. What's the big deal?"

"How much did you eat?"

Herb hid his head behind the newspaper, "Maybe two slices."

"You wouldn't gain two pounds eating two slices."

"I retain water."

Ruth scoffed at him and turned to pick up the coffee pot. She refilled their cups before sitting down at the table next to him.

"Herb, you're pre-diabetic; the doctor said you've got to lose weight."

"I've got a high-pressure job. Need protein to do my work."

"Since when is pizza a good source of protein?" Ruth sighed. "Herb, I'm worried about you. I don't want to be a widow."

"Yeah, yeah, I know."

Ruth placed a half bowl of cereal in front of her husband who looked at it and scowled at his wife. She folded her arms and narrowed her eyes.

"What did you do to Pussy Willow?" asked Jennifer, their nine-year-old daughter, hands on her hips. She had entered the kitchen unnoticed by her parents.

Morrison lowered the paper and looked directly into his daughter's thick glasses. "Where'd you get that name for the cat?"

"Don't change the subject. What did you do to her?"

"What did I do to it? Me?" Morrison's voice rose.

"She came running upstairs and hid under the bed. I can't get her to come out."

"Good! Maybe she won't jump on the table," he said snapping his paper open.

"What did you do to her?" Jennifer asked. She pulled his paper down so she could see his face.

Morrison looked at her over his reading glasses and snarled, "It's not what I did to her. It's what she did to me. Jumped on the table and knocked over the vase. Spilt water all over the table—in my lap. Got dirty water in my cereal."

41

Jennifer laughed. "You probably deserved it." She got a huge bowl, filled it with Frosted Flakes and covered it with the strawberries her mother set out for her.

"How come she eats Frosted Flakes with strawberries and real milk and I get this dog food?"

"Jennifer weighs 74 lbs. When you get down to triple her weight, you can eat what you want, too."

# CHAPTER TEN

"Take off dead flowers so they'll bloom," Morrison told Tori early Tuesday morning. He was stooped in front of the flower bed by Annie Curry's front porch, pocketing the dead flowers as he removed them. "Magnificent hybrids, these," he said.

"Always the gardener," Tori said. She glanced at the cream yellow day lilies. She appreciated their beauty, but had no interest in growing them herself. She disliked getting dirty and sweaty, the two consequences of gardening she dreaded.

Morrison said, "House I grew up in Jersey had a postage stamp-sized front yard. Back yard was muddy when it rained and dusty when it didn't—soil so poor even kudzu wouldn't grow. Living in Florida I grow flowers and vegetables in my yard—it's huge. My dream's to retire and cultivate roses."

"Retire? You're barely in your forties, right?"

"Forty-one." Morrison stood up and they proceeded to the front door.

When Annie Curry answered her doorbell, Morrison was busily removing dead blooms from the geraniums in the pots outside her door. He turned and apologetically handed her the dead flowers. "Take off dead ones—bloom better," he said. "Why they call it a 'green thumb.'" He displayed the green stain on his right thumb.

Annie honored him with a half smile and took the dead flowers as if they would stain her palm. "Margaret was the one who played with flowers." She glided through the living room into the Florida

43

room. Over her shoulder she said, "It's cheerier and brighter in here. Please have a seat." She indicated the wicker chairs covered in bright Florida chintz. "I've just made tea. I'll get it." She went into the kitchen.

"Tea?" hissed Morrison, who drank strong black coffee. "Tea's for old ladies and faggots."

Tori rolled her eyes. "Drink it. I promise it won't affect your sexual orientation."

Morrison growled. Then he chuckled. "More fun being politically incorrect with Dottie. She get's mad. You're not worth the effort."

"Thank God for small favors."

Annie came back carrying a tray with tea and cookies. Morrison frowned. When Tori gave him a dirty look, he picked up the cup of tea with a forced smile. The teacup looked like part of a child's play set in Morrison's hands; his beefy fingers were too large to fit through the dainty handle.

Annie smiled as she placed the plate of cookies on the table next to Morrison. She turned to Tori. "Don't think I'm not upset about my sister's death because I'm not crying. If I start, I'll cry all day. It's better if I pretend I'm all right. I can cry in my pillow at night." Annie said to Morrison, "What do you need to know?"

"Dr. Vincent's got to know about your sister—her and her life."

Annie took a deep breath and looked out into the garden, a blaze of color in the bright Florida sunshine. "Margaret and I grew up in Boston. Our parents were Irish, from the old country. Sent us to parochial schools. Then I went to nursing school and Margaret went to a Catholic girls' college. She met her husband, Edward, at a mixer in college."

"A what?" Morrison asked around the cookie in his mouth.

Annie turned to Morrison with a contagious laugh. "I'm out of touch with the younger generation." Morrison beamed. Tori observed a blush cross his cheeks. "Back in my day colleges used to be all one sex," Annie said. "Women's colleges held dances or mixers for the co-eds to meet 'suitable' young men (her hands mimed quotation marks) from Catholic men's colleges. Margaret and Edward met at a dance. They married after college and moved to Connecticut."

44

Annie picked up the cookie plate and smiled at Morrison. "I'll get more cookies. Then I'll answer more questions."

As soon as Annie left the room, Tori turned to Morrison. "For God's sake, what's the matter with you, Morrison? You're hoovering down those cookies like you haven't eaten in a month. Isn't Ruth feeding you?"

Morrison rubbed his reddening face with both hands, "Ruth has me on one of them fad diets—low carb or some such shit—everything tastes like cardboard and I've had nothing sweet in six days."

"Get over it, Morrison, this is a murder investigation. Buy cookies on your way home." She looked at him. "You've got crumbs on your chin."

Morrison wiped his chin with the tiny napkin Annie had provided. He crumpled the napkin and dropped it on his plate.

A large black cat jumped in Morrison's lap and began to lick his face. He swung his arm back as if to swat the cat away, but looked up as Annie returned. He petted the cat. "Your cat?"

Annie said, "That's Myanmar. She's a black Burmese, so I named her Myanmar. Isn't she beautiful?"

"Lovely," he said. Tori watched him crinkle his nose as he petted the cat with the huge golden eyes.

Annie placed a plate of cookies in front of Morrison. She smoothed her hair. "It's so nice having someone appreciate my cookies."

*Oh God, she's flirting with a man 20 years her junior*, Tori thought. Morrison took a cookie and settled back in his chair smiling.

"Ms. Curry, I wonder if we could see Margaret's bedroom," Tori said.

"Of course, please come this way."

Tori followed Annie. She looked back to see Morrison taking a handful of cookies as he stood up.

Margaret's bedroom was large with French doors leading to the back garden. Purple lilacs decorated the bedspread and matching drapes. There were three silver picture frames face down on the night stand. Tori walked over and picked up one.

"Those are Margaret's," Annie said. "That's a photograph of her and her husband and son. She had 'the perfect Catholic family.'" Again, she did the air quotation marks.

Morrison pointed to a Knicks hat on the other nightstand. "Was Margaret a Knicks fan?"

"No, that's mine. I'm the basketball fanatic."

"Did you see the game last night?" Morrison asked.

Annie said, "Weren't they amazing?"

Tori picked up the second photograph. An elderly couple stood under an arbor. "Your parents?"

Annie nodded.

"Why did Margaret turn the photographs face down?" Tori asked.

Annie straightened the already neat bedspread. "She didn't, I did." She kept her eyes on the bedspread. "I couldn't stand the sight of them. Margaret was always the perfect..." Annie broke off, the muscles in her face tightened as she clenched her jaw.

"It sounds like it was difficult having Margaret for an older sister." Tori commiserated, thinking about the tense relationship she had with her own sister. Her mother thought Cindy was the perfect everything, too.

Annie picked an invisible piece of lint off the pillow sham. "I was never the 'perfect' anything." Tears coursed down her face. Annie daintily wiped them with the lace trimmed handkerchief.

"Anyway, enough about me." Annie turned to face Tori. "Margaret and Edward had a son, Mike." She picked another piece of lint off the spread. Tori noted the edge to Annie's voice— *sibling rivalry still flourishing?* Annie said, "Mike died in a ski accident after he got out of med school. Broke Margaret's heart. She put her energies into teaching and working with those sanctimonious people at her church." She looked at Tori. "Sublimation—isn't that what you call it?"

"That's right."

The cat rubbed against Morrison's leg and Tori observed him clench his jaw.

"You can pick her up," Annie said.

Morrison squatted down and scratched the cat's head. "I need my hands free to examine things," he said.

Annie gave him a radiant smile and picked up the cat. "Myanmar's my only baby, aren't you, sweetie?"

"Ms. Curry, please tell us more about your sister," Tori said.

"Margaret taught school in Wilton, a wealthy town in Connecticut.

Tori asked. "What brought you and Margaret to Gainesville?"

"Right after our parents passed away, Edward had a heart attack. He died. He was 63. I went to stay with Margaret. We became closer than we'd been since we were kids. I convinced her to move to Gainesville to begin a new life."

Tori walked into the adjoining bathroom. It was huge, with wallpaper matching the bedspread. She looked around the room. "There's a big assortment of makeup on the vanity," Tori said. She picked up a tube of eye shadow. "I didn't think Margaret was the type to wear eye shadow."

Annie blushed. "She didn't, that's mine."

"You and Margaret shared this bathroom?"

Annie's color deepened. "No. I'm moving into her room." She paused. "It's bigger than mine."

*Pretty quick move,* Tori thought. *Her sister isn't even buried yet.*

Morrison said, "Margaret was unattached and wealthy. Any guys in her life?"

Annie walked to the window. Morrison took the opportunity to shove Myanmar away from his leg. Annie said, "I guess you might call Jimmie Rafferty a 'man in her life.'"

"Tell us about him," Tori said.

"Margaret met him at church, at a pot luck dinner. He went to the dinner with Lucille Beauregard. Then he started sniffing around Margaret."

Morrison asked, "Sniffing around?"

"Yes, like a dog in heat." Annie huffed.

"You don't have a high opinion of Mr. Rafferty," Tori said.

"I can't stand the man. He wouldn't have looked twice at Margaret, if it weren't for her money."

Morrison asked, "How did Jimmie know Annie had money?"

"From Lucille. She's the world's biggest gossip."

"Give us Jimmie and Lucille's addresses, please," Morrison said.

47

Annie walked to the nightstand, opened a drawer and withdrew pen and paper. She wrote the information on the paper and slipped it into Morrison's hand with a squeeze and a suggestive smile. Tori silently groaned.

"One other question," Tori said. "What did your sister do the morning of the burglary?"

Annie looked up, not speaking for a moment. Then she snapped her fingers. "That's right. She went to interview some people for the Guardian ad Litem program."

"Would you give us their names and addresses?"

"She couldn't tell me that. It's confidential. All I know is her charges were two children. Let me think." She rubbed her chin. After a moment she said, "Their parents were in the midst of a contentious divorce. Father was a banker. Margaret said he was a low-life. He abused the mother. She worried he would use the children as pawns in the divorce."

Tori glanced at Morrison, who nodded.

They walked into the living room.

"What about her will?" Morrison asked. "Did Margaret leave you any money?"

*Investigating the murder or concerned for Annie?* Tori wondered.

Annie snorted. "Margaret didn't forget me, but she didn't trust me, either. She set up a trust fund. The house is mine as long as I live and then it'll be sold. The money will be donated to different charities."

Tori turned to Morrison, "I think we've gotten everything we need, don't you?" She stared pointedly at the empty dish of cookies.

Morrison smiled at Annie, taking her hand in both of his. "Thank you, Miss Curry, for your help."

"Please call me Annie," she said, smiling up at him.

*Good lord, they're flirting again,* Tori thought.

# CHAPTER ELEVEN

As Morrison pulled out of the driveway, he turned to Tori: "Good-looking woman, that Annie."

"Yes, you seemed quite taken with her." She thought, *Watch your step, Morrison, this is how affairs begin.*

Morrison's color deepened, but he kept his eyes on the road. "You don't miss a thing do you?"

"I'm a psychologist. I'm trained to observe people."

"I'd never cheat on Ruth," Morrison said. "But it's a long time since an attractive woman's paid attention to me."

"Even a woman in her 60s?"

"Doesn't look 60."

"I agree," Tori said.

"Ruth's a good wife. But she's a no nonsense woman. Always after me to lose weight. She'd never make me cookies."

"She's concerned about your health."

"Yeah, asshole doctor said I'm pre-diabetic. She acts like I'll drop dead if I eat a cookie."

"At least you have someone who cares about you."

Morrison pulled to a stop at the STOP sign and looked at Tori, "I thought you were seeing your ex-husband."

"Yes and no. He divorced his second wife…"

"The voluptuous attorney?" Morrison turned the car to the right and eased into traffic.

"Yes, her. He comes to see Sean or I take Sean up to see him in Jacksonville. He wanted to date. I wasn't ready."

"And…?"

"Now I'm ready and he's lost interest."

"Dumb shit."

"Him or me?"

"I meant him. But if the shoe fits…"

*He's right,* Tori thought. *I'm a dumb shit. I was trying to play hard to get so Gerry would want me and I lost the whole…*

"What do you think Annie's feelings were toward Margaret?" Morrison asked.

Tori hesitated. "I was wondering that myself. Margaret's body's still warm and Annie's moving into her bedroom."

"Turned Margaret's photos face down."

"She resented Margaret: the perfect child who grew up to marry the perfect husband and have the perfect son. To make matters worse, Margaret inherited a load of money. Annie has emotional baggage related to Margaret."

"She resent Margaret enough to kill her?" he asked.

Tori turned toward Morrison. "In that video of the burglary, could it have been Annie, not Margaret? There's a strong resemblance."

Morrison was stopped at a red light and cocked his head toward Tori without speaking for a moment. He bit his lower lip before shaking his head, saying, "Nah. Couldn't mistake Annie for Margaret. Margaret was heavier, shorter, and had gray hair."

"Those are cosmetic features. You can't tell about an inch or two in height in a video and she could have worn a wig."

"What about the weight?"

"What was the woman wearing in the video?"

"A track suit."

"Maybe Annie was wearing padding under it."

Morrison slowed the car and turned into the parking lot at the police station. "Maybe that's why Margaret said she'd never been in the house."

Morrison parked the car in his reserved place. Tori looked at him. "Herb, thank you for stopping me from hurting Sean last night. I've never hit him."

"You were stressed out."

"That's no excuse," she said. "Thanks for getting Sean's bike for him."

"No problem. I've got a younger brother Shawn, spelt S h a w n. I should've been more protective of him when he was growing up."

"What's he doing now?"

"Twenty years in Jersey State Prison."

As Morrison and Tori walked down the hallway toward his office. Dottie called to them. "How'd the interview go with Annie Curry?

"Good," Morrison replied, opening his office door. "C'mon. We're going to review the tape of the burglary."

"The chief wants to see you," Dottie said.

"I'll see her when I'm ready," Morrison said. "C'mon."

Dottie shook her head. "I didn't hear that."

Morrison ordered Dottie to set up the monitor. He told her about Tori's idea that Margaret's sister might have been the burglar. The three focused on the video. As soon as the burglar started to climb the stairs, Morrison said, "That's not Annie. Look how she moves. Got something wrong with her leg." "I agree," Tori said. "Annie walks with a smooth glide, that woman limps! I don't think she's wearing a wig, either. Her hair's too short. You can barely see it below the side of her cap."

"Not Annie. Nice idea, but back to square one. Margaret burglarized the house," Morrison said. "But, why?"

# CHAPTER TWELVE

As Dottie drove into the neighborhood of aging pastel stucco houses, Tori said, "I feel like I'm in a time machine arriving in 1960."

"Except all the vegetation has been growing un-checked for fifty years," Dottie said. "Look at the mammoth trees and over-grown bushes; they look like they're devouring the houses."

"Yeah, they look like doll houses next to the trees. Not exactly what you'd call a well-heeled area."

"No. Lucille Beauregard is not a wealthy woman."

Tori pointed out the house number on the mailbox and Dottie pulled into the driveway of a small pink house. The lawn was neatly mowed, but, although the shrubs were trimmed, they overwhelmed the house. "She needs a good landscaper," Tori said as they walked the short distance to the door. "Morrison would have a conniption looking at these flowers." She pointed to the plumbagoes. "Look how stringy the flowers are."

An animated Dolly Parton look-alike answered the door carrying a gray Schnauzer. Lucille Beauregard wore spike heels, a spandex top and a short wide skirt straight out of a 1960s dance movie.

Dottie introduced herself and Tori. Dottie and Tori exchanged amused glances as the petite woman, dog in her arms, led them into her living room, her voice trailing behind her. "You want to know about Margaret O'Neal, don't you? Annie told me you talked to her."

Allowing no opportunity for a response, Lucille Beauregard began blathering non-stop. "That's me and Beau dancing," she said pointing to the paneled wall crammed with framed photos. She put the dog on the floor. "Beau, Richard Beauregard, that's my late husband. Handsome, huh?" She allowed the visiting women to nod, but gave them no chance to speak. She tucked one leg under her other thigh as she sat on a worn couch, patting the cushion next to her. The dog jumped to sit beside his owner. "This is Fred— Fred Astaire. I always dreamed of dancing with the real Fred Astaire but that never happened," she said with a sigh. "We would've made a great dance team." She caressed the little dog and kissed the top of his head. "I'm from South Carolina."

*Like we couldn't guess*, Tori thought, listening to the accent.

"People ask me all the time where I come from. I was raised out in the country. My daddy bought him a farm. I helped hoe and stuff. That's what folks did back then."

*Don't Southerners speak slowly?* Tori thought. Even Dottie couldn't get a word in as Lucille nattered on and on.

"Beau was my dance instructor. He was 21. The best looking man I ever saw. I fell hard for him. Wanted to marry him the first time I saw him. Beau and me competed in dance contests when I was 14 or 15. We got married when I was 16. Papa was mad as a wet hen. Thought he was gonna kill Beau."

She jumped up and ran across the room, the little Schnauzer at her heels. She pointed to a framed photograph. "That's me and Beau in Blackpool." She turned to face her visitors. "That's in England. It's where the top dancers compete. We came in third in the Foxtrot."

Tori stood to examine the photo more closely. The woman in the picture was wearing a short dress with a wide skirt, showing off shapely legs as she spun in the dance. The dark haired man and the long-haired blond made a handsome couple. Lucille must have been in her early twenties in the photo. She was beautiful. She could pass for the same age from a distance now. Up close Tori observed a face mistreated by plastic surgery, leaving her permanent smile as her most comfortable expression. *She's probably in her 60s*, Tori guessed.

Lucille shook her head and sighed. "I danced that man to death." She looked up at Tori standing next to her and shrugged her shoulders. "He died two years ago. We were dancing. He fell and broke his hip. Right in our playroom," she said pointing at the connecting room. "I use it for a dance studio, now."

"I'm so sorry," Tori said.

"Life goes on." Lucille half skipped back to her seat. *Where does she get that energy*, wondered Tori. *She acts like she's six years old.* When Fred settled next to her, Lucille put a hand on each side of his head, planting a kiss on his mouth. "We do okay, don't we, Fred?"

The muffled sound of the melody "Can You Feel the Love Tonight" emanated from Tori's purse. She riffled through her bag and pulled out her cell phone, flipped it open and said, "Hi Kiddo, I'm at a meeting. See you about 5:00."

She turned to Lucille and said, "My son. He reports in when he gets home from school."

Lucille said, "A son. How nice."

"I understand you go dancing at the Knights of Columbus," Dottie said, bringing them back to the purpose for the visit. *Good old task-oriented Dottie*, thought a grateful Tori.

"Yes. I used to dance with Jimmie Rafferty. We were an item, that's what the young people call it." She laughed throwing her head back and tossing her long blond curls. "He worshipped me. Jimmie and me went dancing two or three nights a week. He wanted to spend the rest of his life with me. Said we would dance off into the future."

Tori closed her eyes, thinking, *I'm going to barf.*

"What happened to the big romance?" Dottie asked.

For the first time, the smile left Lucille's face. She bared her teeth and scrunched up her nose, her voice higher in pitch and intensity as she spit out the name, "Margaret O'Neal. That's what happened."

"Jimmie Rafferty left you for Margaret O'Neal?" Tori asked in a soft voice.

Lucille sat up and put both feet on the floor, hands on her hips. "He dropped me for Margaret O'Neal's money, not Margaret. Why else would he want to go around with that dumpy old woman with truck driver eyebrows?"

*That was nasty,* thought Tori.

"How did he plan to get her money?" Dottie asked. "Was he going to marry her?"

Lucille sneered. "No, he'd never marry her."

The notes of *The Tennessee Waltz* peeled out. Lucille smiled. "That must be my dance student." She jumped up and went to the answer the door.

Dottie rolled her eyes and Tori nodded.

Lucille breezed by the two women followed by a chunky woman in her late 40s who was a head taller and a foot wider than Lucille. "This is Martha, my dance student." Lucille indicated the woman who trailed behind her. "Come into my studio. I'll get Martha started on some new steps, then we can talk some more."

Lucille danced over to a CD player and started some Latin music. "Martha, let's review the Cuban walk." She looked at Tori and Dottie. "Like to dance, ladies? You can join us."

Lucille stood facing a mirrored wall with her back to Martha and did some steps, counting "quick, quick, slow" as she moved her hips. Tori and Dottie lined up next to Martha who did a clumsy imitation of the graceful dance. "We can dance while I talk to these ladies. They're from the police, you know. They want to know about Margaret O'Neil. That woman that got herself killed by the truck."

Lucille swung her hips as she danced over to where the other three women were dancing. "We're doing a rumba," Lucille said. "You're good," she said to Tori. "You should take lessons."

"You were telling us how Jimmie Rafferty was going to get Margaret O'Neal's money," Tori said.

"Jimmie borrowed money from Margaret," Lucille said. "He told her some cockamamie story about needing it for orphaned boys. A bare-faced lie; he hates kids."

Lucille directed her attention to Martha and said, "Quick, quick slow. Keep the count. That's right. The next piece is slower. You can keep the beat better."

Dottie said, "I thought Jimmie Rafferty taught children's bible classes at the church."

"Only so Margaret would think he cared. I saw him one Sunday and he said the little buggers were a pain in the patootie. I asked, 'Is it worth it to get into Margaret's pants?' That got him. He went bonkers. Accused me of being jealous." She turned to

Tori. "Like I could be jealous of someone with the sex appeal of a washing machine."

*A lot of anger toward Margaret,* Tori thought. She asked, "Why did Jimmie Rafferty need money?"

"I know why," Martha said as she danced around so she faced the others.

Lucille asked, "How do you know Jimmie Rafferty?"

"He was the paid dancer on that cruise I took last fall."

"Why does Jimmie Rafferty need money?" Dottie asked.

"He's got a gambling problem," Martha said. "The cruise line cut off his credit in the casino. He asked all the women for money. Said he could win back what he'd lost."

"Did anyone give him money?" Tori asked.

"Yes, Beverly what's her name? You know, Lucille, the skinny old bird with the wig."

"Beverly Sullivan. She would. She follows Jimmie around the dances like a puppy dog."

"She's the one," Martha said. "We told her she was a fool to give him money, but she wouldn't listen. Jimmie spent the rest of the cruise canoodling with Beverly. She was in seventh heaven."

"Would you give us Beverly's address?" Dottie asked. She wrote the information in her notebook.

"One last question," Dottie said. "Where were you about 6:30 Sunday morning?"

"When Margaret got herself killed? You think I done it?" Lucille frowned at Dottie.

"It's police procedure," Dottie said politely. "We have to ask everyone who knew Margaret where they were."

"I was in bed. I never get up before ten on Sundays," she said. "My Saturday nights are late."

"Is there anyone who can document that?"

Lucille gave her most charming smile, "I never sleep with anyone 'til he gives me a diamond."

Dottie and Tori remained silent until they pulled out of the driveway and turned the corner. Dottie asked, "What would make a woman get that much plastic surgery? Her face is so tight it looks like it hurts."

"Arrested development, poor thing," Tori said. "Did you see the photograph of her and her husband? She was gorgeous as a young woman."

"Lots of gorgeous women mature into lovely older women."

"Lucille gets her sense of identity from her beauty. She does whatever it takes to maintain her youth."

"You think that's why she wears those clothes?"

"She craves attention," Tori said. "Thank goodness Morrison wasn't with us."

Dottie turned to her passenger. "What do you mean?"

"The way he was coming on to Annie Currie this morning."

"You're kidding me."

"No, I'm not. He was following her around like a cat chasing catnip."

"Annie is Margaret's sister, isn't she?"

"Yes, her younger, more attractive sister," Tori said. "Morrison was gaga over her."

"I've never seen Morrison so much as look at another woman. Ruth would cut his balls off."

"I'm not sure how much it was her beauty and how much it was the homemade cookies."

"I'd go with the cookies."

The two rode in silence for awhile, then Tori asked, "You think she could kill someone?"

"Who? Lucille?"

"Yeah, did you see her expression change when she mentioned Margaret? Talk about a woman scorned. I don't think someone would get away with dropping Lucille."

"But wouldn't she go after Jimmie Rafferty, not Margaret?"

"Perhaps, but maybe she wants him back. Maybe she needs him to come back so the world knows no one drops Lucille."

# CHAPTER THIRTEEN

Morrison pulled into the parking lot of the apartment complex in Gainesville's 'Sin City' area, so named by virtue of the wild parties thrown by the university students living there. The complex was decent enough, but somehow he'd expected Margaret's 'man friend' to live in a house or condo or perhaps an apartment complex in a more prestigious section of town. Morrison negotiated tricycles, big wheels, and wagons parked in the hallway to Rafferty's apartment. Morrison would rather live under a bridge in Jacksonville than this child-infested place with its hubbub and clutter. He smiled politely at a young mother setting one jabbering toddler on a tricycle while holding a bawling infant in some kind of sack over her shoulder. *Hell on earth*, he thought, walking quickly to his destination.

Rafferty answered the bell on the first ring, greeting Morrison with a big Irish smile. "Welcome to my humble home," he said with a bow. "You must be Detective Morrison."

Morrison walked past Rafferty into the living area, giving the apartment a once over. He observed a small kitchen to his left and a hallway leading to bedrooms and baths on the right. The large room, serving as living and dining area, was decorated in furniture that looked like it belonged at the Salvation Army. Either Rafferty wasted good money moving worthless furniture to Florida or he'd shopped at a second-hand store after he arrived. There were a couple of banners for the Boston Celtics stuck in a vase. *The guy has no taste in basketball teams,* Morrison thought. The only new object was a large flat screen television dominating the wall opposite a small recliner loveseat designed for two. Morrison sat on the only other chair, a brownish suede rocker. The chair tipped precariously and Rafferty laughed. "I should have tested that chair before I bought it. Good Will doesn't give warranties."

"Damn," said Morrison, balancing carefully on the chair.

"It's a little early for a beer, but I do a mean instant coffee."

"No thanks."

"Suit yourself." Rafferty sat on the loveseat and leaned forward resting his forearms on his thighs. He was tan with the regular features women found attractive and Morrison thought smacked of weakness. "What can I do you for?" Rafferty asked.

Morrison silently moaned and thought, *What did Margaret ever see in this character?* He cleared his throat. "As I said on the phone, I'm investigating Margaret O'Neal's death."

"I thought she was hit by a pick-up."

"Yeah, yeah, but it was no accident."

"What makes you think that?"

Morrison made no attempt to hide his annoyance. He spoke in a strained voice. "If you don't mind, I'll ask the questions."

"Pardon meeee." Rafferty drew out the 'me' to indicate he was offended. Morrison didn't give a flea's ass; he wanted to offend Jimmie Rafferty. Morrison thought people were more likely to slip and tell him something they wanted to hide if they were intimidated or upset.

"Tell me. How did you know Margaret O'Neal?"

"Sure thing." Rafferty flashed his straight white teeth.

*Don't think you're going to charm me*, Morrison thought

"We met at a church function. We hit it off right away. We're both retired teachers. Both went to college in New Rochelle. In New York. I went to Iona College. It's run by the Jesuits." Jimmie puffed out his chest and seemed to wait for Morrison to comment.

"And...?"

"She asked me to teach a Sunday school class. I agreed. I hadn't taught in awhile, so she helped me prepare. We started seeing each other. I drove her to church on Sundays and go for brunch afterwards."

"You plan to drive her to church yesterday?"

"Yes," he looked at his hands in his lap, "but I was so late I couldn't. I called after Mass and Annie told me what happened." He looked Morrison in the eye. "Annie said Margaret was hit by a pick-up truck." He crossed his arms waiting for Morrison's response.

Ignoring Rafferty's implied question, Morrison asked, "What happened you were too late to pick her up for church?"

"I was in bed. I slept late Sunday," he raised his chin as if challenging Morrison.

"Alone?" Morrison asked, looking down his nose.

"No," said Rafferty with a wink.

"You saying you only saw Mrs. O'Neal at church?"

"Of course not. You cut me off before I finished," Rafferty snapped.

Having achieved his goal of annoying Rafferty, Morrison grinned. "Tell me, Jimmie."

"We went dancing at the Knights of Columbus on Fridays."

"Dancing? Didn't Margaret have a bum knee?"

"Margaret and I danced the slow dances. She didn't mind my dancing the faster ones with other ladies."

"Like Lucille Beauregard?"

"Yes, like Lucille Beauregard and Margaret's sister Annie." Rafferty's tone reflected his irritation.

"Go to the K of C often?"

"I used to go to the K of C dances in Connecticut with my wife before she died. When I moved to Gainesville, I didn't know anyone. I thought the dances might be a good place to meet people."

"Women kinds of people?"

"Yes, women kinds of people. Is there something wrong with that?"

"Nah, just want to be clear," Morrison said. "You and Lucille Beauregard used to be a couple, right?"

"Lucille and I used to go dancing before Margaret and I met."

"Where else did you meet women?"

"I went to the Widows and Widowers Meetup. Look, I can tell you don't like me, but I'll be straight with you. I'm retired on a schoolteacher's pension. I don't have much money. I'm a great dancer and not bad looking. Women like me. I go on cruises to meet women."

"How can you afford cruises if you got no money?"

Rafferty lowered his eyes. "Single men can cruise free on some cruise lines if they dance with the single women."

"You're kidding me." Morrison opened his eyes wide. "They let you go free if you dance with women?"

"Women enjoy cruises more if they have someone to dance with. They're more likely to go on future cruises."

"What a racket," Morrison said, shaking his head.

"It's not as easy as it sounds. Most of the unattached women are the size of Volkswagens without the wheels. Dancing with them is like moving refrigerators across the dance floor. By the end of the night I'm exhausted." Rafferty stood up and pointed to a photograph on the wall. "That's me and the widows," he said. "A bunch of blimps wrapped in designer clothes. They shouldn't allow people that fat to wear low-cut gowns. You can't imagine how it feels to hold their bare flab." Rafferty groaned. "It's icky." Then he laughed. "Ain't a pretty picture."

Morrison looked at the photograph of the slim Rafferty surrounded with older women and asked, "What's funny about taking advantage of widows?"

# CHAPTER FOURTEEN

Dottie flopped into the recliner, closed her eyes, pulled the lever raising the foot rest and, taking a deep breath, pushed against the back until she was completely stretched out. She sighed.

Dottie was something of an anomaly—a police officer who championed the poor and down-trodden. A couple of months earlier Dottie had met Bruce Donavan, while she was volunteering at the homeless shelter. He donated his legal services to the residents. They had been together ever since.

Tonight Bruce was preparing dinner. As he picked up the platter holding two huge t-bone steaks, he asked, "Are you up for running in the morning?"

"How far do we have to go?"

"If we want to do the marathon, we need to do a 12-mile run."

"That'll take us over an hour."

"So we start at 4:00 a.m."

Dottie said, "I'm allergic to getting up at 4:00 a.m."

"Whimp!" Bruce walked out on the patio whistling tunelessly. He brushed his special marinade on the huge t-bones steaks. A short time later he called to Dottie as he put two plates on the dining room table; each held a steak, grilled zucchini and squash and a sweet potato. Earlier Dottie had set wine glasses on the table and opened a bottle of Merlot to breathe. Bruce poured them each a glass of wine.

Dottie groaned as she pulled herself out of the lounge chair and navigated to the table. She was not interested in food. She could not get the image of Margaret O'Neal's body out of her mind. *Why would anyone kill a poor old woman who'd never hurt a soul?*

"Great steak," Dottie said absent-mindedly.

"You should taste it before you comment."

Dottie looked at Bruce, "Sorry, sweetie, your steaks are always great, but…"

"Not upset about the Nets losing to the Knicks, are you?"

"Please, don't bring that up. Morrison gloated all day. Every other word was about the Knicks."

"Is that what's upsetting you?"

"Not really, I'm ruminating about my case."

"Are you saying you're distracted?" he asked in an innocent voice.

Dottie looked at him with narrowed eyes.

"Okay. Tell your Bruce what's bugging you."

"It's the school teacher. You know, the one run down by a truck on Sunday. Morrison thinks the hit-and-run is suspicious and I'm sure he's right. Why would someone back over her after she was hit unless he wanted to make sure she was dead?"

"Oh my God! That's horrible! Who wanted her dead?"

"No one. Everybody loved her."

"Look for love or money as motives."

"There's lots of money and love."

"Tell me about the love, I enjoy a good romance," Bruce put a forkful of steak in his mouth.

"Bruce, you're a cynic."

"Moi? How can you accuse me of being a cynic?"

Dottie rolled her eyes. "Margaret O'Neal was dating a man who dropped another woman for Margaret. Tori and I interviewed the castoff woman. You should have seen her—a Dolly Parton double. She was livid her man dropped her for Margaret. Said Margaret had the sex appeal of a washing machine."

"A little bitter, perhaps?" Bruce said. "But I like her imagery."

Dottie sighed.

"Do you think she did it? A woman scorned?" Bruce scratched the beard he was beginning to grow, leaning his elbow on the table.

Dottie scrunched up her face, "Nah. Somehow I can't see Lucille killing a competitor by running her down. She'd want to inflict the pain herself. Besides she didn't think he dropped her for the other woman. She said he was after Margaret's money."

"Aha!" Bruce raised his fist in the air with his index finger pointing to the ceiling. "The money angle! I knew it."

"Yeah, I could more easily see Jimbo…"

"Jimbo? Where do they get these names?"

"Actually, that's Morrison's nickname for him. His name is Jimmie."

"Sorry, go on."

After finishing a piece of steak and taking a sip of wine, Dottie said, "Jimmie borrowed money from Margaret."

"He might've killed her for her money."

"Why kill her if she's 'lending' him money?"

Bruce put a piece of zucchini in his mouth and chewed, deep in thought. He swallowed and looked at Dottie. "Where did she get that kind of money, anyway? I thought she was a retired school teacher."

"She was, but her husband was a broker and left her a bundle."

"Who benefits from her will?"

"We don't have the details, yet. We know her sister gets the house, but she claims to have loved Margaret. Besides, Margaret gave her everything she wanted."

"Maybe she wanted the money with no strings?"

Dottie twirled the stem of her wine glass. "According to the sister, the money she inherits *has* strings. Margaret left her money in a trust fund."

"So you have the scorned woman who wanted her dead." Bruce started counting on his fingers. He paused. "What sixty-something woman would kill to get her lover back?"

Dottie took a sip of wine and looked at Bruce, "You're kidding me, right?"

Bruce shrugged. "Then you have the man who wants her money and the sister. That's three. You need to check out the will."

"There's also the nasty guy Margaret dealt with as a GAL volunteer. She got a judge to take his children away from him."

"Check his record. GAL people deal with some nasty characters. He might have hurt someone in the past."

"I have a call in to Miami."

"Anyone else?"

"Not yet, but I'm still hung up on the burglary. Margaret said she'd never take anything that didn't belong to her. Anyway, Margaret had alibis when the other houses were burglarized. There's something about those burglaries I can't put my finger on. How does the burglar get the key and the alarm code?"

Bruce scratched his chin. "You need to find a connection between the homes being burglarized. What do they have in common? Who goes into the houses?"

"You got it! Maybe the same people do their lawn, dry clean their clothes, deliver their paper…"

"None of those people go inside," Bruce said.

"I'm brainstorming," Dottie said, her voice irritated.

"All right, don't get upset. Let's brainstorm about who goes into houses."

"Repair people."

"Right—plumbers, electricians, carpenters… who else makes repairs?"

"I don't know—painters…"

"People delivering furniture."

There was a pause. Then Bruce said, "But none of those people would have a key to the house or know the alarm code. We need people who go into the house regularly."

"Not necessarily, if they were there long enough, they might see the owner use the alarm code and get a copy of the key."

"Right. Spoken like a true cop."

"Okay, what about baby-sitters, or in this case, nannies?"

"They wouldn't have the same nanny in different homes," he said.

"But the nannies might be from the same agency."

"Yeah. What other services go into houses often or for long periods of time?"

"A cleaning service."

He mused, snapped his fingers, "The man who sprays for bugs. And he has the key and the code."

"Right. Also carpet installers, or floor installers, or carpet cleaners."

Dottie jumped up and got her laptop computer from the corner where she had stowed it earlier. She opened it and started typing.

"Okay, first thing tomorrow, I'll call all the home-owners and find out what services go into their houses regularly."

"Hey. Leave that for later. You aren't doing justice to the wonderful wine I poured you."

# CHAPTER FIFTEEN

Tori and Dottie slipped into the church and sat in the back. Tori stifled a yawn. She had not slept well. Another night filled with nightmares of Margaret O'Neal's body. Dottie elbowed her and pointed to Lucille gliding up the aisle on the arm of a handsome man about her age. He stood aside for her to go into the pew first, but she whispered in his ear and he took the inside seat. She sat on the aisle.

A row of women dressed in white sat toward the front on the right-hand side.

"Aren't you Catholic?" asked Dottie.

"I was."

"Why're they wearing white at a funeral?"

"Members of the Rosary Society—women who pray together," Tori said. "Margaret was probably a member."

"Why white?"

"Many Catholics don't wear black at funerals any more," Tori said, "something about celebrating the deceased going to heaven."

"Happy to see you go?" Dottie asked. "Morbid."

Columns of children filed into the front three rows on the left.

"Must be Sunday school students she taught," Dottie said.

"Where's Morrison?" Tori asked.

"He said he'd see us here."

A dozen young children, most sitting with adult women, were scattered throughout the church. "They must be her Guardian ad Litem charges," Tori said, pointing to two or three groups.

A nice-looking man tried to get into the aisle next to Lucille, but she looked down her nose at him and refused to move. His face reddened. He turned to the other side of the aisle, looking for a seat. Martha, Lucille's dance student, waved him to where she sat with three other middle-aged women. He smiled and joined them.

Tori spotted Seth Rothstein sitting toward the back with an attractive woman half his age. *Who's she,* wondered Tori. *That's not jealousy you're feeling, is it?*

A preteen boy bearing a cross led a choir of children dressed in white from the back of the church to the main altar, singing in voices only children possess. "Amazing grace! How sweet the sound that saved a wretch like me."

A priest with a shock of black hair and a ruddy complexion and dressed in white vestments preceded the coffin down the aisle. Annie walked behind the casket, leaning heavily on the arm of a big man. "Who's that?" Dottie asked. "Oh my God!"

Tori said, "It's Morrison."

"Maybe it wasn't the cookies," Dottie said.

After helping Annie into the front pew, Morrison turned as if to sit somewhere else. Annie's hand shot up and took his arm. He leaned down, listened to her whisper and sat next to her.

The pall-bearers placed the white-draped casket at the foot of the altar near the paschal candle. The priest walked around the casket sprinkling it with holy water and praying for Margaret's soul. Tori tried to listen to his prayers, but found herself analyzing the priest. There was something in his voice—*a tension, anger perhaps.* She noted the prominent blood-red veins on his nose, *a heavy drinker? Not unusual in priests.* The priest laid a cross on the coffin and climbed the steps of the altar to say Mass. The congregation prayed for Margaret and the bereaved in the intercessions. Tori was impressed with the number of people who received communion. She and Dottie remained in the pew.

Ellie Francis offered a brief but poignant eulogy to Margaret. She described her friend, her kindness, her sweetness, and her happy nature. She ended by saying how she would miss Margaret. Tears streamed down her face as she walked into her husband's outstretched arms. Tori wondered why the priest did not add his accolades about Margaret to those of Ellie. *Surely, he knew her personally*, she thought.

After the mass the priest sprinkled the casket with holy water once more and commended Margaret's soul to heaven. The pallbearers rolled the casket out of the church while the children sang, "May the angels lead you into paradise: may the martyrs receive you at your coming, and lead you into the holy city, Jerusalem. May the choir of angels receive you, and with Lazarus, who once was poor, may you have everlasting rest."

Annie walked behind the casket, leaning on Morrison.

Morrison, holding a large cat, answered the door for Dottie and Tori at Annie's house. "Didn't know you were a cat lover," Dottie said.

"Can't have her running out the door." Morrison turned and walked back into the house.

*Isn't he defensive?* Tori thought.

Tori looked around as she entered the living room. At one side was an easel displaying photographs of Margaret as a baby, child, young adult, wife and mother. Annie was in a number of the photographs, as were their parents. Tori noted there were no photographs of Margaret with any man other than her husband. *None taken or politically incorrect to show them?* Tori wondered. Several photographs showed Margaret smiling radiantly as she posed with young children.

The priest was consoling Annie. Lucille and her male friend sat in a corner, deep in conversation. A group of women surrounded the man who had tried to sit next to Lucille at the church. "Who's the man talking to Martha and her friends?" Tori asked Dottie.

"That's Jimmie Rafferty," Morrison said from behind her.

Tori turned to see Morrison holding a tray of cookies. "Are you working or putting the make on Annie?" Tori asked.

Morrison ignored her comment and offered them cookies from the tray he was holding. "Annie makes the best cookies in the state." He brushed some crumbs from his suit.

Dottie turned to Tori. "Told you it was the cookies."

"I wouldn't put money on it," Tori said.

"What're you two going on about?" Morrison asked.

Without answering Morrison's question, Tori said, "Martha, the tall woman talking to Jimmie Rafferty, said he borrowed money from women on a cruise."

"Told me he had no money. Went on cruises free if he danced with women," Morrison said. "He must need the money bad the way he talks about the women."

"Martha said he borrowed money from a 'skinny old bird with a wig,'" Dottie said. "Must be the woman in the unnatural auburn hair—that's got to be a wig."

"Dottie and I'll talk to Jimmie and the women," Tori said.

"I'll chat up the priest," Morrison said. "He'll know all the gossip."

"Yeah, and he's by the wine, too." Dottie reached for the tray. "Let me take the tray as a prop."

Morrison took a handful of cookies before relinquishing the tray to Dottie. She and Tori ambled over to the group of women clustered around Jimmy Rafferty. Dottie greeted Martha and handed her the tray. "Would you mind passing this around?"

"No, not at all." Martha left the group.

Dottie and Tori introduced themselves to Jimmie and the women. Jimmie said, "Please excuse me, ladies."

Tori watched him walk over and sit next to Lucille. *Where's the man Lucille was with at the funeral?* She wondered. *He was there a minute ago.*

Dottie asked the women, "How do you know Margaret O'Neal?"

"Friday dances at the K of C," said a spritely woman with keen gray eyes.

"And you are?" Dottie asked.

"Joyce Sarrubo."

Tori turned to the 'skinny old bird with the wig' and asked, "And what's your name?"

"I'm Beverly Sullivan."

Tori looked into a face as bland and intelligent as a slice of white bread. "Nice to meet you," she said.

"Margaret O'Neal was a dancer?" Dottie asked.

"Not really," Joyce said.

"Don't speak ill of the dead," Beverly said. "We just laid the poor woman to rest."

"Don't be silly, Beverly," Joyce said. "You know Margaret wouldn't call herself a dancer, and she wouldn't care if we said she couldn't dance."

"She only went to the dances to hang around Jimmie," Beverly said. "He lent her money, you know."

*Quick switch from talk nice about the dead to tell all the dirt,* Tori thought.

"Beverly, you're so naïve," Joyce said.

"It's the truth. Jimmie told me himself."

Joyce said, "I hope you didn't lend him money."

The guilty expression on Beverly's face left little doubt that she had.

"You silly old fool," Joyce said. "How much did you lend him?"

"Just $5,000. He was short of cash because he lent it to Margaret."

Joyce shook her head.

Beverly said, "He lent her money. She was hard up. That's why she robbed that house."

"Margaret didn't rob any house," Joyce said.

Dottie said, "There's CCTV of her robbing the house."

"Those things can be altered," Joyce said. "I saw that on *Extra.* I've know Margaret for years. She couldn't keep the wrong change, never mind rob a house."

"What about Jimmie Rafferty?" Tori asked, "Were he and Margaret an item?"

Morrison walked up to the priest and asked, "Mind if I join you, Father?"

"Please do, I'm Father McMahon." He put out his hand and Morrison shook it.

"Herb Morrison."

"Have some wine." The priest took a wineglass off the tray next to him. He tipped the bottle to pour, but there was only enough wine to cover the bottom of the glass. "I'll open another bottle."

"No need," Morrison said. "Don't open a bottle for me."

"I'll join you." The priest uncorked the second bottle, filled Morrison's wineglass and topped off his own glass. Morrison examined the tray of glasses. Only two glasses had been used—his and the priest's. *He must have finished the first bottle himself,* Morrison thought. *Heavy drinking even for a priest.*

71

"You must've known Margaret well," Morrison said. "I understand she was very religious."

"That's what she liked people to think," the priest said.

"She wasn't religious?"

"She went to church and taught Sunday school. She did all the right things."

"But???"

The priest did not answer.

Annie joined them, carrying a tray of tiny sandwiches. "Would you like some sandwiches, Father?" The priest examined the tray before picking up a chicken salad sandwich.

Annie said, "Detective?"

The priest jerked, splashing wine on his jacket. He looked at the stain and put his glass on the table. He pulled some napkins off the tray and wiped at the wine.

Annie put down the tray and gathered some more napkins. "Let me help you."

The priest held up his hand. "It's fine."

"I'm so sorry," she said.

Annie picked up the tray and offered it to Morrison. He helped himself to a sandwich and took a big bite.

"I love a man with a healthy appetite," Annie said before walking toward another group.

Morrison turned back to the priest, "You hinted that Margaret wasn't as religious as people thought."

"Enough said, Detective." The priest pushed past Morrison into the kitchen.

*What was that about?* Morrison thought. *Didn't want to talk after finding out I'm a detective?* He turned and bumped into Seth Rothstein.

"Morning, Detective," Rothstein said.

"Dr. Rothstein. Didn't expect to see you here."

"I'm paying respects to Margaret's sister. She was a favorite client."

"Mind telling me where you were Sunday morning?" Morrison asked.

"Am I a suspect?"

"We ask everyone who knew Mrs. O'Neal where they were."

"I was away all weekend," Rothstein said, "with friends."

"Where's the woman I saw you with in church?" Morrison asked.

"You are observant," Rothstein said. "No wonder you're a detective. She had to leave. She had a client."

"Another psychologist?" Morrison asked.

"No a personal trainer. I recommended her to Margaret. You might consider seeing her."

"What for?"

Rothstein looked pointedly at Morrison's middle. "Do something about that belly." He got his wallet out of an inside pocket, pulled out a card and tucked it into Morrison's breast pocket. He patted him on the shoulder and walked into the other room.

Morrison seethed, *arrogant bastard*. He spotted Bob Francis and his wife, Ellie, and went to talk with them. After exchanging pleasantries, Morrison told Bob what the priest had said. "Any idea what he meant?"

"I can't discuss a client," Francis said.

"Do you mean Margaret or the priest?"

"Both."

"Father McMahon wasn't my client and he's not my favorite person. I'll tell you what he meant," Ellie Francis said. "Margaret told me. The good priest was arrested for DUI. He asked Margaret to pay for his attorney."

"She refused?" Morrison asked.

"She helped him the *first* time," Ellie said. "Bob advised her not to pay the priest's fees, but she did. Margaret was very generous."

"Why's he angry with her?"

"The second time he got arrested, she said she'd give him the money if he went into a rehab program to quit. He swore he would."

"Did he?"

"No, of course not. The third time, she said she wouldn't enable his drinking by helping him get off again. Bob wouldn't handle his case the third time, either. The good priest goes to trial in a couple of weeks."

Morrison felt eyes on him and turned. He saw Father McMahon watching him talking with Ellie Francis. Spotting Morrison looking at him, McMahon walked into the kitchen.

# CHAPTER SIXTEEN

Later the afternoon of the funeral Tori arrived at the Gainesville Police Station to find Dottie hunched over her computer, typing furiously. Tori looked over Dottie's shoulder. "What're you doing?"

"The Fuehrer wants a background check on Jimmie Rafferty. Says he's crafty and would never date Margaret O'Neal when Annie was available."

"Not to mention Lucille," Tori said. "Did you see Rafferty chatting her up at Annie's this morning? I wonder what happened to the man she went to the funeral with."

Dottie said, "I asked Beverly who he was. He's new in town. Lucille brought him to the K of C dance last week. I saw him in the kitchen schmoozing with Annie."

"Left Lucille in the lurch. No wonder she was willing to talk to Rafferty. Those women are worse than junior high girls," Tori said.

Dottie snickered and went back to the computer search. "I'll bring the results in when I find something."

Tori stuck her head into Morrison's office.

"Hi, Doc," he said swallowing the cookie he had been munching, "come in." He motioned her to a seat. "What about them Knicks? What a game."

"I'm not much into basketball," Tori said.

"Oh right. You should get Sean to watch the games."

"He watched the game last night. You converted him to a Knicks fan when you had pizza."

"He's a good kid," Morrison said. "What'd you think about Lucille Beauregard?

"Didn't Dottie tell you?"

"Want your take." He held out a plate of cookies. "Want one?"

"No thanks. Annie Curry's?"

"She gave me the leftovers after the funeral."

*This can't bode well for Morrison's relationship with Ruth,* Tori thought.

"Give me your take on Lucille."

"She's angry about Rafferty dropping her for Margaret, but her anger isn't directed at Margaret," Tori said. "She's egocentric and narcissistic."

"Narcissistic? What? Thinks she's beautiful?"

"Yes, but more than that. She craves compliments from people. She's got a sensitive ego. She'd react strongly to any slight."

"Yeah, yeah, right. Bottom line—would she kill Margaret?" Morrison asked.

"Not likely. If anything she'd kill Rafferty. Having said that, I don't think she loves Rafferty or anyone except herself."

Knock, knock, knock. Before Morrison could answer, Chief Connie Murray marched in. She nodded at Tori and said, "What do you have, Detective?"

Morrison swallowed the cookie he had just picked up and wiped the crumbs from his mouth with his hand. "Got a couple of people of interest, no prime suspect."

"Save the bull for the press," she said. "What've you got?

"Epstein is checking out Jimmie Rafferty, Mrs. O'Neal's man friend."

"Why would he kill her?"

"He borrowed money from her."

"Reason not to kill her," the chief said. "Get me more than that. The press is barking at my heels."

"Epstein says Rafferty's girl friend's got motive," Morrison said.

"To kill Rafferty, he's the one who slighted her," Tori said.

Morrison glared at Tori. "Mrs. O'Neal got a judge to take some banker's kids away from him. He's plenty mad."

"What else?"

"Priest is mad at Mrs. O'Neal."

"A priest? You pulling my leg?" The chief walked to the door. "Get on with it, Detective." She closed the door before he could answer.

Tori turned to Morrison, "Miss Congeniality."

"Ain't that the truth?"

"Did you learn anything from the priest?"

"Father McMahon's got a drinking problem."

"He was hitting the wine hard," Tori said.

"Yeah, arrested three times for DUI. Margaret paid his legal fees first two times. Get this—he's mad at her for not helping him with the third DUI. Stopped talking to me when Annie called me 'Detective.'"

"What about Annie? The man Lucille went to the funeral with spent a lot of time talking with her."

"That so?" Morrison asked. "Wondered why Lucille was talking with Rafferty."

"Did Dottie tell you Beverly Sullivan loaned Rafferty money?"

"Yeah. He's a sleaze ball."

As if on cue Dottie waltzed into the office holding papers aloft. "Wait 'til you hear this," she said. "Our friend Jimmie lied. He's no retired teacher. His wife was a teacher. He never went to college. Didn't live in Greenwich, Connecticut either—couldn't afford it. He lived in a working class neighborhood in Port Chester, New York. Was a book salesman. Traveled to book fairs at colleges in New York and Jersey. He knew Iona College because he sold books there, he wasn't a student."

Morrison jumped up, "Knew he was phony. Trying to charm me."

"Fat chance of that," Dottie said.

Morrison grinned. "Yeah."

"Get this," Dottie said. "Margaret left Rafferty $50,000."

"Lucille said he dropped her for Margaret's money," Tori said.

"Yeah," Morrison said, "went on cruises, dancing with women, conning them out of money."

Dottie asked, "Why would he kill Margaret O'Neal if she lent him money?"

"Couldn't pay it back," Tori said. "Or maybe he knew she left him big bucks."

"Well there's no sense in guessing, let's go talk to the boyo," Morrison said.

# CHAPTER SEVENTEEN

Morrison banged on the door. Rafferty opened the door as far as the chain lock would allow. He looked through the space. "What do you want, Detective?"

"A few words."

"Come back later," said Rafferty. "This isn't a convenient time."

Morrison pushed against the door. "It's convenient for us."

Tori, standing to Morrison's left, had a view into the apartment through the partially open door. She watched as a mass of blond hair poked around the corner near the foyer. When the woman spotted Tori, she scampered down the hall toward the bedrooms.

Rafferty looked toward the vanishing blond. He turned back to Morrison and said, "If you must talk now, come in." He closed the door to unlock the chain, and then opened the door wide. Rafferty was wearing a blue silk bathrobe.

"Nice robe," Morrison said. He stage whispered to Tori, "Gift from some woman, I bet."

"Please excuse the turmoil," Rafferty said. "I've been practicing my dance steps." He swept his arm to indicate the room in which the rug had been rolled up and the furniture pushed to the side.

"Strange clothes for dancing," Dottie said.

Rafferty ignored her comment and said, "Please have a seat," as he picked up a straight-backed chair from a corner to add to the single chair and loveseat already against the wall. Dottie quickly sat in the hard chair and Tori headed for the upholstered chair. Her light frame did not tip the chair the way Morrison's weight had the previous day.

Rafferty smiled at Tori. "What's a lovely psychologist doing involved in a so-called murder investigation?"

Tori briefly explained about psychological autopsies and Rafferty said, "How fascinating. Whatever got you into that?"

"Never mind sweet-talking the good doctor," Morrison growled. "We're here about a murder."

Rafferty grinned. "I didn't mean to irritate you." His tone left no doubt that irritating Morrison was exactly what he'd intended. "Tell me how I can help. I'm at your service." He sat on the loveseat with his arms spread across the back. His posture opened the top of his robe displaying a mass of graying chest hair and leaving little room for the over-sized Morrison.

"Mind moving over a bit?" Morrison asked.

"A little homophobic, are we, Detective?" Rafferty asked.

Morrison glared first at Rafferty and then at Dottie who was trying to suppress giggles.

Rafferty said in a steady voice, "I told you everything I know yesterday. What more do you want?"

"Why'd you lie about your background?" Morrison asked, glaring at Jimmie Rafferty.

Rafferty jerked back as if he'd been hit. He looked stunned for a moment. Then he stood. "Excuse me a minute." Rafferty walked down the hall to the bedrooms. The visitors could hear him close the bedroom door and Tori pantomimed with her fingers about seeing someone go down the hall. She mouthed "woman scampering."

The pantomime was lost on Morrison. "Spit it out, damn it, woman," he said in a loud whisper.

When Tori whispered to him, all he heard was "scampering down the hall."

"He has mice?" Morrison asked.

"You saw mice?" asked Rafferty, who had returned wearing khaki slacks and a blue polo shirt.

"No, I told Detective Morrison I thought this photograph was nice," Tori said, indicating the photo of Rafferty with the women on the cruise.

Rafferty looked at the photograph and back at Tori with a puzzled expression.

Morrison got a chair from the kitchen and set it facing the single upholstered chair in the room. "Doc, would you mind moving? Come sit here, Jimmie, me boy." Morrison said, pointing to the upholstered chair. "I want to ask you some questions."

Tori stood up. Jimmie Rafferty sat where directed, his brows knit and a serious expression on his face. Morrison turned the kitchen chair so the back was toward Rafferty and straddled it. He sat directly in front of Rafferty. Morrison was bigger than Rafferty and sitting astraddle the kitchen chair he loomed over him. Rafferty swallowed and turned to watch as Tori sat on the love seat.

"What's this about?" he asked, covering his mouth with his right hand while wrapping his left arm around his waist as if trying to protect his body.

"So, Jimmie, me boy, why did you tell me you were a teacher, when you never went to college?"

Rafferty gave a nervous laugh. "It was a harmless little fabrication." He winked at Tori. "Women like educated men. I'm self-educated, but they don't know that when they meet me. This way they know I'm intelligent and well-read—which I am."

"Lie all you want to get some broad in bed, but lying to the police is a crime."

Rafferty smirked. "I'm duly chastened, Detective."

Morrison's face turned crimson. "I caught you in a bold-faced lie and you have the gall to say it was harmless. What else did you lie about?"

"Not a thing," Rafferty said.

"What about being in bed with some floozy Sunday morning so you couldn't pick Mrs. O'Neal up for church? Was that a lie?"

Rafferty smirked again. "No. That was the truth."

Dottie took out her notebook, opened it and said, "Give me the name and address of the woman with you Sunday morning."

Rafferty bestowed his most radiant smile on Dottie. "The lady is married. She wouldn't like her husband to know."

"She want to see her lover boy in jail?" Morrison asked.

Jimmie Rafferty sat up straight and turned to Morrison. "What are you accusing me of?"

"Tsk, tsk, an educated man like you ending a sentence with a preposition." Dottie said.

Rafferty frowned at Dottie before saying, "All right, Detective. You've got me in a corner. I'll give you Mary Ann's name and phone number. I only ask you to call her at work, so her husband doesn't find out."

"That's more like it," Morrison said, looking down his nose at Rafferty. He turned to Dottie. "Get the *lady's* name and call. See if she confirms our boyo's story."

After Dottie got the name and address, Morris said, "Now, Jimmie, tell us about the money Margaret O'Neal gave you."

"Margaret didn't *give* me any money; she *lent* it to me," he said. It was a loan."

"How much was the *loan*?"

Rafferty looked down, wringing his hands in his lap. "$40,000," he said in a low voice.

"Forty thousand bucks! You kidding? Margaret O'Neal gave you $40,000? You must be some sex cat under the sheets."

"I never had sex with Margaret," he said, looking directly at Morrison with angry eyes. "And I told you it was a *loan*."

Dottie whistled. "When were you planning to repay the loan? When your horse came in?"

Rafferty blushed deeply. Dottie had stumbled on why Rafferty needed to borrow money. "Where's that money, now?" Dottie asked.

"I paid off debts."

"Gambling debts?" Tori asked.

"Yes, gambling debts," Rafferty said, sticking his chin out.

Tori asked, "Did Margaret know you wanted the money to repay gambling debts?"

Rafferty hesitated too long for Tori to put any faith in the veracity of his response. He said, "Of course. I told her I was in trouble. She offered to get me out of it."

Morrison smiled maliciously and waited a moment before saying, "So, Jimmie, what are you planning to do with the money Margaret O'Neal left you in her will?"

Jimmie Rafferty's eyes flew from Morrison to Tori and back, "What money? What are you talking about?"

"You trying to tell me you don't know Margaret O'Neal left you $50,000 in her will?"

Jimmie Rafferty blanched. His eyes grew big and he said, "What did you say?"

"Nice act, Jimmie," Morrison said. "Is that why you killed Margaret? To get your hands on 50 grand?"

Jimmie Rafferty swallowed hard. "Margaret left me $50,000?"

"Come on, Jimmie, you knew that. That's why you killed her, isn't it?"

"I didn't kill her. I told you I was with Mary Anne Sunday morning. Right here." He pulled out a handkerchief and rubbed the sweat off the back of his neck.

"Will $50,000 pay off your gambling debts?"

"I told you, I paid them off already. Margaret gave me the money a couple months ago."

"That's a nice bonus," Morrison said. "You knock off your moneyed lover and start over with enough cash to woo the woman of your dreams."

"Margaret and I weren't lovers." He looked at Tori, his eyes imploring her to believe him. "She didn't believe in sex out of marriage. She was a religious woman."

"But not a hot little number like your Lucille," Dottie said.

"Margaret wasn't my lover, she was a good friend. I didn't kill Margaret. I had no idea she left me anything." His voice was becoming shrill and he spoke rapidly, clutching the soggy handkerchief.

"Did you do it alone or did Lucille help you?" Morrison asked.

"Lucille and I broke up months ago."

"Did the Mob's debt collector force you to kill Margaret?"

Rafferty's eyes flew open. "Wha..." He looked terrified.

"You don't want to cross the Mob, Jimmie, my boy."

At that point Jimmie Rafferty clenched his fists and said the magic words, "I want an attorney." The questioning was over.

Morrison stood up and pointed a finger in Rafferty's face. "Don't leave town without telling me where you're going and how I can reach you."

"Am I still a suspect? Why would I kill Margaret when she loaned me money?"

"You owed her money you couldn't pay back. She wouldn't lend you any more," Tori said.

"Mary Anne will tell you I was with her on Sunday morning."

"Alibi provided by a lover—useless," Morrison said waving his hand as if tossing away the alibi. "Get yourself an attorney. Bring him with you to the station tomorrow morning at 9:00."

After Jimmie Rafferty slammed the door on his visitors, Tori said, "I saw someone with blond hair like Lucille's running down the hallway to the bedrooms."

Dottie said, "That's why he went to change—so he could close the bedroom door. He didn't want her to overhear our conversation."

"Less than a week after Margaret's death the two love birds are back in the sack," Morrison said.

"So much for Lucille's claim she never sleeps with a man until he's given her a ring," Dottie said.

"Maybe he has." Tori said. "Maybe there was enough of that $40,000 left for a ring."

# CHAPTER EIGHTEEN

The Swamp Restaurant was a popular hangout for students, noted for its boisterous parties, a place the three colleagues usually avoided despite its great food. But today they arrived late enough for the noon crowd to have thinned and too early for the evening onslaught. The waitress in a tight tee shirt and designer jeans flashed a smile and asked, "What can I bring you today?"

Dottie asked for the fish taco and Tori requested one of the healthy wraps with alfalfa and avocado. Herb ordered the steak skewers. The waitress did a double take when Herb said, "Leave off the spinach and give me double steak fries instead."

"Part of your new diet?" Tori raised her eyebrows.

"What Ruth doesn't know won't hurt her."

Dottie shook her head.

Morrison leaned his forearms on the table and glared at his colleagues. "We're here to talk about the case, not what I eat for lunch."

The waitress put their drinks on the table. Tori put her straw in her iced tea and took a sip. Dottie played with her straw, unwrapping it and folding the wrapper.

Morrison grinned. "Nets lost again last night. They don't have a chance at the semis."

"They'll make it up in the next three games," Dottie said.

"Yeah, maybe next year."

A few minutes later the waitress returned with their food. Tori picked up her wrap and took a dainty bite. After chewing for a moment, Tori swallowed and said, "It could be the hit-and-run isn't related to the burglaries."

"Yeah, maybe Margaret was killed for her money," Dottie said.

Morrison swallowed the steak he was chewing. "Think my boy Jimmie has the balls to kill?" he asked. "He's a likely suspect. A smooth liar." He picked up some steak fries dripping with ketchup and ate them. He chewed for a moment, and then wiped his mouth with a napkin.

"And he needs the money," Dottie said. She picked up her taco and held it a moment before taking another bite.

"Yeah, but he'd be better off keeping Margaret alive so he could borrow more," Morrison said. He finished the last of the steak before drinking his soda. .

Tori stopped eating. "More likely she was putting pressure on him to repay the loan. Margaret had no patience for the priest not following through with rehab. She had a touch of self-righteousness, perhaps illusory superiority. She wasn't an easy mark."

Morrison was leaned over the table, slurping his drink. He looked up at Tori. "What's this illusory superiority shit?"

Tori said, "It's a social psychological phenomenon. She'd compare herself to Jimmie. Think he was worse than he was. She'd pressure him to repay the loan."

"There's also Lucille," Dottie said. "If thoughts could kill, Jimmie would be dead for dropping her."

"But she was angry with Jimmie, not Margaret," Tori said. The waitress came to ask if they needed anything. Tori asked the waitress for a box for the second half of her wrap. The waitress turned and left.

"Not going to eat that?" Morrison asked.

"Want it?" Tori asked.

Morrison reached over, picked up the wrap, and took a bite.

"What better way to get even with Jimmie for dumping her than killing his golden goose?" Dottie asked.

The waitress returned with a to-go box for Tori. Dottie pointed to Morrison, "She won't need that. We brought our human garbage disposal with us."

Morrison held up his empty soda glass to the waitress. "You ladies want any more?" Dottie and Tori shook their heads.

Tori said, "Lucille wouldn't run Margaret down with a truck; she'd scratch her eyes out."

Dottie nodded. "There's also the Guardian ad Litem program," she said. "The volunteers deal with the scum of the earth, not the least of them being Delgado."

"Yeah. A creep who beats up on a child would have no qualms about hurting an old woman," Tori said.

The waitress returned with Morrison's glass refilled. He picked up the glass and took a drink.

"Epstein, you checked out that Delgado guy's record, yet?" Morrison asked, finishing the last of Tori's wrap.

"I've got a call into the Miami PD. I'll call again when I get back to the office.

"Doc, let's talk to Delgado's neighbor," Morrison said.

# CHAPTER NINETEEN

Morrison coughed to get the attention of the kneeling woman pruning azaleas in her side yard. She looked up, pushing her mammoth straw hat back to see who was there. "Mrs. Maass?" Morrison asked.

"Yes. Who are you?"

Morrison flashed his badge. He introduced himself and Tori and explained why they were there.

Mrs. Maass asked, "Would you mind if I work while we talk?"

"No. In fact, I'll help," Morrison said squatting down beside her. "Can I?" He took the clippers from her and started pruning the plants. "You got to cut them back about a third of the way after they flower. Like this."

"A detective who gardens—who'd have thought?"

Tori said, "He's a master gardener."

"Got to cut the branch down into the plant so it'll fill out," Morrison explained.

"I'm new to gardening—don't know much about azaleas," Mrs. Maass said. "How do I get them to grow taller?"

"Ain't gonna happen." Morrison laughed. "These're dwarf azaleas. Won't grow more than an inch or so."

Tori sat on a stone wall and observed the gray-haired woman sitting on her haunches. She asked, "What can you tell us about Mr. Delgado?"

"Why do you want to know?"

"We talked to his wife," Tori said, "Did you know she was in a domestic violence shelter?"

Mrs. Maass watched Morrison pruning the plants, then pulled a large black plastic bag from her garden tote. "Here, you can put the branches in this." She turned to Tori. "I wondered where she went. Jennifer and I are close. I worried when I didn't hear from her. Where're the children?"

"They're safe. With a family member."

Morrison stuffed some branches into the plastic bag. "We walked around Delgado's house before we came over here," he said. "Impressive garden. Those bleeding heart vines are something else."

"I don't know anything about bleeding heart vines." Mrs. Maass took off her sunglasses and looked at Tori. "But, I know a good deal about finances. Look at that house—a vice president at a regional bank doesn't make the kind of money it takes to buy that house."

"What're you implying?" Morrison asked. He leaned back on his heels to look at her.

"I'm not implying. I'm telling you," she said in a determined voice. "He's mixed up in something illegal."

"That's a big jump from looking at his house."

"Detective Morrison, I spent 30 years working for Aon in Chicago."

"Where?"

"Aon, a diversified financial company. I know finances. My husband was an economist at the University of Chicago until he retired. We're both convinced Ed Delgado got his money illegally. If you're smart, you'll look for some other source of income." She gathered the rest of the branches Morrison had pruned and put them in the black bag. She pulled off her garden gloves and sat on the stone wall next to Tori.

"Where do you think he got his money?" Tori asked.

"Did Jennifer tell you about his 'friends?'" Mrs. Maass asked. Tori said, "Yes, she said he had tough friends."

"Yeah, I'd guess they were involved with the Mob."

"Why?" Morrison asked. He took a large handkerchief out of his back pocket, wiped his hands on it, brushed off his slacks and stood in front of the women who were sitting on the stone wall.

89

"Expensive cars. Flashy jewelry—Rolexes, pinky rings."

"You met them?" Morrison asked.

"No. I saw them going in and out," Mrs. Maass said.

Morrison looked at the neighboring house. "You saw their watches and rings from here?"

"My husband's a birder," Mrs. Maass said. "He has high-powered binoculars. We worried about Jennifer, so after she told us about the men, we checked them out. The guys looked like Mafia to me. Enforcers, you know. I saw enough of them in Chicago to recognize thugs when I see them."

Morrison said, "Tell us about Delgado."

"He's a bully. He tried to intimidate me."

Morrison sneered. "Successfully?"

Tori assumed he knew full-well what the answer would be.

Mrs. Maass lowered her head and looked at him over her sunglasses. "I've had experts try to intimidate me."

"What was he trying to achieve?" Tori asked.

"He wanted to isolate Jennifer. She was becoming too independent for his druthers."

"What else can you tell us about Delgado?" Tori asked.

"He can be charming when he wants to. He tried to convince me that Jennifer was psychologically unbalanced. I pretended I agreed with him so I could continue to see her."

"Mrs. Delgado said her husband threatened you," Tori said.

She smirked. "He told me to stay away from his wife and to stop filling her head with 'crazy' ideas."

"What crazy ideas did he mean?" Morrison asked.

"I was encouraging her to go back to college."

Morrison asked, "Why'd he think that was crazy?"

Mrs. Maass turned toward Tori. "Haven't you explained to him about abusive husbands and how they isolate their wives?"

Morrison's voice did not hide his irritation. "Why don't you explain it to me?"

"Eduardo beat …"

"Hold on a minute," Morrison said. "Eduardo? I thought his name was Edward."

"He goes by Edward, but his birth name is Eduardo."

Morrison said, "Go on."

"He beat Jennifer. He kept her from seeing her family, didn't let her work and tried to keep her from talking to me."

"The typical abusive spouse," Morrison said.

Mrs. Maass inclined her head. "Right."

# CHAPTER TWENTY

Immediately after lunch Dottie developed a spreadsheet. She listed all the homes burglarized in the last three years in one column and every possible type of service across the rows at the top. She completed the matrix and checked her watch, 2:30. She drummed her fingers on her desk, then went to Starbucks and got a café latté with skim milk. She was back at her computer by 3:05.

Ten minutes later Morrison stopped by her desk. "Find anything on this Delgado creep?"

"They've got nothing on him in Miami."

He stomped off. "Damn!"

Dottie continued the tedious process of contacting the homeowners. Her café latté was long gone before she found a pattern. "Eureka!" She pumped her fist in the air with a wide grin.

Dottie burst into Morrison's office without knocking. "Lookie here, Morrison! I've found the connection."

Herb Morrison was tilted back in his huge executive chair, feet on the desk, head resting on his chest, catching a snooze. He had a big smile on his face. Dottie saw the telltale jerk of his head as he woke up. *He'll be roaring mad*, she thought. *He was probably dreaming about sitting in Annie Curry's Florida Room eating plate after plate of homemade cookies. I'd better convince him before he wakes up completely and chews my head off.*

Looking groggy, Morrison put his feet on the floor.

Pretending she hadn't noticed he had been sleeping, Dottie walked behind her boss' desk and spread the printout in front of him. "Look at this. Most of the burglarized homes use the same house cleaning service, Heavenly Maids."

Morrison took the printout from Dottie and grumbled. "This better be good."

Dottie pointed to the column listing the cleaners. Morrison took a deep breath and tried to understand the paper in front of him, wiping the dreamt cookies from his mouth. It took a moment for his mind to reorient before he observed the pattern Dottie had discovered.

"Good job, Epstein. Let's go interview the Phillips." Suppressing a moan, he leaned on the desk pulling his body onto creaky knees.

"The Phillips the people got the CCTV video of Margaret O'Neal?" Dottie asked.

"Yeah, get the file. Refresh my memory on the drive." The phone interrupted their conversation. "Morrison."

"Yeah, Don. Thanks for returning my call." Morrison sat again and grinned into the phone. He leaned back in his chair and turned it around so he was looking out the window. "How do you like Miami?"

After a pause, he said, "Me, too. Can't beat the weather."

Dottie took a deep breath and crossed her arms. She leaned against the wall, gritting her teeth. Morrison was jawing with an old crony. This could take forever.

"Just fine. How's Marianne?" Morrison asked. He waited for an answer before asking, "What do you have on our friend?"

There was a long pause. Morrison swung his chair around to his desk and picked up a pen. He held the phone with his shoulder and took notes.

"Great. Thanks, Don."

Morrison stood. "We're going to interview Delgado. Call Tori. Tell her to meet us there. I want her to watch his body language."

"Now? Before we interview the Phillips?"

"Right now."

Knock! Knock!

An officer stuck his head around the door. "Chief wants you in her office."

"Shit, not now," Morrison muttered. Out loud he said, "I'll check in later."

"She said, now."

"Tell her I'm on a hot lead."

"It's your head." The officer closed the door.

Dottie asked, "Who was on the phone?"

"Old buddy from Paterson. I phoned him a while ago and left him a message asking about Delgado. He gave me info."

"Delgado's got no record. I checked it out."

"It's off the record," Morrison said. "Don dealt with Eduardo when he lived in…"

"What's this Eduardo, shit? I thought his name was Edward."

"He goes by Edward, but his real name is Eduardo. Don tried to arrest him umpteen times. Back when he lived in Miami before he came up here to college. Don says Eduardo was an enforcer for the Cuban mob that runs the gambling game."

"Yeah, but they never caught him doing anything illegal."

"What if he's working with the same group, now?"

"We've got no proof."

"What if he collected the money Jimmie owed in gambling debts?"

Dottie opened her eyes wide. "Hot damn, Morrison, that's the connection! Delgado wanted Mrs. O'Neal dead and Rafferty owed him money. Rafferty paid off his debt by running Mrs. O'Neal down."

"You got it."

## CHAPTER TWENTY ONE

Morrison stormed through the bank lobby, nodded at the receptionist, and barged into Delgado's office with Dottie and Tori close behind him. The receptionist jumped up and followed the detectives, calling to them to stop. Delgado's head jerked up and he reached for the drawer handle on the left side of his desk. He stammered, "Who…? Wha…?"

Dottie flashed her badge at the receptionist as she closed the door in her face.

Morrison watched Delgado reaching for his desk drawer. "Got a gun in there?" Morrison asked as he showed his badge.

"I have a license," Delgado said, putting his hands on his desk. "Banks get robbed, you know. The way you forced your way in here, I thought you were bank robbers."

"Bet you know a few bank robbers," Morrison said.

"What the hell does that mean?"

"Tell us about your relationship with Jimmie Rafferty," Morrison said.

Tori observed Delgado's eyes flick to the side. He said nothing. She asked, "Is he a bank customer?"

"I don't know all the customers."

"He's a private loan customer," Morrison said.

"The bank doesn't have private loan customers."

"Not a bank customer," Morrison said. "Your private customer."

Delgado's eyes narrowed and his hands gripped the desk. "What are you implying?"

"How well you know Juan Pablo Iglesias?" Morrison asked.

Tori noted the same eye flick to the side.

"Who?" Delgado asked.

"C'mon," Morrison said. "You worked for Iglesias in Miami."

"That was 20 years ago, for Christ's sake."

"Was it?" Morrison asked. "I think you're working for him now."

The phone on the desk rang and Delgado reached to answer it. Morrison slammed his hand on top of Delgado's, keeping him from lifting the phone. "Let it ring."

Morrison released Delgado's hand. Delgado rubbed his reddening hand. "What do you want?"

"You're working for Iglesias, aren't you?" Dottie asked.

"I ran errands for Mr. Iglesias when I was in high school."

"Yeah right!" Morrison said. "Collecting loans?"

"I don't know what you're talking about."

"Iglesias ran a gambling racket, right?" Morrison towered over Delgado's desk.

"All I did was run errands—got him coffee, went to the store, that kind of stuff. Nothing illegal."

"Remember Detective Tomlinson?" Morrison asked.

"Can't say I've had the pleasure." Delgado's eyes were flitting from Morrison to Dottie to Tori.

"He remembers you," Morrison said. "Thinks you were an enforcer for Iglesias—you collected gambling debts."

"I've never been convicted of any crime."

"Collecting debts for Iglesias was good training for becoming a wife beater and child abuser," Tori said.

"That's it. I'm not talking to you without my attorney."

Tori whispered to Morrison. He nodded and looked at Delgado. "Right. Be at my office tomorrow morning at 9:00—sharp. Bring your lawyer." Morrison flipped his card onto Delgado's desk. "We'll find our way out."

Dottie said, "You unnerved him."

"Did you see his eyes flicker when you mentioned Rafferty?" Tori asked.

"So what?" Dottie asked.

"People do that when they're lying," Tori said. "He knows him all right."

"He did the same thing when Morrison asked about Iglesias," Dottie said.

"You noticed it, too?"

"Why'd you want him at the department at the same time Rafferty comes tomorrow?" Morrison asked Tori.

She explained.

"Brilliant," Dottie said.

Morrison said, "I can't wait to interview them tomorrow."

"His attorney won't let him answer any questions," Dottie said.

"I can still get his knickers in a twist."

Dottie rolled her eyes and looked at Morrison, "Where do you come up with those expressions?"

"That came from my dear old granny."

Dottie shook her head. She almost bumped into Morrison as he stopped suddenly. He squatted down with his back to Dottie and Tori.

"Are you all right? What's the matter?" Tori asked.

"These day lilies."

Dottie grasped her head with both hands and moaned. "Morrison, this is a murder investigation. Can't you do your gardening on your own time?"

Morrison stood and brushed his hands together to get rid of the dirt. He stood silently, looking into the sky with unfocused eyes. "I'm trying to remember something." He snapped his fingers. "Annie's."

"Morrison, have you finally cracked?" Dottie asked.

He looked at Dottie over his sun glasses. "Annie Curry has some of these day lilies in her yard."

Dottie threw her hands in the air. "So…" Her voice demonstrated her exasperation.

"So I've been trying to buy these day lilies for months. They're hybrids. They're Holy Spirits—creamy yellow color. Can't get them anywhere."

Dottie shrugged. "What? Delgado and Annie Curry shop at the same nursery."

"No one sells them around here."

"What's your point?" Tori asked.

"I saw some at Delgado's. I've been trying to remember where else I saw them. Don't you see? It's the connection between Margaret O'Neal and Delgado. Annie said Margaret was the one who 'played with flowers.' If Rafferty wanted to get on Margaret's good side, you know, he'd give her rare flowers."

"He got them from Delgado!" Dottie said.

"You're not as dumb as you look."

# CHAPTER TWENTY TWO

"Call the Phillips. Tell them we're coming," Morrison said to Dottie as he pulled his unmarked car out of the bank parking lot. Tori waved from her car as she pulled out of her parking space.

When Dottie completed the call and put away her phone, Morrison asked her to refresh his memory about the Phillips. She opened the file on the burglary and went through it. "The Phillips are self-made millionaires. They own the College Pizza chain.

Morrison stopped at a red light. He turned to his colleague. "Any sign of dirt?"

"Nah. So clean they sparkle."

"Get their mortgage through Delgado?"

"Bought the house before Delgado started at the bank."

Morrison turned into the gated community in the northwest outskirts of Gainesville. He stopped at the guardhouse, opened his window and showed his ID to the guard. After going through the gate, he drove through meandering streets with overhanging live oaks and impeccable lawns surrounding huge mansions. The Phillips' traditional brick house sat on a large expanse of property. Morrison was as impressed by the size of the house on this visit as he had been when he interviewed the Phillips after the burglary.

Dottie whistled. "The pizza business has done well for them. The house looks like one of the mansions along A1A. You know the ones, between Jacksonville and St. Augustine."

"More land. Got three acres."

"Wow!"

"Eight bedrooms, ten bathrooms. Could run a hotel. Even have a media room."

"How many people live there?" Dottie asked.

"Two."

"A little pretentious for Gainesville, don't you think?"

"I don't know." He shrugged. "If you've got it, flaunt it."

"Yeah, but then don't be surprised if someone burglarizes your house."

Brian Phillips answered the doorbell and led them into the living room—which he pompously called the "drawing room." *He's been watching too many British films*, Dottie thought. It was eerie going into the house she had seen being burglarized on video.

Mavis Phillips stood as the detectives entered. Her dank brownish hair accentuated the narrowness of her long face and angular neck. The Phillips, in their mid to late 50s, were both tall and thin, almost too thin, and awkward in their bearing, as if they would be more comfortable making pizzas than entertaining people. Both wore expensive, yet unflattering, clothes. His outfit was on the loud side. *Some salesman saw him coming,* mused Dottie, taking in his plaid jacket and bright colored pants. Mavis' clothes were more conservative, neutral colors and classic lines. *Her clothes look like hand me downs from an older sibling with a different shape.*

A fireplace consumed a third of the east wall, drawing Morrison's attention. He commented on the photographs displayed on the mantelpiece.

"Those are our sons." Mr. Phillips beamed. "They're both attorneys. They went to the University of Florida and to Harvard Law. Only the best for our boys."

"They're bright boys and worked hard. They deserve everything we give them," said his wife.

He said, "They have such influential friends; we're taking night courses at the university, so we won't embarrass them."

"There's nothing to be embarrassed about," Mrs. Phillips said, standing straighter. "My husband and I studied art on our own for years. You can see we collect modern art." She waved her arm to indicate the paintings and sculptures. "We're learning about antiques and architecture at the university."

Dottie thought, *did they really pay good money for that junk?*

100

"Nice collection," Morrison said. "Can we sit?"

"Of course, please forgive me," Mavis Phillips said.

"Have you found our jewelry?" her husband asked.

"No, but we're working on it. My colleague discovered connections between the burglarized houses. Epstein, tell the Phillips what you found."

Dottie reminded Mrs. Phillips about her phone call earlier that morning. "Oh, yes." She turned to her husband. "I told you about that, Brian."

He nodded at his wife. "What'd you find? Has someone been in all the houses?"

"Well, not every house, but someone's been to most—Heavenly Maids."

"One of the maids went back to rob the houses?" he asked.

"No, the maids don't have access to the keys. It must be someone higher up."

The Phillips looked at each other. Mrs. Phillips said, "I don't think there is anyone except Carlos in administration."

"Who's he?" Morrison asked.

"The owner."

"He has access to the keys and the alarm codes," Dottie said.

Mr. Phillips frowned. "You're barking up the wrong tree with that one, my dear. Carlos Sanchez is an honest man. A few years ago he returned a ruby ring my wife never noticed was missing."

"I would have noticed the next time I wanted to wear it," she said.

"Honey, I'm not faulting you." He patted her hand. "I'm saying he could've kept the ring. We'd never've been the wiser. Instead, he brought it back."

She said, "He found it in one of the maids' lockers. He fired her on the spot and returned the ring."

"He was concerned there was no taint of dishonesty to blemish his company's reputation. I recognize his entrepreneurial spirit. It's the same hard-working honesty that got me and my wife where we are today," Mr. Phillips said. "Carlos Sanchez is not the sort of man who robs houses."

"Perhaps, there's someone else who works for him who has access to the keys?" Dottie suggested.

"No, not a chance," Mr. Phillips said. "He emphatically told us he was the only one with access to keys or information about the houses. He hands out the keys immediately before the women go to clean and collects them when they finish."

# CHAPTER TWENTY THREE

"Over there." Tori's partner Kevin Cunningham pointed. "There're two seats next to Gladys."

"No. Let's sit here by the center."

"Why not sit with Gladys?" Kevin asked.

Gladys waved.

Kevin said, "See, she's waving us over."

Tori waved to Gladys. "She's waving to us, not waving us over."

"Why don't you want to sit with Gladys?" Kevin asked. "You're friends, aren't you?"

"We are friends—that's why I don't want to sit next to her."

"You're talking in code," said Kevin. "What do you mean?"

"Excuse me," Tori said to the man on the aisle as she climbed over him to the empty seats.

Kevin stumbled over the man's feet. "Sorry."

"No problem," the man said. "The seats are too close together."

Tori put her purse on the empty chair next to her and pulled out her iPad.

"So what's with you and Gladys?" asked Kevin."

"I think Gladys has the hots for Seth Rothstein."

"No way." Kevin craned his neck so he could see Gladys sitting next to Rothstein on the other side of the room. "He's sleazy."

"God, Kevin, you men are all alike," Tori said. "You think there's something wrong with any man who dresses nicely. Rothstein's suave, not sleazy."

"That's what my wife says."

"Aha! Do I detect a hint of jealousy about Edie?"

"Edie is gaga over Rothstein." Kevin stretched to look again. "Gladys and Rothstein are awfully cozy."

"Stop staring."

A young woman in a beige suit brought their attention to the podium. She said, "Our speaker tonight is our own Dr. Michael Silverman. He's going to present his research on false memory."

Ten minutes into the talk, Kevin leaned toward Tori and whispered, "What tripe! You'd do a better job on that topic."

Tori elbowed him. "Hush. Take your CEUs and be grateful."

After the talk Gladys walked over to where Tori and Kevin were standing. "Why didn't you come when I waved you over?" Gladys asked. "I saved you seats."

"I thought you wanted to be alone with the handsome Dr. Rothstein," Tori said.

Gladys looked over her glasses at Tori. "Do I detect some projection?"

Tori blushed.

Kevin asked, "What's with the blushing? What aren't you telling me?"

"Let's get some coffee," Tori said.

"I can't. I've got an early appointment," Gladys said. "Maybe you can join Dr. Rothstein."

Tori pulled the handle on the urn and filled the Styrofoam cup under the spout with coffee. "Is that decaf?" a male voice asked.

"I sure hope so or I'll be awake all night." Tori turned toward the speaker.

"The lovely Dr. Vincent," Seth Rothstein said.

"Good evening, Seth," Tori said. "Let me introduce you to my partner, Kevin Cunningham."

Seth extended his hand. "Edie's husband. She's my client."

Kevin shook Seth's hand. "She's very impressed with you."

"A delightful young woman."

Tori asked, "Seth, Annie Currie said her sister had become friends with one of your clients—a woman you saw right before Mrs. O'Neal. Do you know who that is?"

"As much as I'd like to help you, Tori, you know I can't reveal a client's name."

"Of course. I understand you can't give me her name because of confidentiality." Tori pulled out a business card. "I wonder if you would be willing to ask her to contact me." She wrote on the card. "My home number is on the back. I'd like to talk to her."

Rothstein took the card. "I'm sure I can find a use for your home number."

Tori smiled. "Please give your client the card."

"I'm not sure I know who she is. If someone comes to mind, I'll ask her to contact you. Can you give me any more information about her?"

"No. Annie never met her. She couldn't give me any description. She thinks her name's Karen."

"Okay," Seth said. "Excuse me, I see a colleague I need to speak to." He gave Tori a kiss on the cheek. "I'll call you."

Kevin watched Seth walk away. He turned to Tori. "You two seem rather intimate. Is there anything you aren't telling me?"

"He's one of those men who think they're so good-looking, women want them to touch them."

"You don't?"

Tori said, "I didn't say that."

Kevin watched Seth walk over to another man. "I think Rothstein breached confidentiality," Kevin said. "He shouldn't have told us Edie is his client."

"We both knew she was seeing him," Tori said.

"Are you defending him?"

"No, I…"

"His confidentiality was strong enough when you asked about a client," Kevin said.

"You're jealous."

"I say he's sleazy."

"Suave is the term Gladys uses," Tori said. She felt her cell phone vibrating and pulled it out of her purse and flipped it open. "Tori Vincent."

"Dr. Vincent, this is Annie Currie. Herb Morrison… he…he's… had an attack. Please help…"

"Calm down, Miss Currie. What happened?"

"Herb's at my house. He's unconscious."

"Call 911."

"He told me not to. He doesn't want his wife to…"

"I'm on my way. Call 911. I'll cover for him."

Tori heard the ambulance sirens in the distance. Kevin's car careened around the corner and skidded to a stop in the driveway. They raced to the house. Annie was standing in the front door, her hair disheveled, tears streaming down her face. "He's in here." She led them into the bedroom. Morrison lay on the floor. He was shirtless and his pants belt unbuckled. His eyes were closed. He was a pasty shade of gray.

Kevin bent over Morrison and checked the pulse in his neck. "He's alive."

"What happened?" Tori asked Annie.

"Herb came by and we were…were talking…" She started to weep. "I never do anything right." She collapsed onto the bed and buried her face in her hands.

Tori clutched Annie by her shoulders. "Get a grip, Annie," Tori said. "There's no time for this. We need to call Herb's wife. Tell me what happened. We've to get our act straight. When did he collapse?"

Annie looked up at Tori. "We walked into the bedroom." She gulped. "We kissed. He took off his shirt and then…"

"Okay. Listen up," Tori said. "I came over with Morrison. We came into Margaret's bedroom because we wanted to search it again. He collapsed. You're a nurse. You told me to take off his shirt and loosen his belt. Right?"

"Right," Annie said. She rubbed her face with her hands.

The ambulance screeched into the driveway, sirens blaring. Kevin opened the door. He led the EMTs to the bedroom where they encircled Morrison. They checked his vital signs, inserted an IV and started fluids.

"When did he collapse?" The head EMT asked.

Tori turned to Annie who sat on the bed sobbing. "Annie, when did he collapse?"

"I don't know. Maybe 10 – 15 minutes ago." Annie got up and stood over the EMTs wringing her hands. "If I'd known he was sick, I'd never have…"

Tori said, "Sit down and get out of their way."

Tori pulled out her phone and dialed Morrison's home number. "Mrs. Morrison?"

Ruth said, "Yes."

"This is Tori Vincent. I work with your husband."

"He's not home."

"I know. I'm with him. We were interviewing a witness and he collapsed. The ambulance is here."

Ruth told Tori that Morrison was pre-diabetic. Tori relayed the information to the EMTs.

Annie sprang up. "I'll get some orange juice."

Tori said into the phone, "Hold on. They're getting him orange juice."

Annie handed the orange juice to the EMT kneeling next to Morrison. He gave Morrison a couple sips. Morrison moaned. The EMTs lifted him onto a stretcher.

Tori said, "I'll go with him. Kevin, would you pick up his wife?" She handed Kevin her phone.

Kevin got Morrison's address from Ruth over Tori's phone and handed it back to her.

The EMTs wheeled Morrison toward the door. Tori followed them, stuffing the phone in her pocket.

"I'll go with you to the hospital," Annie said.

Tori glared at her. "You stay here. His wife is going to the hospital."

Annie stood in the doorway, whimpering.

# CHAPTER TWENTY FOUR

Tori leaned back in her chair and rested her feet on the stool next to her desk in her home office. It was 7:30 a.m. She liked to get a head start on the day and finally had slept all night without nightmares about Mrs. O'Neal. She was reading a dissertation on Munchausen by Proxy, the syndrome in which a caregiver makes a child ill in order to get attention for himself or herself, usually the latter. Marilyn, a talented student, had correlated the attention-getting behavior of the mother when she was a child to the syndrome when she was grown and had children. It was a fascinating research project.

Tori reached for the ringing phone, not bothering to check the caller ID. "Tori Vincent."

She dropped her feet to the floor, silently cursing when she heard her mother's voice. "I've been trying to get hold of you for days. Where've you been?"

"Hello to you, too, Mom," said Tori, chiding herself for her brittle tone.

"You don't need to be snide. I've been worried."

"I'm sorry, Mom. I didn't mean to snap. I've been busy."

"Too busy to talk to your mother? Or your sister? Cindy's been calling, too."

"You would hear from me more often if you learned to use the internet. I could email you."

"So now it's my fault you won't answer the phone?"

Tori took a deep breath. She counted to ten. *I'm a psychologist,* she reminded herself. *Why do I let my mother unnerve me?*

"Mom, I'm sorry. I've started a new case and haven't been home much." It was an outright lie. She was home Sunday evening when her mother called, but that time she'd been smart enough to check caller ID. Bless Sean—he had warned her that Gran had called earlier, and was on the warpath about something.

"A new case? Another psychological autopsy?"

*Oh, drat.* Tori closed her eyes and winced. She had stepped onto a minefield. She'd forgotten her mother hated her little girl dealing with death and murder.

"Yes, Mother. That's what a forensic psychologist does—psychological autopsies."

"Don't call me Mother—you only do that when you're angry."

"Sorry, Mom." *Why did every sentence spoken to her mother start with "sorry?"*

"Doesn't that university pay you enough? You don't need another job. If you're tight for money, ask your father. He seems to have plenty."

"How is Dad?"

"He's fine. But don't change the subject. Why are you doing a psychological autopsy?"

"Moth...Mom. I've explained before—I do psychological autopsies because it's good for my career. It's also a service to the community."

"If you say so."

"Mom, why are you calling me? Is something wrong?" Tori hoped her voice did not betray her irritation.

"Yes, something's wrong. Cindy's going to divorce Derrick. She needs to give the marriage a chance."

"Derrick abused Cindy. She should divorce him."

"He said some ugly things—we all do when we're angry."

*You sure do,* thought Tori. "He did more than say ugly things. He threatened her and threw things at her. She was afraid for her life."

"Everyone throws things when they're mad. I've even done it."

"I know you've thrown things, but most people call that abuse." Tori picked up a pencil and threw it at the photograph of her mother on the bookcase. The pencil ricocheted off a book and fell to the floor.

"Your father used to throw things, too."

Tori looked at the ceiling. "I don't remember Dad ever throwing anything."

"He hit me, too."

"Mother, that's not true. You're imagining things." Tori picked up another pencil and sent it following the first one. Ping. It hit its mark, but had no impact on the photo.

"Don't you talk to me like *that*. Remember I was the one who stood by you when Gerry left you alone with a baby."

"Actually, I took Sean and left Gerry." Tori did not add Gerry was so glad to see her go; he'd filed for divorce while she and baby Sean were still en route to her new job in Gainesville.

"I told you from the beginning he was no good for you."

"Mother, you're reconstructing history. You told me you thought he was good looking and a nice catch—a future attorney."

"I never said that. I said all along he was a Romeo and would never settle down."

"Whatever."

"You need to talk to Cindy. If I'd been more attentive when you started dating Gerry, I might've been able to stop the marriage."

Tori took a deep breath, "I'll talk to Cindy."

"Good. I wish my mother had been more involved with me when I got married. I might have married Robert Baker. He's a well-known doctor, you know, wealthy now."

Tori closed her eyes and counted to ten. She was still boiling so she counted to 20 in Spanish, which took more concentration.

"Victoria! Are you there?"

"Yes, Mom, I'm here. Mom, stay out of Cindy's life. It won't do any good and could push her in the wrong direction."

"What about you? Who are you seeing now?"

Tori thought, *you've got to be kidding. You want me to tell you about my personal life so you can berate me for it?* "I told you I'm busy. I don't have time for dating."

"A beautiful young woman like you should have lots of dates. You need someone in your life, especially now that Sean is getting older. Your sister wants to remarry."

110

*Yeah, maybe Cindy's third marriage will stick,* thought Tori. She said, "Mom, I'm sorry, I have an appointment at the police station. I'll call you next week."

"You're always in a hurry to get off the phone."

*Why do you suppose that is?* "Bye, Mom, give my love to Dad."

# CHAPTER TWENTY FIVE

A pretty Latina in jeans and an apron embroidered "Heavenly Maids" answered the door to Dottie who walked in past the open-mouthed woman. Carlos Sanchez, yelling in Spanish, stood amid a gaggle of women wearing similar jeans and aprons. He was what Dottie's grandmother would have called a "dandy." Average height, he had the slim-waisted physique of a bullfighter. His thick wavy black hair was slicked back. He looked over at Dottie with sensuous brown eyes—*most women would kill for his lashes*, she thought.

He exuded sexuality. He looked Dottie up and down, then gazed into her eyes for a moment too long. He flashed brilliant white teeth, winked and said, "I'll be with you in a minute, Sweetheart. I'm giving the girls their instructions for the day."

Ignoring the wink, Dottie said, "No problem. I'll wait."

The three women with their backs to the door turned at the sound of Dottie's voice. They opened their eyes wide then asked Sanchez something in Spanish. He cut them off. "De nada." The women kept whispering among themselves until Sanchez shouted at them, "Corta! Corta!" Dottie knew enough Spanish to understand "shut up" and to realize the women were worried about immigration.

All the women were young and attractive, Dottie noted. *Typical male*, she thought, *only hiring pretty young women when others needed the job more and would be better qualified.*

112

Dottie leaned against the wall, and crossed her arms while scrutinizing Sanchez. The cuffs of his pleated slacks broke on his highly polished loafers at the precise point required by fashionistas. His yellow silk shirt had a designer logo on the pocket. What caught Dottie's eye were the Rolex watch and diamond pinky ring.

Dottie left her spot against the wall to look around the office while Sanchez finished with the workers. She could feel Sanchez's eyes on her back as she strolled to the wall map with red pins indicating the houses Heavenly Maids cleaned. She lingered at the map, pretending to examine it while she watched Sanchez from the corner of her eye. He seemed more intent on Dottie than on the women he was ordering around. Dottie wandered over to his desk and looked over the papers on it. She was an expert at reading papers upside-down.

Sanchez shooed the women out of the office and sat behind his desk. He turned the papers Dottie had been perusing face down. He smiled at her. "Every morning's like this. I organize the day for four teams of women."

"I know how a maid service works," Dottie said.

"What can I do for you?" Sanchez asked.

Dottie flashed her badge and slowly pulled out her notebook. "Tell me if your service cleans the following houses…" She listed one by one the houses that had been burglarized. Sanchez confirmed the first two before he seemed to have second thoughts. He spoke calmly, but Dottie observed beads of sweat breaking out on his upper lip. When she mentioned the Phillips' house he looked toward the ceiling and hesitated before saying, "I'm not sure about that one. I'll have to check the files."

"Go ahead. I'll wait." She was positive he remembered. How could he forget going to the Phillips' house to return a ruby ring? But she sat calmly while he went to the cabinet and shuffled through the files. He brought one of the files back to his desk and said, "Oh, of course. I'd forgotten. I found a ruby ring in one of the women's lockers. I confronted her and she admitted stealing it from the Phillips' house. I fired her then and there, but I had to return the ring and apologize to the Phillips. You can't imagine how embarrassed I was."

He smiled broadly. "They're nice people, very gracious. They didn't know the ring was missing. They were grateful I brought it back personally."

"They must have been impressed you returned something they didn't know was missing."

Sanchez took a deep breath and once more displayed his perfect teeth. "All in a day's work."

Dottie asked, "Do you clean the Winslow house on north 114th Way? Or the Levine house on NW 100th?" The owners of those burglarized houses did not list Heavenly Maid as their cleaning service.

"I don't recognize those addresses. I'd have to look them up."

"Go ahead." Dottie crossed her arms.

Sanchez stood and went to the file cabinet. He pulled out a drawer. After a few minutes, Sanchez said, "No, we don't clean either of those houses."

"Did you ever clean them?"

"I don't know. We've cleaned lots of houses. I'd have to look in the archives."

"Go ahead, I've got time."

"I don't keep those files here." Sanchez patted his top lip with a monogrammed linen handkerchief.

"Check on them and let me know." Dottie handed him her card. "Do you know if any of the houses you clean were robbed recently?"

Sanchez wiped his forehead and said, "I only know if the homeowner tells me."

Dottie narrowed her eyes and stared at Sanchez. "All the houses I asked about have been burglarized in the last couple of years."

Sanchez opened his eyes wide. "What has that got to do with my service?"

"We're trying to find a connection between the houses. You have keys to the houses, don't you?"

"How else would we get in?" Sanchez sat back behind the desk and started straightening the papers again. His fingers left damp marks on them.

"What if the house has a burglar alarm? Do you have the code?"

"Of course we have the code. We need it to get in. But the keys and codes are kept under lock and key. I only give them to the girls when they're going to the house."

Sanchez ran his hands through his perfectly coiffed hair. He wiped the sweat off his brow and upper lip with his wrinkled handkerchief.

Dottie looked at Sanchez's wrist and said, "That's a great watch. Is it a Rolex?"

Sanchez blanched. He stammered, "It…it's… it's a knock-off. I got it on the street in Miami."

Dottie nodded and smiled a knowing smile. *Like hell you did,* she thought.

# CHAPTER TWENTY SIX

Tori walked into Morrison's office a few minutes before 9:00 am. "How're you feeling, Herb?"

Morrison looked down. "Had a reaction to sugar—all those cookies. Kept me for observation. Let me go early this morning."

"You look awful. I hope you learned your lesson."

"I did," Morrison said. He looked at her. "Tori, thank you for covering for me. You know, Annie and I didn't do anything…"

"Only because you went into a diabetic coma."

"Yeah, right." Morrison nodded.

"You were lucky. You got a wake up call."

"I don't know what came over me. I'm an old fool. I love Ruth and would never hurt her."

"That's good."

"As soon as this case is over, I'm taking some time off. I'll take Ruth on a second honeymoon. She's always wanted to go a Caribbean cruise."

"I'm glad to hear that," Tori said. "You deserve some time off and you need to show Ruth you love her."

"Yeah, right. I told her I'd take ballroom dancing with her," Morrison said. "She's been after me for years to take lessons."

"She must be thrilled."

"Yeah." Morrison picked up a folder. "Epstein is keeping Rafferty in a front office. Delgado's in the interview room with his attorney. C'mon. Watch me interview him."

He led Tori to the observation room before going into the interview room. Tori watched through the one-way mirror as Delgado drummed his fingers on the metal table. When Morrison entered, Delgado scowled at him. "Is this supposed to make me crack and confess? It won't work. It makes me more determined than ever."

His attorney placed his hand on Delgado's arm. "Take it easy, Ed."

Morrison switched on the recorder. "Let the record show that at 9:13 am, Thursday April 17th, Detective Herb Morrison is interviewing Eduardo Delgado with his attorney Joseph Lavanderos."

Delgado snapped, "My name is Edward."

Morrison said, "Not on your birth certificate, it isn't."

"Mr. Delgado goes by Edward," Lavanderos said.

Morrison shrugged. "Mr. Delgado, we're interested in your interactions with Juan Pablo Iglesias. How do you know him?"

Delgado leaned toward his attorney and whispered in his ear with his hand covering his mouth. Morrison sat back in his chair, staring at Delgado. The attorney whispered something to Delgado who said, "I worked for Mr. Iglesias in Miami a number of years ago."

"Collecting gambling debts?"

"No," Delgado snapped. "I ran errands for him after school. I was in high school, for God's sake."

"That's when you had a run in with Detective Tomlinson?"

Delgado had another whispered conversation with his attorney. Delgado said, "Detective Tomlinson stopped me while I was running an errand for Mr. Iglesias. He did not arrest me or file charges."

"You were an enforcer for Iglesias, weren't you?"

"No. I told you, I never did anything illegal."

"What about Jimmy Rafferty? Did you collect a gambling debt from him?"

Delgado glared at Morrison, his hands clutching the edge of the table so tight his knuckles were white. "I do not collect gambling debts. I am a banker." He spoke slowly and harshly.

"Mr. Delgado, how well do you know Jimmie Rafferty?"

"I don't know him."

"How much did you lend him?" Morrison asked.

"Is he a customer of the bank?" Delgado asked, "I don't know all the customers."

"We know you loaned him money personally."

Delgado said, "I never lend money to people except through the bank."

"Mr. Delgado, how well do you know Carlos Sanchez?" Morrison asked. Lavanderos leaned toward Delgado and they had another whispered conversation.

"Mr. Sanchez is a bank customer and a personal friend," Delgado said.

"What's your working relationship?" Morrison asked.

"I told you. He's a customer of the bank."

"When'd you last see him?" Morrison asked.

"I don't know. Maybe a week ago."

Morrison asked, "Where?"

Delgado conferred with his attorney. Then he said, "At my house. We have a weekly poker game."

Morrison's cell phone rang. He pulled it out and flipped it open. He read the text message, flipped the phone closed and said, "The record will show the interview ended at 9:59." Morrison stood. "This way, gentlemen."

Morrison opened the door and waited while Lavanderos and Delgado walked ahead of him into the hall. Then he stepped in front of them to lead the way.

# CHAPTER TWENTY SEVEN

As Morrison guided Lavanderos and Delgado along the corridor, Dottie and Tori approached from the other direction with Jimmy Rafferty. Stone-faced, Morrison watched as Rafferty glanced up and caught sight of Delgado. Rafferty flinched and then averted his eyes. No one in either group said a word, but the nonverbal reactions were not lost on Morrison and the two women.

When Morrison rejoined Tori and Dottie in the observation room, they congratulated each other on the results of the plan.

Dottie said, "Tori, that was brilliant having us walk Delgado and Rafferty by each other."

"Rafferty was shocked all right," Morrison said.

"There's no doubt Delgado knew Rafferty," Tori said. "His eyes widened for a nanosecond and then he glared at Rafferty before looking away. They know each other and don't want us to know about it."

A loud knock interrupted. An officer stuck his head in the door. "Chief wants to see you, Morrison."

"Tell her I'm interviewing suspects," Morrison said. "Close the door."

Dottie turned to Tori. "Your idea that Delgado might know Sanchez was inspired."

"Yeah, Tori" Morrison said. "You nailed this one. Looks like Delgado and Sanchez are mixed up with the Cuban Mafia in Miami."

"I think it's more interesting that Delgado's attorney knows Sanchez," Tori said.

"What makes you think Lavanderos knows Sanchez?" Dottie asked.

"When Morrison asked Delgado how well he knew Sanchez, it was Lavanderos who reacted. The attorney initiated the discussion, not Delgado. He was disconcerted."

"So what?" Morrison asked.

"The attorney represents Delgado. I bet he also represents Sanchez. Check with your colleague in Miami, I wouldn't be surprised if Lavanderos is an attorney for the Cuban Mafia."

"Right," Morrison said.

"Delgado was cool until I mentioned Sanchez," Morrison said. "After Dottie interviews Rafferty I'll call my contact in Miami. Find out what he knows about Sanchez. Bet he was involved with Iglesias, too."

"Wish me luck," Dottie said as she went to the interrogation room. Rafferty was squirming at the table when she entered. He started to talk, but Dottie raised her hand like a traffic cop while she turned on the recorder and gave the specifics about the interview. Then she looked at Rafferty and asked, "Where's your attorney?"

"I can't afford one. The Public Defender won't represent me unless I'm charged."

"Eduardo Delgado collected gambling debts from you, didn't he?" Dottie asked.

Rafferty looked at his hands in his lap and nodded.

Dottie said, "Please answer out loud so your response will be on the recorder."

"Yes," Rafferty said in a small voice.

"Did Delgado threaten you?"

Rafferty looked up with sad eyes. "He said he'd break both my knees. I'd never dance again."

"So you had to run over Margaret O'Neal to repay your debts."

"No. No. I didn't hurt Margaret. I'd never do that. I…"

"You what?"

"I'd never hurt anyone," he said.

"What about your late wife?"

"What about her?"

"You abused her," Dottie said. "There're records of domestic abuse calls to your house in Port Chester, NY."

"You got it wrong way around," Rafferty said. "I didn't abuse her. She out-weighed me by a hundred pounds, for Pete's sake. She beat me. I'm the one called the cops."

"We can verify that."

"Go ahead. It's true."

"Let's get back to Delgado. He threatened you if you didn't pay your debt," Dottie said. "He wanted you to run over Margaret, didn't he?"

"No. He never mentioned Margaret until I gave him the money." Rafferty said.

"What did he say about Margaret?"

"I told him I got the money from a friend. When I gave him the $40,000 he wanted to know about the friend. I told him about Margaret."

"He gave you day lilies for Margaret."

"How'd you know that?"

"Just answer the question," Dottie said.

"Yes, he gave me flowers for Margaret."

"Why?"

"I don't know," Rafferty said. "Months after I paid off the debt he came to see me. I was terrified. I told him I didn't owe any more money. He laughed and said he was just visiting a friend. He brought a bottle of expensive scotch and suggested we have a drink. After we'd had a few he asked me about Margaret. I told him how she had money and loved flowers and stuff.

"A couple days later he came by again and gave me day lilies for Margaret. Said they were very special. He asked me about Margaret. What her habits were—that sort of thing. I told him how she walked before church on Sundays. He asked me where she walked." He lowered his head. "I didn't know he would hurt her."

Back in his office, Morrison asked, "What do you think, Doc?"

"He's telling the truth about his wife beating him. No man likes to admit that sort of thing."

Dottie asked, "What about Margaret?"

"I think he's projected his hatred for his wife on other women," Tori said. "That's why he uses women."

121

"Would he run Margaret over with a truck?" Morrison asked.

"He might use a truck to hurt a woman. He sees them as objects to be used. But, he wouldn't kill the woman giving him money."

Morrison said, "Epstein, check out that poker game Delgado talked about. Rafferty's a gambler. He might have lost money to Delgado or someone else at the weekly game."

A loud knock on the door drew their attention. The door started opening and Morrison shouted, "I told you to tell her I'm busy."

Chief Connie Murray slammed open the door and marched into the room. "And I said I wanted to see you."

Morrison stood. "Sorry, Chief. We were interviewing suspects."

"I don't see any suspects."

Dottie said, "They just left."

"Don't be so quick to defend him, Detective Epstein," Murray said. She nodded at Tori, then turned back to Morrison. "What've you got, Detective?"

"We've got a couple of people of interest. They're involved with the Cuban Mafia in Miami."

"What's that got to do with a retired school teacher burglarizing a house and being killed?"

"Mrs. O'Neal lent money to a friend. He used the money to pay off his gambling debts to the Mafia," Morrison said.

"Who else of interest?" Murray asked.

"The father of Mrs. O'Neal's charge in the GAL program. The one I told you beat his wife and broke his kid's arm. Mrs. O'Neal had the judge take his kids. He's furious. He's a debt collector for the Cuban Mafia."

"That's interesting. Anything else?"

Dottie said, "All the burglarized houses used the same cleaning service—Heavenly Maids."

"And?"

"And the owner is Cuban and knows both the people of interest."

"Is the owner involved with the Cuban Mafia?" Murray asked.

"We're checking that out," Morrison said.

"Get on with it, Detective," Murray said and strode out of the office.

Morrison turned to Dottie, "I'll tell you what to tell the chief."

"Sorry, Morrison. Most of the houses had Heavenly Maids as their cleaners."

"Most! Not all of them. Unless they're all connected, we don't have anything." Morrison said.

Dottie said, "I called Mrs. Levine this morning. She said they had the Heavenly Maids but stopped using them because she suspected they were stealing."

"Did they have them when they were burglarized?" Morrison asked.

"I didn't ask," Dottie said in a lower voice.

"Damn it, Epstein, don't waste time chasing false leads. You heard her. Chief's on my ass. Phillips swears Carlos Sanchez is honest."

"Come on, Morrison. You know how good con artists are," Dottie said. "And what about that woman the state troopers picked up outside town?"

"What woman?"

"The illegal alien the troopers picked up two weeks ago. She said she cleaned for Heavenly Maids."

"What's that got to do with the price of tea in China?"

"Maybe Sanchez is trafficking in illegal aliens."

Morrison closed his eyes and groaned. "Epstein, you're going off the deep end." He gritted his teeth.

Morrison paced the office, taking deep breaths. Finally he sat behind his desk, formed his hands into a steeple and said in a reasonably calm voice, "Epstein, look at the facts. There's no connection between Margaret O'Neal and the cleaning service."

Dottie leaned across the desk facing her superior officer, "I am looking at the facts. Most of the houses used Heavenly Maids." She glared, hands on her hips.

Morrison's face contorted, brows forming a deep trench down the middle of his forehead as he stood and pointed a huge finger in Dottie's face, matching glare with glare. "Epstein, I'm telling you—check out that poker game. Check out the connection between Delgado and Rafferty. Check on Margaret's other Guardian ad Litem charges. That's an order. Got it?"

Dottie's teeth were clenched and her face flushed, but she did not escalate the argument. She did not tell Morrison she had already interviewed Sanchez. She would check out the Rolex and ring on her own.

Tori was impressed with Dottie's gumption. She was tenacious, didn't back down. Tori asked, "Morrison, why are you making such a big deal of this? What's wrong with Dottie pursuing a lead? She might find something. It's not like you to be so rigid."

"You said you wouldn't pull rank on me," Dottie added. "I thought we were partners."

Morrison sat back in his chair and took a deep breath. "Okay, okay, hear me out. Chief's on my ass, you know. Maybe there's a connection with the Heavenly Maids' and the burglaries. But, I'm convinced Margaret was killed because of her work with Guardian ad Litem. I talked to Annie Curry yesterday. She confirmed Rafferty gave Margaret the day lilies just before she was killed. We need to pursue the connection between Delgado and Rafferty and Margaret. Find out if Delgado loaned money to Rafferty. That's a better lead."

Dottie gave Morrison an exaggerated salute, "Ja, mein Führer."

# CHAPTER TWENTY EIGHT

Sanchez burst into the office, "I've got to talk to you. NOW!! It's urgent."

The man behind the desk scowled at the intruding Sanchez. He smiled at the woman sitting opposite him and asked her if she would mind stepping out to the reception area for a short time. He walked her to the door, apologizing for the inconvenience. As soon as the door closed, he turned to Sanchez and said in a harsh voice, "What the hell is so important? I told you never to come here."

"Por favor, Giovanni, you've got to help me."

"Don't call me Giovanni."

"My sorry, I forgot," Sanchez said. "You told me no one would ever know."

"Know what?"

"Know about the burglaries."

"No one will find out if you keep your cool. What the hell's the matter with you?" Sanchez clasped Giovanni by the shoulders.

"A cop came to the office this morning."

Giovanni pushed Sanchez's hands away. "Sit down, you idiot. What happened?"

Sanchez backed into the recently vacated chair. "Some black bitch came to see me. She had a list of the houses we robbed. Wanted to know if we cleaned them." Sanchez rubbed his sweaty hands on his slacks.

"What'd you tell her?" Giovanni stood over Sanchez, his piercing eyes burning so hot Sanchez could not look at them. He lowered his eyes.

"I said I couldn't remember. Files were in the archives," Sanchez said in a quaking voice.

"Good! That's good," Giovanni said, "Nothing connects us with the thefts. We've stopped the burglaries. They can't prove we've had anything to do with the old ones."

"She asked if I had keys to the houses and codes for the alarms." Sanchez stammered, his shirt soaked with sweat.

"What'd you say?"

"The keys are kept locked in the office. The codes are given to the girls the day they clean a house." Sanchez hesitated. "She seemed suspicious."

"So what? She can't prove anything."

When Sanchez ran his hands through his disheveled hair. Giovanni spotted the Rolex on his wrist. Giovanni grabbed Sanchez's wrist, twisting it. Giovanni was bigger and more muscular than the slim Sanchez. Sanchez grimaced. Giovanni's voice was menacing. "She saw the Rolex, didn't she?"

Sanchez nodded and Giovanni let go of him. Sanchez rubbed his red wrist before dropping his head into his hands.

"You fucking idiot. Didn't I warn you not to keep stolen stuff? You fucked up the perfect scheme."

Sanchez raised his head. "Don't blame me. You got the cops involved—with that damned school teacher."

"You didn't tell me there was a motion activated video in the house."

"How the fuck was I supposed to know?"

"You cased the place."

"You didn't tell me to check for surveillance cameras."

"Lower your voice." Giovanni took a deep breath and sat behind his desk. "Let me think," he said lowering his chin onto his right hand, his elbow resting on the desk.

In a few minutes Giovanni looked up, rubbed his chin and said, "Okay, here's the plan…"

# CHAPTER TWENTY NINE

Tori looked around at the eight graduate students in the seminar she was teaching on criminal and violent behavior. The class met weekly. "Today I want to discuss an actual case. As I told you at the beginning of the semester, everything we discuss in class is confidential. You cannot discuss it outside this room."

The students looked at her with increased attention. "Earlier this week a retired school teacher was hit by a truck," Tori said.

Tom said, "I saw that in the paper. It was a hit and run."

"That's right. But the police don't think it was just a hit and run. They think the woman, Mrs. O'Neal, was murdered."

A murmur went through the class. Marcie asked, "What makes them think it was murder?"

"A couple of reasons. After the man hit Mrs. O'Neal with his truck, he backed over her."

"Couldn't he have panicked and backed up not knowing he would hit her?" Frank asked.

"That might be possible, but a witness heard the man laugh."

"That's sadistic," Sharon said.

"What kind of person would laugh after running over a retired schoolteacher?" Tori asked. "Sharon, you said it was sadistic. Do you think the person has a sadistic personality disorder?"

"Definitely."

"Why?"

"People with sadistic personality disorder like seeing others suffer. They enjoy causing pain. That's why they do sadistic things."

"Sadistic personality disorder has a high level of comorbidity to other psychopathological disorders," Tori said. "What other disorders would you expect in this person?"

"Anti-social personality disorder, for sure," Mike said.

"Good. Others?"

"Borderline personality disorder," Terry said. "And maybe alcoholism."

Marcie said, "Narcissistic personality disorder."

"Conduct disorder," Mike said, "when he was an adolescent."

"Good point, Mike," Tori said. "That brings us to the factors influencing sadism. What might those factors be?"

"The man's upbringing," Terry said. "He might have been abused when he was a child."

"Very good." Tori said. "Is anyone familiar with the research on the MAOA gene?"

Sharon asked, "Is that what they call the 'warrior gene?'"

"That's right," Tori said. "People with a mutation leading to low activity in their MAOA gene tend to be aggressive. These people feel little or no empathy for others. They're likely to hurt others.

"As with most behaviors, there is a nurture factor as well as the nature factor. In other words, people who have this MAOA gene do not automatically attack other people. Some trigger in their environment is necessary to set them off. What do you suppose the trigger might be?"

Terry said, "abusive parents?"

"Right. Scientists think that being exposed to trauma when they are young triggers aggression in people with low activity in the MAOA gene. For example, if when these people were children they were abused or witnessed violence they would be more likely to be aggressive as adults."

"What kind of violence?" Marci asked. "Like a violent neighborhood?"

"Right," Tori said. "Or in the family."

"Like the sadist," Mike said.

"Exactly," Tori said. "What do you think the implications of this research are for the courts?"

"Lawyers use psychology. They twist everything," Marcie said. "They get people off who belong in prison."

"Right. Bradley Waldroup was tried in Tennessee for the 2006 attempted murder of his estranged wife Penney and the murder of Leslie Bradshaw. Penny dropped off their four children for a weekend visit with Waldroup. When Penny and Leslie Bradshaw began to leave, Waldroup shot Bradshaw and sliced open her head before attacking his wife with a machete. Defense attorney Wylie Richardson used the defense that Bradley Waldroup had the MAOA mutation and had been abused as a child. According to forensic psychiatrist William Bernet, this combination meant Waldroup had diminished responsibility for shooting Bradshaw and attacking his wife."

"That makes me so mad," Terry said.

"Nigel Barber describes the defense as "a germ of scientific truth combined with a hefty dose of junk science, including clever labeling. However, this defense kept Waldroup from being convicted of first degree murder."

"So he was let go?" asked Mike.

"He wasn't let off completely." Tori said. "He was sentenced to 32 years in prison."

After class Tori drove to the Reen E Dance Studio. She had time to do some ballet exercises before meeting Morrison and Dottie. She pulled her Boxster into the strip mall parking lot and found a space not far from the studio entrance. She went to her car trunk, retrieved her bag with her dancing paraphernalia, and strode into the studio.

"Hi, Tori," said Grace. "I haven't seen you for awhile."

"I've been busy."

"You need to make room in your life for dance. It's good for your soul."

Tori smiled. "My soul needs to dance today." She went to the dressing room and changed into her black leotard and dance shoes. She thought, *I feel the tension lifting just putting on my dance clothes.*

Tori walked into the mirrored room with the barre along one wall. There was another barre that extended into the room. Reen was conducting a private session with a talented teenage girl at one end of the room. Tori watched the teenager dance for a moment. She thought back to when she was a teenager dancing in the Stamford ballet. *It was so easy then.* Reen said, "Hi, Tori. Glad to see you."

The teenager continued her dance without appearing to notice Tori.

"Thanks, Reen. Nice to be here." Tori walked to the barre and executed her stretch exercises to warm her muscles. She felt as if her anxiety was floating away. She directed every thought to the movement of her body. Images of Mrs. O'Neal's body and concerns about the murderer evaporated. She went through the five positions of her feet. Next, she completed a series of pliés to increase the flexibility of her joints and tendons. *Pliés get more difficult each year. I'm stiff. I haven't been conscientious enough about doing my exercises on a regular basis.*

By the time she completed her exercises, Tori was relaxed and ready to face Morrison and talk about the murder investigation.

# CHAPTER THIRTY

That evening Morrison's car squealed into the parking lot of the Pomodoro Café. He jammed on the brakes. He pounded his fist against the steering wheel. "Damn, Damn. Damned bastard." He pulled his hefty body out of the car and slammed the door. Dottie got out of the passenger side. She did not say a word as they walked into the Pomodoro Café. It was their favorite Thursday night haunt since the Purple Porpoise closed. Tori, whom they had invited to join them, was sitting at the table reserved for the duo on Thursdays. Tori felt Dottie look her over. Tori was particularly well-dressed this evening. *She thinks I'm going on a date*, thought Tori, determined to avoid the topic.

A scowling Morrison ignored Tori's welcoming smile. He signaled the waitress and ordered a pitcher of beer before taking a seat. He pointed at Dottie. "You drive me home. I'm drinking the whole pitcher in one gulp."

Dottie pulled out her cell phone, flipped it open, and walked to the door so she could get better reception. Tori watched her speak into the phone, looking back at Tori and Morrison every so often. She flipped the phone closed, stuffed it in her pocket, and walked back to the table. Dottie looked at Tori, who raised her right shoulder.

Tori turned to Morrison. "Bad day?" Morrison frowned at her. He called the waitress. "I want a pizza. The super special, extra large, with extra cheese."

131

Dottie asked Morrison, "Is that pizza all for you or are you willing to share?"

"How the hell do you stay so skinny? You eat twice what I do."

"I also run every day and usually eat salads—healthy food."

The waitress arrived to take Tori's and Dottie's orders. Dottie ordered a Coke and a small veggie pizza.

Dottie turned to Tori, "How about you, Tori, want some wine?"

"No, thanks. Club soda for me." Before anyone could comment on her choice of drinks, Tori asked, "Why are you in such a foul mood, Morrison?"

"That Rafferty guy is too smooth by half. Who's got an alibi for 6:30 Sunday morning? He's hiding something, I can tell," Morrison said. By now he had downed a large portion of the pitcher of beer and it was not helping his disposition.

"Could be he's telling the truth," Dottie said.

Morrison's scorching look silenced her.

"Jimmie Rafferty's little love bird returned Epstein's call on our way here. Gave him an alibi," Morrison said. "She was in bed with him Sunday morning. She's the one hiding in Rafferty's bedroom when we interviewed him."

"It wasn't Lucille?" Tori asked.

"Not according to Rafferty or Mary Ann," Dottie said.

Jason Nolan ambled over to the table. Morrison looked at the technician and grumbled, "What're you doing here? You and Epstein don't date no more."

Jason slapped Morrison on the back. "Aren't you in a great mood, Morrison. This grouchiness because your Knicks are sure to lose tonight?" He kissed Dottie on the cheek and hugged Tori as he reached for a chair. He turned the chair backwards, arms crossed on its back, dismissing the waitress who tried to take his order with a shake of the head.

"The Knicks aren't going to lose," Morrison said.

"Everyone's predicting the Bulls will win."

"In your dreams."

"How do you know Jason and I aren't dating?" Dottie asked.

Morrison looked at Dottie and took a deep breath. "No secrets in the department." He took a big swig of beer and swiped the back of his hand across his mouth. "I only tolerated Nolan for your sake."

Dottie shot daggers at Morrison. "If you want me to drive you home after you drink yourself under the table, Jason needs to follow and drive me to my car."

Morrison grumbled. "Okay." He looked at Tori. "So what's with the club soda? Want me to look like a lush?"

"No, Herb, my drinking club soda has nothing to do with you. I have a meeting this evening."

The others looked at her, questioningly. "Where're you going?" Morrison asked.

"I'm going to a meeting of the Florida Psychological Association, if you must know." Tori felt a hint of a blush cross her face. *Why can't I control my blushing?*

"Who you going with?" Morrison asked.

"What makes you think I'm going with anyone?"

He waved his hand to indicate Tori. "Way you're dressed."

"I'm dressed for the meeting, but Seth Rothstein is driving me."

"You dating Rothstein?" Dottie asked.

"No. We discussed FPA when we had coffee after the CEU presentation the other evening. He suggested we go together. He called this afternoon to arrange to pick me up."

Morrison took another gulp of beer and shook his head. "Rothstein makes my skin crawl."

"I saw a photograph of him in an old FPA newsletter," Tori said. "His hair and beard were grayer. He looked older than he does now."

"You think he dyes his hair and beard?" Jason asked, rubbing his mustache, so blond it was barely noticeable.

"Don't even think about it," Dottie said. "Men who dye their hair are… are…"

"Faggots," Morrison said.

"I was going to say conceited." Dottie gave her boss another dirty look.

Ignoring the bickering, Tori said, "Dottie's right. Rothstein is narcissistic."

# CHAPTER THIRTY ONE

Squeezing a drunk Morrison into the passenger seat of his patrol car was no easy chore. After drinking a pitcher of beer, Morrison thought he was invincible and insisted he could drive.

"Where's Tori?" Jason asked. "Maybe she can convince Morrison to let you drive him home?"

"She's gone," Dottie said.

"Dang."

Dottie said, "My sentiments are a lot stronger than 'dang.'"

Jason and Dottie were in good shape, but they were dwarfed by the massive Morrison.

"I feel like I'm trying to squeeze a sumo wrestler into a Volkswagen," Jason said.

"A drunk sumo wrestler with an attitude," Dottie said. She put her hands on her hips, looked Morrison in the eye and said, "If you don't get in and let me drive you home, I'm going to call Ruth."

Morrison looked at Dottie, eyes wide. "You wouldn't do that, would you?"

"And, I'll tell her about Annie's cookies and the pizza you scarfed down."

"No, no. You wouldn't."

"If you don't get into the car, I sure as hell will."

Morrison lowered his head and folded himself into the passenger side of the car, his shoulders slumped. Jason stuffed Morrison's legs under the dashboard.

"Will you be all right driving him home?" Jason asked, leaning across Morrison to latch his seatbelt as Dottie climbed into the driver's seat.

"Yeah, he'll probably fall asleep. He's too drunk to be a problem."

A short time later Dottie pulled Morrison's car into his driveway. Jason swung his jeep into the driveway behind Morrison's unmarked police car. Dottie jumped out of Morrison's car and opened the passenger door for her boss. She and Jason had to pull him out of the car.

Morrison groaned as he stood. "Damn knees."

Dottie handed the car keys to Morrison who staggered to his front door without so much as a thank you. She got into the passenger seat of Jason's car and said, "Thanks."

"Herb's been in some dark moods, but tonight was the worst," Dottie said. "I've never seen him drink like that."

"He really tied one on," Jason agreed, pulling into the road

"This case is getting to him. He was captivated by Margaret O'Neal. He wants to find her killer."

"What was that about cookies from Annie?" Jason asked.

"Annie's Margaret's sister—good looking woman. Tori says Morrison has the hots for her."

"For the cookies, maybe."

"That's what I said," Dottie said, "but he collapsed in Annie's bedroom last night, half naked."

"No way! His wife would kill him."

"Ruth will cut his balls off, if she finds out," Dottie said.

They drove in silence for a few minutes, then Jason said, "I thought you found a connection between the burglaries and some cleaning service?"

"I did, but Morrison won't let me follow up on it."

Jason turned to Dottie. "You gotta be kidding."

"Wish I were. Because every single house didn't use the service, he thinks there's no connection. You know, he has no concept about inferential statistics. He can't get his little brain around probability."

"Wait a minute! Wait a minute! What kind of statistics?"

"It doesn't matter."

"I thought he valued your expertise."

"Only if it fits his preconceived ideas. He wants data if they support the case as he sees it. Otherwise it's bullshit."

Jason patted Dottie's knee, "Dottie, you're being too hard on him. He's a cantankerous old blowhard, but he does listen to you."

Dottie glared at her former lover. "Yeah. Right."

"What's his problem with this issue?" Jason asked.

"One of the homeowners swears the cleaning service owner, Carlos Sanchez, is the most honest person on the face of the earth."

"Why's he say that?"

"Carlos returned a ruby ring the homeowner didn't know was missing. Morrison bought the story. He'll never change his mind about investigating Sanchez unless I get concrete evidence."

"Are you going to sit by and not follow up on a lead?"

"What makes you think I'd do what the cantankerous old blowhard orders me to do?"

He grinned. "Atta girl."

"I interviewed Carlos Sanchez this morning. I'm sure he's involved. He was so nervous he was sweating, wiping his forehead with a handkerchief. Get this, his handkerchief had his initials embroidered on it. Damn, he was such a glamour boy he kept winking at me with his long dark eyelashes."

"And you said a man dyeing his beard is narcissistic."

"I didn't say Sanchez wasn't conceited. He was wearing designer clothes—silk shirt and slacks. He kept looking deeply into my eyes like I'd drop the case and fall into his arms. He thinks he's a lady-killer."

"But he's no match for this lady."

"He was wearing a Rolex watch. The thieves stole a ton of those. When I asked him about the watch he almost fainted. Stammered—said he bought it on the street in Miami. Probably where he sends stolen goods to be hocked."

"Have you told Morrison about the interview?"

"Are you kidding? I can't. He'd bite my head off. He ordered me not to continue the investigation of Heavenly Maids."

"How are Heavenly Maids and this Sanchez connected to Margaret O'Neal?"

"I don't know. First of all I have to connect Sanchez and Heavenly Maids to the burglaries. Then I can pursue how Margaret was involved with them."

# CHAPTER THIRTY TWO

Tori purposely had not told Morrison and Dottie that she and Rothstein were going to dinner before the meeting. She was not sure where their relationship was going and did not want her colleagues to quiz her about it. Tori told herself she was seeing Rothstein so she could find out more about Margaret O'Neal and thought this was a good way of doing so. She asked herself, *Am I really only interested in Margaret O'Neal?* She was putting the last minute touches to her make up when Rothstein rang the bell.

Sean looked out the window and called, "Wow! Look at his car!" He ran to the door and opened it. "Is that yours?" he asked pointing to the red Jaguar convertible parked in the driveway.

"Sean, where are your manners?" Tori asked as she joined him at the door. She turned to Rothstein, "This is my son, Sean. Please excuse his behavior. Sean, this is Dr. Rothstein."

"Sorry. Glad to meet you." Sean glanced quickly at Rothstein and returned his gaze to the car.

"Don't worry about it," Rothstein said. "I'd have done the same thing when I was your age. Are you old enough to drive?"

"I wish."

"I don't have time tonight, but next time I'll give you a ride. Maybe we can find a parking lot where you can drive it."

"Really?" Sean looked back at Rothstein, his eyes shining.

"Sure. Now, if you don't mind, your mother and I need to get going. Come out and look the car over before we leave."

Sean ran to the driveway and caressed the front hood of Seth's car. "Sweet!"

Rothstein walked Tori to the passenger side and opened the door for her, before climbing in behind the steering wheel and starting the car. He said, "See you soon, Sean."

Rothstein turned to look out the back window as he drove out of the drive, "Nice young man, your son."

"Thanks. He's nothing if not exuberant."

It was 20 minutes into their dinner when Rothstein patted his lips with his napkin and asked, "How is the investigation going on Margaret O'Neal?"

Tori stopped her forkful of tilapia half way to her mouth. "I'm not privy to the investigation. I'm only doing the psychological autopsy."

"Have you decided whether she committed suicide?"

Tori ate a bite of fish. "You knew her better than I do. What do you think?"

"Typical psychologist." Rothstein twirled the stem of his wine glass and smiled. "Turning the question back to the questioner."

"And that's a typical psychologist who doesn't answer the question."

"Touché."

"Well? What do you think?" Tori asked as she sipped her Pinot Grigio.

"I didn't see her the week before she died. Up until then I'd have said she would never commit suicide." He rubbed his beard. "But she was concerned about that Delgado character she met through the Guardian ad Litem program."

"She told you Edward Delgado's children were her charges?"

"Yes. And she was worried."

"I thought she was careful about confidentiality with her charges."

Rothstein picked up his wine glass and took a sip, looking at her over the rim. "She was. But she was afraid of Delgado and knew I'd keep it confidential."

"What did she say about him?"

"Delgado threatened her." He sipped his wine and sighed. "I can't remember exactly—something to the effect she'd regret

138

taking his children away from him. I might have more details in my notes."

Tori bit her knuckle. Rothstein reached across the table and took Tori's hand. "Come back. You need to separate your feelings from this case. What does the macho detective think?"

Tori looked at Rothstein, "Morrison?"

"Yes."

She said, "He doesn't share his thoughts." Tori smiled at Rothstein. "You said you'd tell me about your partner, John Rodriguez."

"Did I tell you his name?"

"No. I saw it on a photo in an old FPA newsletter. They had your names reversed in the photo." She smiled. "Dr. Rodriguez doesn't look Hispanic."

Tori noticed a flash of emotion cross his face before he smiled at her. She asked, "About your partner?"

Rothstein looked into the distance, as if he could see the events he described, sadness defined his face. "John was a gentle and caring psychologist. He saw clients for the department of corrections. We both did. I kept warning him they could be dangerous and he needed to get a gun. Of course, he refused. He said no one would hurt him." Rothstein looked at Tori. "He was wrong. One of our clients flipped out and beat him to death."

Tori gasped. She reached for Rothstein's hand. "Seth, no wonder you don't want to talk about it. It must have been traumatic."

# CHAPTER THIRTY THREE

*Seven years earlier*

The burly man with tattoos running from the edge of his short sleeves down his muscular arms to his wrists fidgeted in the waiting room under the careless eye of the guard. The tattoos depicting weapons, blood, hatred, and slaughter were an accurate reflection of Dominick's temperament.

The guard asked, "What's up, Dominick? I thought you liked seeing the shrink."

"I like getting outta that dump. Hate touchy-feely shit. The shrink's a pain in the ass."

"You ain't seeing that shrink today. You're seeing his partner."

"Still hate it."

"Listen Dominck, the judge ain't letting you loose on society until you complete 12 therapy sessions with a psychologist."

"Crock of shit!"

"Take it easy. You gotta go along to get along."

The new psychologist smiled as he welcomed Dominick into the office. "We're going to meet here so you're familiar with the room."

His partner had reached an impasse with Dominick and asked him to see the client. The psychologist had a soothing voice. He did some preliminary introductions.

"You ain't like that other shrink," Dominick said. "You listen."

"I'm sure he listens."

Dominick noted the new guy was older. He looked like a couch potato whereas his regular shrink was muscular and athletic.

The psychologist asked Dominick, "Please tell me why you went to prison."

"You got it in them notes." He pointed to the file on the therapist's lap. "I told the other shrink already."

"I realize it must be irritating to repeat, but I would like to hear your description."

"It weren't my fault. I done nothing wrong. My buddy and me was at the shore. We met these chicks in a bar. Went to their motel room to party. We was having fun and they were getting real friendly, know what I mean?" He paused for the psychologist to nod. "We run out of booze. The chicks went to this ABC down the street to get more. They come back, said the guy called them 'whores.' They was upset so we said we'd take care of the fucker—teach him how to treat ladies."

He shrugged. "We beat the crap outta the kid. Put him in a coma." He shrugged again. "He's a vegetable—won't never walk again." He looked at the therapist with a bland expression. "Then these broads tell us he ain't the right fucker. It was some odder guy."

He threw his hands in the air. "The bastard went off duty before we got there. Whatcha goin' do? We got the wrong guy."

"Do you feel responsible for this young man's injuries?"

"Ain't my fault. Them chicks shoudda told us he weren't the right fucker. I'll make it up to him."

"How do you intend to do that?"

Dominick said, "When I get out I'll rob a bank or something and give him some dough."

Taken aback, the psychologist looked down at his notes to regain his composure. A moment later he asked, "How did you get along in prison?"

"It ain't bad. It's not like I never been there before. I been in and out since I was 14. It ain't bad if you foller the 'rules' and show them cons you're tough. I got myself a shank."

"A what?"

"A toothbrush. I sharpened the end like a knife. I was ready when trouble come. I got him 'fore he got me. No one picks on you after that."

"Did someone try to do something to you?"

"Yeah, this con tried to take my radio. I used the shank on him. He didn't never try nothing again." He chuckled. "No one else done either. They's all afraid of me."

"Were there any witnesses?"

Dominick said, "Nobody sees nothing in the joint, not if they wanna live to get out. 'Do your own time.' That's what ya gotta do."

His violence was not the reason the psychologist was seeing Dominick. According to his colleague, the client had issues with his mother and was not able to address them with the other psychologist. When he believed the client was comfortable with him, the psychologist approached the topic of the client's mother. The psychologist was making notes on his pad when he heard a noise and looked up to see Dominick standing over him with a metal bookend shaped like a horse's head. The horse's head was the last thing the therapist saw as it smashed into his face, over and over again.

The police detective leaned over the body and cringed when he saw the dead psychologist, his face beaten to oblivion. If the murder had not taken place in his own office, it would have been difficult to identify the dead man. The detective went to the reception area where the victim's partner was waiting. The partner was sitting slumped in a chair, staring at the wall. The detective sat next to the psychologist. "I know this is tough for you, doctor, but would you please tell me what happened?"

The psychologist bit his lower lip and said, "I was in my office catching up on paper work. John was seeing a client in his office," he said in a quivering voice. "I heard some thumping noises and then John called for help." He put his hands over his face. Then he looked up and bit his lip. Tears streamed down his face.

The detective sat quietly, too used to sitting with survivors, and having heard too many stories about finding murder victims. He waited.

142

The psychologist pulled out a handkerchief and wiped his eyes. "I'm sorry."

He paused before saying, "When John called I got the gun out of the desk. We have adjoining offices. I went in. The client was beating John with a book end." He bit his lip again. "I shot the client; but I was too late to save John."

"Do you know who the client was?"

"I only know he was ordered by the court to see us."

"It seems unusual for a psychologist to keep a loaded gun in his desk. How do you happen to have one?"

The psychologist said, "My partner counseled inmates from the work release center and jail. I warned him one of them would become violent one day." He choked up, his voice coming out trembling, "I couldn't convince John to protect himself, so I got a gun to protect him."

The funeral for the psychologist was not well-attended. He'd been in Baltimore for fewer than three months and spent most of his time with his friend and partner, Dr. Seth Rothstein. His partner requested a closed funeral; he wanted to mourn in private. He did not even want his own friends to attend and console him.

Within a week the office was closed and for sale. The surviving psychologist left the state.

# CHAPTER THIRTY FOUR

It was 6:30 a.m. Morrison, wearing a tattered plaid bathrobe, sat hunched over the kitchen table, clutching his bowed head as if he could keep it from splitting open. His disheveled hair made him look like a sandy haired Albert Einstein.

Ruth clanged dishes and slammed the cupboard doors, making as much racket as she could while unloading the dishwasher. She glowered over her shoulder at her husband. "I hope you feel as bad as you look. I haven't seen you that drunk since college."

Morrison groaned, looking up at his wife. The bags under his bloodshot eyes were so brown and puffy it looked as if he had a beat-up boxing glove under each eye. Gray stubble covered the chin of his greenish-gray face.

Ruth said, "I've no sympathy. You look like one of the homeless men hanging out at the Greyhound bus station in Jacksonville." She shook her head. "Men! I thought you'd outgrown drowning your problems with alcohol. You of all people—you saw what alcohol did to your father and your family."

She finished unloading the dishwasher and started loading the dirty dishes. She made no attempt to be quiet; in fact, she went out of her way to be noisy.

Morrison turned to look at his wife, moaning with the effort and pain. "At my age, I should've learned."

"Yes, you should have."

Ruth dried her hands on her apron and walked to Herb's chair. She kissed his forehead and sat next to him. "Want a Bloody Mary? I've heard they're good for hangovers."

Morrison moaned again. "Don't want alcohol for the rest of my life."

"Or at least the rest of this week," Ruth said. "I hope you remember this."

"You laugh, but I got to go to work. Epstein'll know I'm hung over. She'll play loud rock music, torture me, like you."

"What's so bad you drank half the beer in Gainesville?"

Morrison sighed. "Got a case I can't figure out. Retired school teacher doesn't up and rob a house for no reason. I know crooks. She's not one."

"What makes you so sure she wouldn't do it?"

"She's as close to being a saint as anyone on earth."

"Bah! You and your Catholicism! You don't believe that malarkey about saints."

"Don't talk so loud," Morrison said. "If I believed in saints, I'd pray to Margaret to help solve this case."

"Herb, get a grip."

"Hear me out. This woman was so religious she said the rosary when she walked, for God's sake. She was a Sunday school teacher in a black church, bought the kids snacks, took them to museums and the zoo on her own dime. She even took them to Disney World—and that costs a small fortune. It almost broke me taking you and Jennifer there last year."

"Okay, okay, she was Mother Teresa reincarnated. Even saints need money. Maybe she ran up a huge debt feeding all those poor families. Or maybe she thought she was a female Robin Hood stealing from the rich to feed the poor."

"She didn't need money. Husband left her a bundle. No kids. She got all the dough." Morrison paused. "And she didn't rob the other houses. Out of town with her sister when the burglaries were done last summer. So who burglarized those houses?"

"I see the problem. Have you found any of the stolen articles?"

"One ring in Miami. Got no leads from that."

"What happened to this Margaret's money after she was killed?"

"She took care of her sister. Left a chunk to her 'man friend.' Gave the rest to charity."

"Maybe she was being blackmailed?"

"Why blackmail a retired school teacher who's religious?"

"For her money."

"Yeah, but what would they blackmail her about?"

"How do I know? You're the detective," Ruth said, as she leaned her hands against the table pushing herself to her feet.

# CHAPTER THIRTY FIVE

Before dawn on a moonless night, Carlos Sanchez parked his car and hurried toward his office, head down, shoulders tense. A layer of clouds blocked the faint light morning stars might have provided, but Sanchez was familiar with the area and walked hurriedly. Fumbling with his keys, Sanchez did not notice the truck parked on the far side of the lot like a panther waiting for its quarry. He paid no heed until the truck was bearing down on him. By then it was too late. The truck plowed into him, tossing him into the air like a wide-eyed rag doll. He might have been alive when he hit the ground some thirty feet away, but the truck driver ran over him two more times.

The killer jumped out of the truck and removed something from the dead man. He climbed back into the driver's seat, backed up, almost hitting the arriving paper delivery man's car, and paused. He stomped on the gas, careening out of the parking lot past an old beat-up Toyota pulling in. The Toyota's driver, one of the Heavenly Maids, discovered the body of her boss and called 911. The investigating officer notified Herb Morrison because the incident was similar to the one in which Margaret O'Neal was murdered.

Dottie was at the scene hunched over the body when Morrison arrived. She looked at her boss but refrained from commenting on his appearance. She had to proceed carefully. His eyes looked like road maps and there was a patch of gray stubble on his right jaw that his shaver had missed.

"The victim is Carlos Sanchez," she said.

"Who?" Morrison's voice was gravelly.

Dottie stood up and looked at her superior officer. "Carlos Sanchez, you know, the owner of Heavenly Maids."

"I.D. on him?"

"Didn't have to check his I.D., I interviewed him yesterday." How could she not recognize that slicked back hair and those long eye lashes, beautiful even in death?

Morrison's face clouded. "What?"

"I know, I know. You told me not to follow up on Heavenly Maids, but I came here before work yesterday." Dottie might circumvent her boss's orders, but she could never tell him an outright lie. She saw thunder clouds amassing in his eyes and waited for the reprimand.

"And...?" His eyes drilled into hers.

"He was wearing a Rolex watch and a diamond pinky ring—items reported stolen from the burglarized houses."

"Get tech to check the I.D. on them. Make sure they're the stolen ones," Morrison said as he turned toward the coroner.

"He's not wearing them today."

Morrison slowly turned back to face Dottie and raised his eyebrows. "Oh?"

Dottie felt as if she were walking across a firing range, ducking bullets. At any minute Morrison could verbally shoot her. He was never in a particularly good mood, but today he was hung-over and she had disobeyed his direct order not to interview Sanchez.

"Look, I know I didn't get your stamp of approval. I did it on my own time. I had a gut feeling about him and Tori always says to go with gut feelings. It's not like I don't have a model for that behavior." Dottie was speaking at a New Yorker's pace, a hundred miles a minute and sounding guiltier with every word. She jutted her chin defiantly and stopped talking.

Morrison scowled. "He wore them yesterday and they're not there now? That what you're saying?"

Dottie looked her superior officer in the eye. "Yes. He was nervous when I interviewed him, so I pushed him. I asked about the burglarized houses and about the watch and ring. He was unnerved—sweating all over his silk shirt. Told me the watch was a rip off he got on the street in Miami."

Dottie hesitated. Seeing she had Morrison's attention, possibly even his approval, she said, "At least one of the houses that hadn't listed Heavenly Maids as their cleaning service, used them at the time of the burglaries. The owners didn't remember until I asked them specifically."

"Okay, Epstein. Good job. See if anyone saw him with the watch. Find out if someone can confirm where he got it." He looked at the body. "And when he got it."

Tori slipped under the crime scene tape and joined Morrison. "You look like you're the one hit by the truck," she observed. "Are you suicidal, Herb? Last night you drank yourself into oblivion. The day before you ate enough cookies to put yourself into a coma. Then you cheated on your wife."

"I know. I know. I'm an idiot. Don't tell Ruth. You know, about Annie. She'd kill me."

"She won't have to," Tori said. "You're doing a pretty good job of killing yourself."

"I feel as bad as I deserve," he said.

Dr. Nguyen joined them. "You okay, Morrison?" The medical examiner asked.

"Bad night," Morrison said. "Fill us in about the incident."

"Hit by a vehicle," Nguyen said. "Pretty heavy one—truck or SUV. First hit sent him flying. Then the killer drove over him a couple of times. What one might call 'overkill.'" The ME grinned. "I'll know more when I do the post mortem."

"Same vehicle that hit Mrs. O'Neal?"

"Yes, probably. I'll have to have the lab compare the paint flakes."

"When will we get results?"

"Later today. I'll call you." Nguyen walked away.

"What do you think, Doc?"

"If it's the same vehicle, it's the same person who killed Mrs. O'Neal," Tori said. "The murderer doesn't just kill. He inflicts pain, likes to see the victim's suffering. This is at least his second murder. He'll kill again."

"He?" Morrison asked.

149

"Yes, serial murderers are almost always men. This one's a sadist as well as a serial murderer," Tori said. "He's probably got that gene for violence, MAOA-2R."

"Tell me about the gene," Morrison said.

"The research is controversial. Supposedly, if a male is genetically susceptible to aggression and is exposed to violence as a child, he'll become violent when he grows up."

"Say that in English," Morrison said, rubbing his head.

"The murderer probably was abused as a child or witnessed a lot of violence. He might have grown up in a violent neighborhood. Maybe his father was abusive to him or to his mother or both," Tori said.

"My father beat me and my mother. I never killed anyone," Morison said.

"You probably don't have the gene that predisposes you to violence."

Morrison turned away and asked the cop behind him, "Anyone see the hit-and-run?"

"No, but one of the women who works here said she saw a red pick-up truck leaving the parking lot. She came in early to …."

"Put out an APB on the truck," Morrison said to Dottie.

"Done."

"Anyone else see it?"

"Yes," Dottie said. "The paper delivery guy saw the truck leave. He said the truck backed up to his front bumper and stayed there a moment. He didn't get the whole license number, just the first three digits. Said it's registered in Marion County. He was born there. Recognized the license plate."

"The killer wants you to find the truck," Tori said. "That's why he paused—so the paper man could see the license. Otherwise he would have covered the license or made sure no one saw it."

Dottie said. "The woman who works here saw the truck before. Sanchez was talking to the driver a week or so ago."

"Any description of the driver?" Morrison asked.

"No, it was dark and the truck was speeding out of the parking lot this morning. When she saw it last week, she couldn't see the driver."

# CHAPTER THIRTY SIX

Alberto saw the blue lights in his rearview mirror, but he didn't worry. He was driving below the speed limit. He always did. He knew how southern cops treated Latinos and he never gave them the chance to find him doing something illegal. The cops were after someone else. He looked again and felt a rush of adrenalin. Something was wrong. The blue lights were flashing right behind him. The cop was saying something into a megaphone. Alberto's heart beat rapidly. He was legal—had a green card. Sweat broke out all over his body. His hands were slippery on the steering wheel.

Alberto pulled the truck over to the shoulder and started to get out. The State Trooper yelled and leveled a gun at him. Alberto trembled. The trooper waved his gun, indicating Alberto should get back in the truck. He prayed to the Virgin of Guadeloupe as he climbed behind the steering wheel. He reached for the rosary beads hanging from his rearview mirror, but the trooper shouted at him again. Every word of English Alberto ever knew was erased by fear. He sat like petrified wood.

Later that morning, Morrison and Tori watched through a one-way mirror as Dottie questioned Alberto, the driver of the truck which had run over Sanchez. Alberto Paredes rattled on in Spanish, or more accurately Spanglish, to the interpreter.

Alberto made the sign of the cross. "Dear Mary, mother of God, pray for me. As God is my witness, I got green card," he said.

151

Dottie told Alberto through the translator, "We're not from Immigration."

"Blessed be God. Thank you Mother Mary," he said kissing the medal hanging from the chain around his neck.

"Okay. Enough," Dottie said. "Ask Alberto about the truck he was driving."

"I buy truck. I got receipt. I swear on lives of my dear children I no steal truck."

Dottie asked. "Where's this receipt?"

Before the interpreter could translate the question, Alberto started gesticulating and talking even faster. "Hablo mas despicio, por favor," the translator said. "Speak more slowly, please."

"Police have receipt," he said waving his arms and pointing in the direction of the police desk. "They take everything. They take pictures of my children and my wife. Mother of God, what I do?"

"Just answer the questions," Morrison grumbled.

"That man is scared out of his wits," Tori said. "He's not a hardened killer."

"Then why was he driving that truck an hour after it ran over Sanchez?"

"Why don't you ask him?"

Morrison frowned, but relayed the question through the speaker to Dottie's ear phones.

"Ask him when and where he bought the truck," Dottie said clenching her fists in her lap.

"I buy truck last night. Man from Miami," the translator reported Alberto saying. "Ad for truck on window. 7-11 store in Hastings. I call man. We meet."

"Where were he and the truck at 6:30 this morning," Dottie asked.

"Julio drive me to get truck." Alberto looked at the interpreter like she was crazy. "Why?"

Dottie said, "I thought he said he bought the truck last night."

"He says he bought the truck last night, but picked it up this morning," the interpreter said.

"That truck ran over a man at 6:30 this morning," Dottie said. "When and where did he get the truck?"

Alberto wrung his hands. Then he blessed himself and began praying.

"Have him answer the question." Dottie spoke through gritted teeth.

"I pick up truck early. Man sell truck say he leave in parking lot of bar. I worry not get it right. He give me spare key and title. He say I pay tonight. I need truck. Need get to work. Mother of God. How will children eat?"

Tori turned to Morrison. "Alberto didn't kill Sanchez. He's not a murderer."

"Might be a good actor," Morrison said.

"He's not acting. He's frightened."

"What time did you pick the truck up?" Dottie asked Alberto through the interpreter.

"Muy early—little after 7:00."

"What did the owner say when you picked it up?"

"He no there. Oh, Mother of God, protect me." The litany to all the saints in heaven continued.

"Don't translate his prayers, damn it," Dottie said. "Ask him what he meant when he said the owner wasn't there."

"She not understand? I buy truck last night. He need use it. Give me keys and title. Say get this morning after 7:00. We meet tonight in bar. I pay cash. I got receipt."

Dottie took a photograph of Sanchez out of the folder. "Ask him if he knows this man?"

Alberto was excited. "He's guy! He's guy! Thank God, that's him."

"What guy?"

"Guy sold me truck. Guy I see at bar last night."

Morrison and Tori looked at each other. Dottie managed to keep her face neutral as she asked him the man's name.

"Giovanni Romero," Alberto said, a big smile across his face.

"Giovanni Romero?" Morrison asked. "Who the hell's Giovanni Romero?

# CHAPTER THIRTY SEVEN

Morrison shook hands with the attorney. "Mr. Lavanderos, I'm sorry for calling you back. We had some new developments this morning and we have some additional questions for your client."

Edward Delgado drummed his fingers on the metal table and glared at Morrison.

Morrison switched on the recorder. "Let the record show that Detective Morrison is interviewing Eduardo Delgado and his attorney, Joseph Lavanderos, 9:00 am. April 18."

"Mr. Delgado, how well do you know Carlos Sanchez?" Morrison asked.

"You asked me that yesterday. The answer is still the same. He's a friend." Delgado leaned back in his chair as if he were not concerned about being interviewed.

"When was the last time you saw him?"

Delgado turned to Lavanderos. "Do I have to answer these questions again?"

Lavanderos said to Morrison. "My client answered those questions yesterday."

"There have been some new developments, Mr. Lavanderos," Morrison said. He turned to Delgado. "Mr. Delgado, did you have any contact with Mr. Sanchez yesterday?"

"No. Is that all?" Delgado asked.

"Mr. Delgado, where were you between 6:00 and 8:00 this morning?"

"I don't get up until 6:30. I was at home. I left about 7:30 for the bank. I opened it at 8:00." Delgado turned to his attorney. "Why do I have to explain my whereabouts to him?"

"Carlos Sanchez was murdered about 6:30 this morning," Morrison said.

Delgado sat up straight. His face went ashen.

"Let the record show that Mr. Delgado reacted strongly to being told of Mr. Sanchez's death."

"What happened to him?" Delgado asked.

"He was run down by a truck this morning."

Delgado covered his face with his hands.

"How did you know him?" Morrison asked.

"He worked for Iglesias in Miami."

"And you renewed your acquaintance here in Gainesville?"

Delgado nodded.

"Let the record show Mr. Delgado nodded in response to the question."

"When?"

"A couple years ago. We were friends."

"Friends who worked together?"

Lavanderos whispered in Delgado's ear. Delgado sat staring ahead. He shrugged.

Morrison waited a moment then asked, "Who is Giovanni Romero?"

Delgado gasped. He leaned toward his attorney and they had a whispered conversation. Lavanderos nodded.

Delgado said, "Giovanni Romero is a friend of Carlos Sanchez."

"Do you know him?" Morrison asked.

"No, I've only heard about him."

After the interview Morrison joined Tori in his office. "What do you think, Doc?"

"Delgado acted upset about Sanchez's death," she said.

"Was it an act?"

Tori said, "Delgado has an anti-social personality disorder and..."

"Cut the psychobabble. What the hell's an anti-social whatever?"

"Sorry, Morrison," Tori said. "You've probably heard the old terms 'psychopath' or 'sociopath.' Those terms are used interchangeably now. Psychologists prefer the term anti-social personality disorder."

"Yeah. So?"

"It's hard to tell if someone with an anti-social personality disorder is lying," Tori said. "Most people who lie get caught because they feel guilty and show signs of nervousness. People with an anti-social personality disorder don't feel guilt. They aren't nervous, so it's hard to catch them lying."

"So Delgado might be upset or he might have killed Sanchez?'

"Yes. But once again Mr. Lavanderos reacted strongly—this time to Giovanni Romero's name. He knows him."

"Think Delgado knows him?" Morrison asked.

"It's hard to say. Mr. Lavanderos doesn't have an anti-social personality disorder, so he's easier to read," Tori said. "Delgado admits he knows the name."

"My friend in Miami is checking on Romero."

"It's possible Carlos Sanchez used Giovanni Romero as an alias when he worked for Iglesias," Tori said.

# CHAPTER THIRTY EIGHT

The house was similar to the other houses on the street: small, flat-roofed cinderblock squares with peeling paint and lawns more dirt than grass. The house had been white at some point in its history, but now splotches of black mold spilled down from the windows and eaves and the paint had aged to an unappealing gray. Broken slats on the blinds attempted to shield the small house from the outside world.

Three black and whites were parked in the street when Morrison pulled into the driveway, which was barely long enough to hold his car. He greeted the uniformed officer who was keeping the curious neighbors at bay. He looked up to see Dottie emerge from the house.

"Strange home for the owner of a successful company," Morrison said, walking to the front door to join Dottie.

"He didn't live here."

Morrison looked at her quizzically, "You said he did."

"It was his house. He **owned** the house, but kept it for the women."

"The women?"

"The Heavenly Maids."

"You're nuts. Bosses don't provide housing for the help." Morrison rubbed his temples. *When will the Advil kick in and stop this damn headache?*

"He wasn't being benevolent."

Morrison asked. "What?"

"You'll see," she said as she opened the door. They entered a small unfurnished room.

The two detectives were engulfed by pandemonium. A dozen women spoke animatedly in Spanish to four police officers. The police did not understand a word the women said. Three women huddled in a corner, weeping. A woman walked toward Dottie. She stopped when she saw Morrison.

Dottie raised her finger. "Un momento."

"What the fuck's going on?" Morrison asked.

"Lower your voice. They'll panic."

Morrison repeated his question in a lower voice through gritted teeth.

"Sanchez conned these women into coming to the U.S.," Dottie said. "Human trafficking. He got them in Columbia. Promised to marry each woman. They got here. No marriage, no jobs, they're stuck. Illegal immigrants—couldn't complain to the authorities. Nowhere to go—virtual slaves."

Morrison ran his hand through his hair. "Notify INS."

"You nuts? They'll deport them. We'll never find out what happened to Sanchez."

"I'm not interested in your libertarian ideas," Morrison said. "Too bad, but these women're illegal. Notify INS. I'm not abetting a crime."

"I'm not saying don't notify INS," Dottie said. "Just delay notifying them. Once we notify them, these women are theirs. We can't interview them. Just delay."

"What good'd that do?"

"We find out about the burglaries. Show them Margaret's photo. Mention INS and they'll clam up."

Morrison observed the mayhem in the house, sighed, and after a moment said, "All right, all right. Interview them. Show them Margaret's photo."

"Thanks, Morrison."

"Anyone else speak Spanish?"

"No one here. I've called Maria Perez. She's on her way."

"I didn't say don't contact INS." Morrison pointed his beefy finger in Dottie's face. "You got 'til 4:00." He lowered his voice, "Call them then. They won't get out here 'til morning."

"Thanks."

Morrison looked around, hands on his hips. "God! Must be a hundred of them. Where do they sleep?"

Dottie motioned with her head for her superior officer to follow her down the dark hallway. She opened a door on the right and flipped the light switch. A single bulb hanging from a cord illuminated half a dozen mattresses on the floor. Each mattress, covered with a single crumpled sheet, harbored a small collection of prized possessions—photographs, makeup, plastic bags stuffed with belongings. A small teddy bear nestled on the bed nearest the door. Morrison shook his head, mumbling curses under his breath. Dottie took him to see the scene repeated in two rooms further down the hall.

"Looks like slave quarters or… or a prison," said Morrison.

"Florida's a leader in human trafficking," Dottie said. "Went to a workshop. Lots of sex trade, but some working slavery."

"Where did Sanchez live?"

"In a better section of town. His favorites lived with him. They drove the women to clean. Spoke enough English to get by. Kept the other women in line."

Morrison was still shaking his head when he asked Dottie, "What's the address for Sanchez's house?"

After Dottie gave Morrison the address, he left, looking over his shoulder and muttering to himself.

Dottie took a deep breath. She'd spoken Spanish a lot when she lived in New York. Now her opportunity to use it was limited to "real" Mexican restaurants or on her infrequent trips to south Florida or back home. She turned to the women who had been watching her talk to Morrison. She smiled and tried her rusty Spanish, slowly explaining to the women that she was going to ask them some questions. "Preguntas."

They nodded and gathered around her. She knew they were wary, but preferred to talk with her rather than the uniformed officers. Her halting Spanish was comforting. She pointed to the kitchen and waved her hand. "Vamos, por favor." They followed her and sat around the table. "Gracias."

Dottie showed the women Margaret O'Neal's photograph. "Have you seen this woman?" she asked. Two of them got excited.

"I see her. I see her."

159

"Donde? Where did you see her?" asked Dottie almost as excited as they were.

"On television," they said in unison.

*Great,* thought Dottie, her shoulders sagged.

She showed them the photograph of the house in which Margaret was video-taped on CCTV.

They all spoke at once. They recognized the house.

"Bien. How do you know the house? One at a time, por favor."

"We clean."

"You know the house was burglarized? Si?"

"Si."

Dottie asked, "Did you see the Rolex watches and the diamond tennis bracelet? The things stolen?"

"Si, si. Carlos say look. No want nothing missing."

"Did Sanchez go to that house?"

"Si."

"Before or after the jewelry—la joyeria—was stolen?"

"Before casa robbed."

Dottie showed them another photograph. It was of the house burglarized before the Phillips' house.

Clara said, "I clean house."

Dottie described the items stolen from the house.

"I remember," Clara said. "Mrs. Reynolds cry. Padre gave pearl necklace. He die last year." Her mouth lowered into a sad frown.

"Where was the necklace kept?" Dottie asked.

"Top drawer."

As Dottie went through the photographs of the other houses. The young women became more comfortable with her and began talking voluntarily.

"When did Sanchez go to the houses? Did he check up on the cleaning?"

Juanita said, "Dios, he don't care cleaning. He want know where la joyeria. When people on vacation." The others sneered and nodded.

"Si, si," Juanita said, "he check Phillips' house. It rob when they on vacation."

A light bulb flashed in Dottie's head. Sanchez planned the burglaries so no one was around to intercept the burglar. Now all she needed was to figure out who the burglar or burglars were. Where did Sanchez get the people who burglarized the houses?

# CHAPTER THIRTY NINE

Morrison's head throbbed. *Those Advil aren't helping.* He strained to concentrate as he drove across Gainesville to one of the golf course developments with manicured lawns and large, well-cared for houses. Sanchez had lived in a pricey neighborhood. Morrison spotted the street number on a wrought iron sign imbedded in the stone column at the end of the drive. He pulled into the driveway of the two-story house with a three-car garage. The first floor was brick with a large entranceway composed of two white columns, supporting an archway. The second floor was pale yellow with black shutters matching the double front doors.

An attractive young woman answered the doorbell. She had long black hair and big brown eyes framed by thick eye-lashes. Morrison thought, *those are 'dark Spanish eyes;' no wonder people write songs about them.* He identified himself to the woman, flipped open his badge and asked to come in.

"I legal," she said, lifting her chin.

"I'm not with INS. It's about Carlos Sanchez."

"Not here," she said, attempting to close the door.

Morrison jammed his foot into the door. "Please let me in. I need to talk to you."

Her dark eyes blazing, she stepped away from the door, and motioned for Morrison to follow. She walked into a family room. French doors in the far wall opened onto a pool and displayed a view of the golf course. She sat on the edge of a hassock and nodded toward the curved cream colored leather couch.

"What is your name, please?"

"Irma Sanchez."

"Carlos Sanchez's wife?"

"Yes."

"Anyone else here, Mrs. Sanchez?"

"My sister. She resting," she said.

"Please, bring her here."

"I tell you, she resting," her voice was sharp.

"Get her!" Morrison's voice was so stern the young woman blanched. She stood and silently walked out of the room. He checked his pockets for Advil. He fished out the bottle. It was empty. *Damn.*

A few minutes later Irma Sanchez returned leading a trembling girl by the hand. Except for coloring, the girl bore no resemblance to Irma. She was at least four inches taller than her 'sister.' *Sister, my foot*, thought Morrison. "What's your name?"

The girl turned to Irma, who said, "No speak English. Her Adrianna."

*Damn, I wish I'd paid attention in Spanish class,* Morrison thought. He said, "Please sit down, Mrs. Sanchez, Adrianna."

Irma Sanchez said something in Spanish to Adrianna and they sat on the sofa.

Morrison sat on the hassock opposite the two women. He rested his forearms on his thighs and leaned toward them. He clenched his hands to keep from wringing them. "Mrs. Sanchez, I have bad news. Carlos was hit by a truck this morning."

Irma's hand went to her throat. All color drained from her face. "How he is? In hospital?"

"I'm sorry, your husband is dead."

Irma Sanchez gasped and toppled off her seat onto the carpet. Morrison rushed to her, saying over his shoulder to Adrianna, "Get her some water."

Adrianna looked from Morrison to Irma, eyes wide. Morrison laid Irma on the floor. He checked the pulse in her neck. He looked at the sister. "Water," he said louder. *What the hell's the Spanish word for—ah*, "Agua." He could not fathom how he'd come up with the word but was grateful he had.

Adrianna rushed out of the room. In a moment she handed Morrison a glass of water. Morrison lifted Irma's head to help her take a sip. She swallowed a little water and started shaking.

Morrison asked, "Can you sit on the couch?"

Irma nodded and he assisted her to the sofa. Tears streamed down her face. Adrianna stood next to her, patting her shoulder, confusion on her face. Between sobs Irma said, "I tell him he dead if work with Giovanni. I tell him."

She dropped her head into her hands and wept.

"Giovanni Romero?" asked Morrison.

"No," she said between sobs, "Giovanni El Grande."

Adrianna asked Irma something in Spanish. Irma said, "Carlos es mort."

Adrianna stared at Morrison with wide eyes. She paled. Morrison watched her. He did not want another woman fainting. Adrianna slowly backed away and sat in a chair.

Morrison walked to the foyer and phoned Dottie. "Come to the Sanchez house. I need…

Dottie said, "Chief wants to see you."

"She can wait."

"I didn't hear that."

"Listen, there're two females here. One says she's Sanchez's wife."

"Doubt it," Dottie said.

"Me, too. A girl—looks 14—doesn't speak English. Older one says they're sisters. Don't look alike." He paused. "Epstein, get some Advil on your way. Extra strength."

Morrison had barely hung up when the doorbell rang. He admitted two technicians. He put his finger to his lips and they nodded. He led them upstairs and opened the door to a bedroom decorated in pink with lots of frills and ruffles. *Adrianna's?*

When Morrison opened the next bedroom door, the head technician whistled. The room was decorated in swinging bachelor mode.

The technician said to his colleague, "Hey, Rusty, get a load of this."

Rusty said, "I ain't never seen a round bed before." He paused. "Look, there's a mirror over it."

"Guess we know what he did here."

164

"Okay, keep your comments to yourselves," Morrison said. "Look for information about Sanchez and his operations. Look for jewelry—something might've been stolen." Morrison stood for a minute looking at the black and silver decor before walking into the en suite bathroom. It contained a huge circular Jacuzzi surrounded with half burnt candles of all colors and sizes and two champagne glasses next to an ice bucket with an empty bottle of champagne. *Not what you'd call subtle*, he thought.

"Okay. See what you can find. Stay up here until I finish talking with the women. Then you can check downstairs."

Morrison returned to the first floor and sat waiting for Dottie. Patience was not one of Morrison's strong traits. He got up and paced the floor, then noticed the young girl had tears running down her face. "Oh shit," he muttered to himself. *Where are you, Epstein?*

"Morrison, come up here," Rusty said.

Morrison bounded up the stairs and into the master bedroom. His eyes followed Rusty's pointing finger.

# CHAPTER FORTY

Tori leaned toward the mirror over the sink in her bathroom to apply eye liner. She took particular care. Gerry was picking up Sean and she wanted to look her best. She leaned back to survey the finished product. She sighed. Crows feet seem to overshadow the green eyes she considered her best feature. *When did I start wrinkles?* She wondered. Her 38th birthday loomed.

"Mom! Mom!" Sean called.

"I'm in here," she said. "What is it?"

"Dad wants to know if you can go to dinner with us tonight."

"Is he here already?"

Sean walked into the bathroom carrying the cordless phone in one hand and orange juice in the Knicks glass Morrison had given him in the other.

"He's at the airport."

Tori reached for the phone, but Sean pulled it away. "Can you or can't you?"

Tori put out her hand and gave Sean a mother's look that said it all. He handed her the phone. He took a gulp of orange juice.

"Hi, Gerry, I have to meet Morrison and Dottie in 30 minutes."

"Hi, Beautiful. Can you cancel them?"

"I wish I could. I'm working on a case and they have new info. I can do a late dinner."

"That won't work for me. I need to get back by 8:00. Maybe next time."

Disappointment filled Tori's gut. *When will Gerry and I be in sync?* She wondered.

Gerry said, "I'll pick Sean up in 10 minutes. Ciao!"

Tori went back to applying her make up.

"Mom, can I talk to you?"

"Sure, Sean, what is it?"

"It's about Frank."

"Who's Frank?"

While Tori dabbed on eye shadow, she thought, *Maybe the next time Gerry picks up Sean I should invite him to dinner. Is that too obvious?*

"Mom? Mom? Did you hear me?"

"I'm sorry, Sean. I was thinking about something."

"Never Mind." He stormed out of the room.

"Wait, Sean." She caught up with him and took his arm. "Sean, I was upset about not going to dinner with you and Dad." She looked in his eyes. "Forgive me?"

He nodded.

"Please tell me again." She led him to the couch and sat next to him. "Who's Frank?"

"The bully. He stole our bikes—Randy's and mine."

"I remember. And?"

"His father's beating him," Sean said. "Real bad."

"Tell me about it."

"He's got big red cuts all over his back. They're all bloody and full of pus. He hurts real bad. His father whipped him."

"That's awful, Sean. Has he told anyone?"

"No. I saw his back after soccer. He waited to change until everyone else left. He didn't see me."

Tori took her son's hand. "Did you tell anyone? A teacher? Coach?"

"No. Frank said his father would kill him if he told anyone."

"Sean, that's my concern. His father might kill him."

"You won't tell anyone, will you?"

"Sean, I have to call DCF. The law requires me to."

Sean stood up and faced his mother. His face was contorted with rage. "I knew you'd get me in trouble."

"Sean, Frank is a bully. Sometimes kids become bullies because they're abused."

"He's going to hate me."

The doorbell rang and Sean started toward the door.

Tori caught his arm. "Sean, this isn't about you. This is about protecting Frank."

"Dad will know what to do." He ran to the door and opened it for his father.

"Dad, tell her she can't do that. Tell her."

Gerry asked, "What's going on?"

After Tori explained, Gerry put his arm around Sean's shoulder. "Son, what you described is child abuse. Your mother has to report it. If she doesn't I will. It's the law."

"You don't understand…"

"The law was put there because people don't want to report child abuse," Tori said. "I won't mention your name."

"Frank will know."

Gerry said, "Frank will be grateful if someone stops the abuse."

# CHAPTER FORTY ONE

Morrison looked into the bottom drawer of the big dresser. Under a stack of shirts, the technicians had uncovered a Rolex watch and three men's rings—one a diamond ring. "Lookie, lookie, what have we here?"

With gloved hands, Rusty took the jewelry out and placed the items in a bag.

"Check if they match stolen items," Morrison said.

Rusty said, "Rolexes have serial numbers, it'll be easy to trace."

"Good work," Morrison said. "Keep searching."

Morrison heard a car in the driveway and looked out the front window. He ran down the stairs and opened the door for Dottie. She motioned him to join her on the front porch for a quick consult.

"Epstein, got the Advil?" Morrison asked.

"Yeah." She searched through her backpack and pulled out a CVS bag and handed it to Morrison.

Morrison reached in the bag, took out the box and ripped it open. He pulled out the bottle.

Dottie said, "I checked with Juanita. She said Irma isn't married to Sanchez; she's his number one lover. Been with Sanchez for years."

"For years? She can't be more than 22." Morrison opened the bottle and tapped out four or five pills. He stuffed them in his mouth and swallowed.

"He likes them young."

"Perverted bastard."

Dottie said, "The girl isn't Irma's sister. Sanchez brought her from Columbia. Liked her. Doubt she's a legal immigrant."

"Not legal age, either." Morrison clenched his fists. "Wish that son of a bitch were alive. I'd get him for child sexual abuse." Morrison's face was red, a purple vein pulsed in his forehead.

Dottie told Morrison about her interviews and he brought her up to date on the watch and rings.

"Great! That ties Sanchez to the burglaries," Dottie said.

By the time Morrison and Dottie went into the house Irma had regained her composure. She was sitting on the sofa comforting Adrianna. Morrison picked up the glass of water he had given Irma and downed the remnants. He sat to one side while Dottie introduced herself.

"Irma. May I call you Irma?" Dottie asked.

The petite woman nodded but kept her arms around the girl, her face turned away from Dottie.

"I'm sorry about Carlos' death," Dottie said. She waited, but there was no response. "Irma, we want to find who did this to Carlos."

Still no response.

"Irma, Carlos was using the Heavenly Maids to rob houses."

Irma sat up straight, took one arm from around the girl, and turned to face Dottie. "Women no rob."

"Who did the robbing?"

Irma shrugged, "Carlos tell me nada."

"How do you know about it?"

Irma took her other arm from around the young girl and moved to one side. She put both her hands under her thighs, rocked forward and took a deep breath. "Carlos drink como una esponja. When tomado...drunk, talk."

"Who robbed the houses?"

Irma rocked faster. "Giovanni get people."

"Who's Giovanni?" Morrison asked.

Irma looked at Morrison and stopped rocking. Dottie frowned at Morrison and he stopped talking.

Dottie asked, "Who's Giovanni?"

"Morrison, come up and listen to this," Rusty called.

Morrison and Dottie ran up the stairs. Rusty showed them into an office. On the desk was an answering machine. Rusty said, "Listen to this." He pushed the play button.

A man's voice said, "Carlos, the big *kahuna* says you kept a watch. The cops are on to you. Get rid of it—now. I'll send it to Miami."

"That's Delgado," Dottie said. "I'd swear to it."

# CHAPTER FORTY TWO

Dottie and Morrison returned downstairs and Dottie continued the interview of Irma.

"Sorry for the interruption, Irma," Dottie said. "You told us about Giovanni. Who's Giovanni?"

"Carlos know Giovanni in Miami," Irma said. "Giovanni is *el alborotado*."

"A troublemaker," Dottie said. "Is Giovanni still in Miami?"

"No. Carlos see Giovanni picture in …" She made a circular motion with her finger indicating she did not know the word in English. "periodico."

"Newspaper? *Gainesville Sun*?" Dottie asked.

"Si. He el pez gordo in Gainesville."

"What the hell is pass gordo?" Morrison asked.

"Big shot," Dottie said. "Stop interrupting." She turned back to Irma. "So Giovanni is el pez gordo?"

"Have otra name. Carlos laugh. Say he el estafador."

"Giovanni is a con artist?" Dottie asked.

"Si. I beg Carlos no see Giovanni. No listen." Irma sighed. "He happy. Have new chanchullo. Rob houses. He got keys."

Dottie asked, "Did he rob the houses himself?"

"No. Otras people rob houses. Give sustantivo—you know, jewels, Giovanni. Giovanni give jewels someone in Miami."

"Did you ever see Giovanni? Did he ever come here?"

"No, I see in Miami."

"Can you describe him to me? Would you recognize him?"

"Long time. He same tall as Carlos, bigger." She stretched her arms out at shoulder height.

"Fat? Gordo?"

"No. He have…" She tensed her arm and pointed to her bicep. "You know."

"He was muscular?"

"Si. Si. Carlos say Giovanni in prison. Lift…you know…there." She pantomimes lifting weights.

"Lifted weights."

"Si. Si."

"What about hair, eyes?"

"Dark curly hair. Down here." She indicated her shoulder.

"Hispanic?"

"I think." She shrugged. "He and Carlos no speak Spanish. Speak English and mine no so good then."

"Irma, Marcella told me Carlos was involved with prostitution in Miami."

"Marcella have big mouth." She bared her top teeth. "Big ideas. No think. No moral."

"Marcella was immoral?" Dottie asked. "Was she a prostitute?"

Irma scoffed at the idea. "Marcella was…" she looked at Morrison. She lowered her voice. "She la tortillera."

"She made tortillas?'

Irma shook her head. "She like women, you know."

"She's a lesbian?"

Irma put her hands out, confused.

"She likes women, not men?"

"Si. Si. She and Juanita…you know." Irma blushed.

"Lovers?"

"Si."

"Carlos found out and sent her to the other house?"

"No. Carlos no know Marcella like women. He punish her because want free. She get Juanita and Paula out. Paula Juanita's sister. They walking on road. Marcella and Juanita go woods to pee. Paula get caught. Cop see Paula. Pick her up. Juanita scared. Come back. Marcella, too. Carlos punish her."

"Irma, you told Detective Morrison you were married to Carlos." Dottie said. "That's not true is it?"

Irma sighed. "No, we say married so I get green card." She looked down at her hands folded in her lap. "He want marry me." She looked up.

"Was Carlos afraid of Giovanni?"

"Yesterday he afraid. Say he go somewhere for Giovanni. He say Giovanni kill him if screw up again."

# CHAPTER FORTY THREE

Morrison, with Dottie in his wake, plowed through the after work crowd enjoying "Sundowner" at Emiliano's to the back of the café where Tori was sitting at a table sipping red wine. As he plopped in a seat, Morrison said, "How can they tolerate this racket and confusion?"

"They're here for the cheap beer and 2 for 1 drinks," Dottie said.

Tori added, "Not to mention the opportunity to hook up with someone. The more singles here the better chance they have. It's the '2 am beauty queen' phenomenon."

"The what?" Morrison asked. He fiddled with his keys. The TV over the bar suddenly went black and the clientele stopped talking mid-sentence to turn toward the blank screen. Blessed silence lasted a few seconds before the chattering resumed.

Tori glanced at the TV, then turned back to Morrison and explained. "When bars get close to closing time, people who haven't paired off with someone perceive potential dates as better looking—thus the 2 am beauty queen."

The bartender turned the TV back on and Dottie looked at Morrison, "Are you using that thing to turn off the TV, again?"

Morrison grinned. "The TV B Gone clicker, I'm never without it."

"You'll get us killed one of these days, Morrison." Tori said.

"I'll protect you." He pointed the gadget toward the TV again.

The bartender looked at Morrison and winked. He told the complainers that the TV was on the fritz. He meandered over to their table and said, "Detective, I'll leave the TV off for 20 minutes. When I turn it back on, I expect it to stay on. I don't want to ban you."

"Okay, okay," Morrison said. "How about getting me a Corona? Keep my second one cold." He turned to the women and asked, "What do you want?"

Dottie ordered a Mojito.

Tori avoided eye contact with the bartender. "I'm fine."

After the bartender left, Dottie asked Tori, "Where's Sean?"

"He's spending the weekend with his dad. We had a big fight." Tori described the incident.

Morrison said, "I'll check on Frank over the weekend."

"Did you call DCF?" Dottie asked.

Tori nodded.

Morrison asked, "Didn't Gerry use to stay and go out with you and Sean on Friday evenings?"

Tori nodded. "Tell me what you found at Sanchez's house while we still have a modicum of quiet."

"We'll discuss the case, but I know you're avoiding talking about Gerry," Morrison said.

Dottie described the scene at the house where the women were kept.

"My god, they were slaves," Tori said. "Where did he find the women?"

"He brought them from Columbia. Promised to marry them," Dottie said, mirroring Tori's frown.

"My contact on Miami PD said Sanchez has been bringing in illegal aliens for years, most of them underage. He furnished whorehouses. The authorities were about to clamp down on him when he disappeared—apparently, to move to Gainesville and start Heavenly Maids. Brought a couple of the women with him. Got more in Columbia."

"Bastard," Dottie said.

"Those women are going to need psychological help," Tori said.

"INS doesn't provide counseling for illegal immigrants," Dottie said. She glared at Morrison.

176

Tori turned to Morrison, her eyes wide. "You didn't turn those poor women over to INS, did you?"

"What could I do? I swore to uphold the law when I took this job. Can't hide a crime."

"This country has too many laws," Dottie said. "Victimless crimes shouldn't be illegal."

"Don't start that libertarian bunk, again," Morrison said.

"Prostitution should be taxed and supervised, like in Europe—in Germany and Belgium," Dottie said. "Then people like Sanchez wouldn't be able to force women into prostitution."

"We don't make the laws," Morrison said. "We enforce them whether we like them or not."

Tori knew Dottie was libertarian. She didn't know that Morrison was aware of it. He was strictly law and order. She asked, "Sanchez was running a prostitution ring?"

"Not here," Morrison said. "He provided women to brothels in Miami."

"None of the women were legal?" Tori asked.

"A couple were," Dottie said. "Would you counsel them?"

"Of course."

"We can't pay you."

Tori waved Dottie's concern away. "I'll call you over the weekend and set it up."

"Thanks," Dottie said.

"Was Delgado involved with the Heavenly Maids and the burglaries?" Tori asked.

"Can't prove it," Dottie said. "But, I swear his voice was on Sanchez's answering machine about a Rolex. Probably the one I saw Sanchez wearing."

"He knew Sanchez in Miami—they both worked for Iglesias," Morrison said.

"The one who runs the Cuban Mafia?" Tori asked.

"Yeah, Delgado collected gambling debts for him."

"Can't you arrest him for that?"

"Got no proof."

"Why did Delgado move to Gainesville?" Tori asked.

"Iglesias needed legitimate people in banking. Someone to launder money. He paid for Delgado to go to UF."

Dottie said, "Delgado collected debts like Rafferty's for Iglesias."

"We can tie Delgado to Rafferty and Rafferty to O'Neal, but can't connect either of them to Margaret O'Neal's murder," Morrison said. "It was just a coincidence Delgado collected a debt from Rafferty."

"I don't believe in coincidences, especially ones that big," Tori said. "Not to mention that Margaret and Sanchez were both run down. And by the same man."

"Yeah, yeah," Morrison said. "Can't prove a connection between Delgado and the burglaries."

"What about that Giovanni Romero, Alberto mentioned?" Tori asked.

Morrison snapped his fingers. "Reminds me. Irma said his last name was El Grande. Romero might be an alias. Epstein, check that name out on the computer."

# CHAPTER FORTY FOUR

Later that evening, Tori sat in her university office with her feet up, sipping a glass of iced tea, while grading papers. She usually graded papers at home, but with Sean visiting his father, the house felt cold and empty. The alone times she used to savor were no treat when they occurred every other weekend. As quiet as the university office was, it somehow did not seem as lonely. She was evaluating a tediously written paper describing a worthless research project. She attempted to make positive suggestions but found little of value to build upon.

The ringing phone felt like a reprieve. *Maybe it's Gerry.* Disappointment gripped her when she checked the caller ID. It said "Curry." It took a moment before the name registered—Annie Curry.

At least it was an excuse to stop reading drivel. After exchanging pleasantries, Annie asked, "How is Herb doing?"

"Don't go there. It's none of your business."

Annie said, "I understand. That's not why I called." She paused. "I received the sweetest note from Karen Baker. Margaret had been a good friend and was kind to her." Annie rattled on about how sweet the note was and Tori, distractedly said, "Yes, she seems nice." Finally, Tori asked Annie why she was calling.

"I thought you were missing the point," Annie said. "Karen's the woman Margaret met at Dr. Rothstein's office. She had an appointment with him right before Margaret's appointment."

Annie now had Tori's undivided attention. "What's her name, again? Does the envelope have her return address?" Tori wrote them on a notepad. She looked at her watch, 7:30. *Not too late.* She found Karen's phone number on the internet and called.

Karen said, "Please come over. I'd like to talk about Margaret."

Karen lived in a predominantly black area on the north side. The flat roofed house was a faded burgundy with dark trim encircled by a freshly painted slat fence. A live oak with Spanish moss dangling from meandering limbs shaded the yard and dirt driveway.

The woman answering the bell was shorter than Tori, maybe 5'3". She appeared to be in her mid to late 60s, a dark-skinned woman with a neat gray Afro. She invited Tori in but said, "The house is a mess." She was not exaggerating. Although clean, the small house was so cluttered Tori felt claustrophobic. The disorder was not the result of sloppiness, but artwork. Every level surface was covered with pottery. One living room wall was lined with shelves brimming with pottery of varying artistic value. An étagère loaded with more pottery squeezed between the couch and an archway. Through the archway Tori observed a table laden with a hodgepodge of pottery in various stages of completion: wet and dry clay, green ware, bisque ware, and glazed pieces. Tori's head spun from over stimulation.

Karen said, "My husband and I planned to join the Peace Corps when we retired. But God took him the last year I taught."

"How unfortunate," Tori said. "What did you teach? Looking at the pottery and photographs, I'd guess art."

"No, pottery's my new avocation; I taught mathematics for 28 years. My husband was the artist, a photographer." She pointed to extraordinary photographs of Florida over the couch on the opposite wall. "God gave him great talent."

"He was good." After viewing the photographs, Tori asked if Karen's husband died suddenly.

"Yes and no." Karen rubbed the silver cross hanging around her neck as if it were a good luck charm. "He had stomach cancer. Was sick for a year, but I never believed he'd die. So, even though

180

I had lots of warning, to me his death was sudden. It seemed he was here one day and God took him the next."

"Is that why you're seeing Dr. Rothstein? For grief counseling?"

"Yes and no." She massaged the cross. "It isn't exactly for grief counseling." Karen folded her hands in her lap and looked down. "I assuaged my grief with alcohol."

After a moment Karen looked up. "Losing my husband was the most horrible thing ever happened to me. He was my best friend, my only real friend. In the evening I was lonely and I could hear him talking to me. If I drank, I heard him better."

She hesitated then said, "I began drinking a glass of wine with dinner. Then I'd have a night cap before going to bed." She emitted a mirthless laugh. "When I stopped teaching, I'd have a glass of wine with lunch. Then I'd have some Margaritas in the afternoon. When I felt bad the next morning, I'd have some Bloody Marys. I probably would have drunk myself to death, if I hadn't been caught.

"After the first DUI, I decided I could drink as long as I didn't drive. I thought God would help me." Karen looked at her hands clenched in her lap. "That worked for awhile. One night I craved pizza." She turned to face Tori. "They don't like to deliver here—a black area." Karen's hands were shaking. "The shaking isn't alcohol. It's embarrassment. Before I joined AA, I would have lied.

"Anyway," Karen said, "I went to get a pizza. I drove through a STOP sign. Thank God, no one was coming the other way." She shook her head. "I guess it was God's way of getting my attention." She looked to the heavens. She made the sign of the cross.

"The cop was parked on the cross street. He knew right away I was drunk as a skunk. When I went to court they allowed me to stay out of jail provided I went to AA meetings. I started the next day."

The tune "Can You Feel the Love Tonight" alerted Tori. She searched her purse and pulled out her cell phone. She flipped it open and said, "Can I call you back? I'm with someone."

She laughed. "No, it's not a date. A woman who knew Margaret O'Neal."

181

"Your husband?" Karen asked.

"No, actually it was Dr. Rothstein."

"Don't tell him what I say."

"Whatever you want," Tori said. "What made you decide to see Dr. Rothstein?"

"I go to AA meetings at my church. Dr. Rothstein spoke one night. He said he helped people with drinking problems. I thought it couldn't hurt to see a psychologist."

"Did he help you?"

"I'm a recovering alcoholic. I'm not sure how much my recovering is due to his therapy and how much because of AA or my addiction to pottery." Karen shrugged.

"My daughter was furious. She wouldn't let the twins, my granddaughters, stay with me." Karen pointed to a photograph of two toddlers in identical white dresses and sighed. "I love those little angels more than life itself." She smiled. "Certainly more than alcohol."

"They're adorable."

"That's an old picture. They're 10 now. I keep the photo because it reminds me of when Thomas photographed them a few months before he died. We had a wonderful day with the little loves. God protect those little angels." She blessed herself and grasped her cross.

"Tell me how you met Margaret O'Neal."

Karen's voice quivered. "I had to sit in the back of the bus when I was a youngster. I vowed never again. Sherry, my daughter, makes me take the bus to Dr. Rothstein's. She picks me up. Sometimes she gets out of class late. I'd be waiting when Margaret came for her appointment. Margaret looked familiar, but I couldn't place her. Then it clicked. She taught Sunday school at my church. I was about to introduce myself when she snapped her fingers and said 'Sunday school.' We laughed.

"We'd a lot in common—retired teachers and Catholic—really Catholic, not just in name. We both were trying to lose weight. She took me to Curves. Sometimes we walked together, not often. She liked to walk in the early morning and I don't do mornings. I promised myself I'd sleep in every day when I retired." She chuckled.

"What do you think about Margaret burglarizing a house?"

"Preposterous. Margaret would never rob anyone. Besides, she was seeing Dr. Rothstein when the robbery occurred."

"How do you know?"

"I saw her."

"You're sure you saw her the day of the robbery? In the office?"

"Absolutely positive. I saw the video of the woman who broke into the house on the morning news. When they said the burglary occurred the previous afternoon I knew it wasn't Margaret. I'd seen her at Dr. Rothstein's office."

"Did you tell Dr. Rothstein?"

"Yes, I told him yesterday. He said I was confused." She huffed. "I'm not confused. Margaret and I always see Dr. Rothstein on Thursday."

"What about the video they showed on TV? Didn't you think the woman in the video was Margaret?"

"It looked like Margaret. But, I knew it wasn't. God rest her soul."

Driving home, Tori was perplexed; something did not compute. Karen was adamant she'd seen Margaret at Rothstein's. Yet, Seth was just as insistent Margaret was a no-show that afternoon. Tori thought it more likely Karen Baker got the days confused than Rothstein—he kept records. *She's a recovering alcoholic and in her late 60s. Her memory's probably fading. Maybe she started drinking again and confused the days,* Tori thought.

Tori knew eyewitness identification was notoriously inaccurate. Hundreds of men convicted by it later were proven innocent by DNA. *Could they have misidentified Margaret on the CCTV? But a video tape's not the same as eyewitness identification.* Tori saw the video herself. It was Margaret. The woman was wearing the same clothes Margaret wore when the truck hit her. *I need to ask Karen what Margaret was wearing when she saw her at Dr. Rothstein's.*

The question still remained, *why did Margaret O'Neal burglarize a house? And how did she get the key and alarm code? She must have gotten it from Sanchez, but how? Why?*

An inkling of an idea began to form in the back of Tori's mind. She needed to review the video tape of the burglary again. If she was right, she might have solved the puzzle. As soon as she got home she'd call Seth and tell him her idea. She'd also ask him to help counsel the women Sanchez kept as slaves. Seth had told her he spoke Spanish.

# CHAPTER FORTY FIVE

Kevin Cunningham's MG would not start Saturday morning. Not an unusual occurrence; but it necessitated him driving his wife's SUV to the office he shared with Tori. Edie Cunningham teased her husband about his MG. She said it spent more time in the shop than on the road. He was beginning to think she was right. But while the body of Kevin's MG was in pristine shape, Edie's late model Toyota SUV looked as if it had spent the past year taking part in crash tests. His wife was easily distracted by their hyperactive twin sons. She had never been in a serious accident, but he worried about her. She was always denting or scratching the car. Even so, Kevin was careful because Edie would notice if he added any new scratches to her prized SUV. He muttered curses at his MG and at the large Lexus sedan extending into his reserved parking space. If he'd been driving his MG he could have fit in the space even with the Lexus taking more than its fair share. As it was he had to park the SUV across the parking lot.

Two hours later, a daydreaming Kevin looked out his office window while waiting for a late client. Something caught his attention, snapping him out of his reverie. An old Honda SUV in even worse condition than his wife's was parked in Kevin's reserved space. The driver sitting in the SUV was fiddling with something. Kevin looked intently. The driver was pulling something over his head—*a ski mask? a stocking?*
"What in heaven's name…?"

185

Kevin heard the back door close. *Good God Tori's on her way out.* Kevin ran to catch her. As she walked to her car he shouted. "Watch out! Behind you!"

Tori turned. The Honda SUV was heading directly toward her. The SUV blocked Kevin's view of Tori. He didn't see it clip Tori, sending her bouncing onto the hood of a car. Her body careened off the hood and fell between two cars. She banged her head on the door handle and again on the pavement. Kevin was quick-witted enough to catch the make, model, and part of the license number of the SUV. The ski-masked driver stopped to check the traffic. Kevin shouted at him, but the SUV sped out of the parking lot, tires screeching.

"I've got the first part of the license number," Kevin said. "Did you get the end of it?" He was busy writing the information on his palm.

"Tori, did you hear me?" She did not respond.

Kevin spotted Tori lying between two cars. When Kevin reached her, he could see Tori was bleeding from a head wound. There was blood on the handle of the car door on Tori's right. There was more blood on the pavement next to her head.

Kevin pulled off his shirt and pressed it against Tori's head wound to stop the bleeding. She moaned, the only sign she was alive. He told her she would be all right, almost believing it himself. "I'll call 911," he said, reaching for his phone.

With one hand trying to stop the bleeding, Kevin called 911 with the other hand. He asked them to send an ambulance immediately. "And notify Detective Morrison that Dr. Vincent has been hit."

The dispatcher asked, "Who do you want to notify?"

"Detective Morrison."

"Why? Who's he?"

Exasperated, Kevin said, "Forget it."

Still holding his shirt to her head, Kevin reached for Tori's purse with his free hand and dug out her cell phone. He cursed the ambulance, the SUV driver, the amount of stuff in Tori's purse and the small buttons on her cell phone. Finally he located Tori's direct dial to Herb Morrison.

Up to his elbows in dirt, Morrison was planting impatiens around the live oak in his back yard. He whistled, enjoying the early spring weather and the peacefulness of gardening before the heat of summer descended. Ruth was at the synagogue for Saturday service. Morrison was not Jewish so he never went with her. In fact, he did not practice any religion. The only time he bent his knees in worship was to something that grew in the ground.

Growing up in urban New Jersey, his family barely had a yard, never mind a garden. When he moved to Gainesville, Morrison planted tomatoes and zucchini. His delight was unbounded when the plants thrived and the vegetables were edible. He presented his first home-grown vegetables to his wife with a wide grin. Ruth's smile was almost as big as his. She wanted him to enjoy a hobby to take his mind off his job. Gardening was everything she had hoped for and more. He lost himself in it. He came from working in the garden covered in dirt and euphoric.

Morrison still had a good-sized vegetable garden, but he now grew plants and flowers as well. He had taken a course to become a master gardener. His passion for gardening amused his daughter, Jennifer. The idea of this great big, hard-nosed cop weeding flower beds tickled her.

Morrison looked up from his plants and made a mental note to prune his roses on the trellis behind the gazebo. He was contemplating the best way to prune them when the phone rang. Jennifer was reading a book in the gazebo, and she answered the cordless phone that accompanied her every move. The typical preteen, she could not bare to miss a friend's call.

She shouted to her father. "Dad, it's an emergency call."

Morrison said, "Damn it. Only day to relax and someone has to go and get himself killed." He stood up and brushed off his pants. "Second time this week my gardening's been interrupted."

Jennifer looked at her father. "I don't think someone 'got himself killed' just to keep you from gardening."

"Yeah, don't bet on it." Morrison took the phone from her.

# CHAPTER FORTY SIX

Morrison's car tore into the parking lot. He jumped out and sized up the situation. Kevin said to Morrison, "A guy in a ski mask. He hit her with an SUV."

Morrison asked, "Where's the ambulance?"

"I called 20 minutes ago."

Morrison was livid. It was a toss up whether he was more furious with the SUV driver or the ambulance driver for taking so long. Neither one would have survived an encounter with Morrison unscathed. He dialed 911. "Where the fuck is the ambulance for 23rd street? He called over 20 minutes ago."

The dispatcher calmly explained. "I thought it was a crank call."

"You what???"

"The caller said, 'forget it,' so I didn't notify the ambulance."

Morrison was apoplectic. He turned deep purple. He shouted. "You god damn idiot. Is that how you've been trained? Get that fucking ambulance over here now if you want a job tomorrow!"

Dottie's car barreled into the parking lot and squealed to a stop. She hopped out and looked around. Kevin shouted to her from where he was wedged between the two cars. He was still pressing his shirt to Tori's head. Dottie took over stopping Tori's wound from bleeding. She evaluated where Tori was lying. Dottie said to Morrison, "Move Tori's car so the EMTs can get to her."

Morrison retrieved Tori's keys from her purse, but was unable to squeeze into the front seat with the limited space between it and the car in the next parking space. Kevin, slimmer and more agile, got into the car on the passenger side, climbed across to the driver's seat and inched the car out of the parking space. Morrison directed him while Dottie leaned over Tori, protecting her with her own body.

Kevin got out of the car and said to Morrison, "The SUV was a beat-up old Honda CRV."

"How old?"

"Ten – 12 years. I got the first part of the license number." He showed Morrison the number written on his palm.

Morrison pulled out the police radio. "I want an APB for a ten or twelve year old Honda CRV." He gave them the partial license number.

Sirens and screeching tires announced the ambulance's arrival. Morrison signaled the driver to park near where Tori lay. "Over this way," he shouted at the medics. The medics went to work to stabilize Tori.

"We need patrol backup for the emergency on 23rd," Morrison called into his police radio. He went to watch the medics working on Tori. One bandaged her head and put a brace around her neck. Another EMT started an IV. A third EMT checked for broken bones and wrapped her leg in cushioning material. By the time they completed the initial preparations, the sound of a helicopter could be heard overhead.

Three black and whites, sirens blaring, pulled into the parking lot. Morrison shouted. "Block the entrance with your cars." When the cars were parked where he wanted them, Morrison said, "Keep the gawkers out of the parking lot. We got to have room for the helicopter to land."

The officers moved the expanding group of on-lookers out of the way just as the helicopter touched down.

Morrison watched like a doting father as the EMTs lifted the stretcher and placed Tori gently in the helicopter. He gulped when he heard Tori moan. She wasn't conscious, but she was alive.

Not until the helicopter took off with Tori did her friends become self-conscious about their appearances. A shirtless Kevin went to get a tee shirt from the athletic bag in his wife's SUV. Dottie looked Morrison up and down. Morrison followed her gaze, realized his pants were covered in dirt and brushed them off. "I was gardening," he said.

Dottie nodded, looking down at her own shorts and tank top stained with sweat.

"I was paying bills on the computer."

"Pretty sweaty job?"

"I was cooling down after my five mile run."

Morrison nodded.

Kevin rode to the hospital in the police car with Morrison driving, siren blaring and tires squealing. Kevin held on for his life—even Edie didn't drive that recklessly. Dottie sat in the back seat with Tori's cell phone. She used it to call Gerry Arroyo and tell him about his ex-wife's "accident."

"Where is she?"

"They're life-flighting her to Shands."

"What's her prognosis?"

"Gerry, I've told you everything I know. Just bring Sean to Shands."

By the time they got to the hospital, Tori was behind closed doors in the Emergency Room. The ER staff was not responsive to an overweight middle-aged man in dirty jeans, a thin black woman in sweat-stained shorts and tank top, and a youngish man wearing casual khakis and a bright fuchsia tee shirt with "I'm the Queen" emblazoned across the front. Kevin saw the clerk raise her eyebrows and was grateful the tee shirt was one of the large ones Edie kept to throw over her bathing suit. If it had been her size he would have been shirtless.

Flashing his badge did not get Morrison in to see Tori; however, it did get the ER physician's attention.

"Detective, we are working on Ms. Vincent and no one except family can go in."

"It's Dr. Vincent," Morrison said. "How is she?"

The doctor raised his eyebrows on hearing Tori's title, then said, "She's unconscious and we can't give her anything for pain until we check for brain injuries."

"How serious are her injuries?"

"Too soon to say. She has a sprained ankle, but no broken bones. Our first priority is the brain. She needs an MRI so we can evaluate the level of trauma."

"Is that where she is?"

"No, I'm sorry. As you can see, the ER is extremely busy. We have a backlog of serious cases. They should be able to get her in for an MRI in an hour."

Kevin said, "Dr. Vincent and I are professors here at the university."

The doctor met Kevin's eyes and said, "I understand."

He glanced at Kevin's tee shirt and suppressed a grin. However, the speed of Tori's care improved somewhat. The police presence reinforced the importance of this patient and everything seemed to be getting a higher priority.

# CHAPTER FORTY SEVEN

Less than an hour later Gerry Arroyo rushed into Shands Hospital with Sean at his side. "How did you get here so fast?" Dottie asked. "Even speeding I couldn't make it in that time."

"I flew." Gerry said and went to confer with the hospital staff. His dark suit and FBI badge convinced the E.R. staff that Tori was a VIP. Suddenly, the MRI was available in 20 minutes and nothing was too good for their patient. While Tori had been receiving adequate care, there were other patients in the E.R. and the staff and doctors were spread thin. Nevertheless, Tori became top priority.

Meanwhile, Dottie took Sean to the waiting room. She asked him, "How'd your father get a flight?"

Sean said, "Dad's a pilot. Flying's his hobby."

"He has his own plane?" Dottie's interest was piqued."

"Third interest in a six passenger Piper in Jacksonville," Sean said.

Kevin said, "Keeps an old clunker at the Gainesville airport so he can get around when he's here."

Gerry joined the others in the waiting room. He hugged his son. "I'm going to try to see your mother." He left to plead to see Tori.

Gerry persuaded the overworked E.R. physician to allow him to see his "wife." He barely recognized Tori with her reddish hair covered in bandages, eyes unfocused and tubes providing blood and nourishment to the small frame on the ER bed. He was shocked to see how pale and fragile she looked. Tori appeared to be conscious but did not seem to be functioning well. Gerry leaned over her bed, took her hand, and asked, "Honey, do you know where you are?"

"Of course," she said in a weak voice, "I'm at Kentucky Fried Chicken."

Her eyes wandered away from Gerry and she said no more.

Gerry asked, "How are you feeling?"

It seemed to take an inordinate amount of effort for Tori to return her gaze to Gerry. She said, "My head hurts and so does my ankle. Actually, everything hurts. I feel like I fell out a window and down 20 stories. What happened?"

Gerry explained about the hit-and-run. Tori listened closely then told him again her head hurt and so did her ankle. "Actually, everything hurts. I feel like I fell out a window and down 20 stories. What happened?"

Gerry looked at the doctor. His heart pounded. The doctor was engrossed in reading a chart at the nurses' station and did not respond to Gerry's non-verbal query. Again, Tori asked what happened. Gerry no sooner explained one more time than she asked what happened again.

A nurse interrupted Gerry's anxious thoughts. "Mr. Arroyo, I'm sorry you will have to leave. We're taking Dr. Vincent for an MRI."

"May I walk with her?"

"No, it's just a short distance. We need to keep the hall clear. I'll let you know when she's back."

Dottie had gotten a Coke for Sean and was sitting with her arm around him talking in whispers in the waiting room. Kevin and Morrison silently sipped coffee from Styrofoam cups. The three adults and Sean stood when Gerry walked into the room, his teeth clenched and his face ashen. He walked to Sean and hugged him. He spoke over Sean's head to the others. "I think she suffered brain damage. She keeps saying the same thing over and over. She told me everything hurts and asked what happened. As soon as I told her, she said everything hurts and asked what happened again." His voice was strained.

Morrison and Dottie looked at each other with fear in their eyes, but Kevin said, "Tori's reaction is not unusual. Frequently, concussions interfere with short term memory even when there's no permanent brain damage. A friend of mine did the same thing when he fell off his horse. It took awhile, but he regained his memory. He's back teaching philosophy and doing fine."

Gerry's eyes drilled into Kevin's, the muscles in his face relaxed slightly, "Are you saying Tori has no brain damage?"

Kevin placed his hand on Gerry's forearm and responded gently. "No, I'm not saying she has no brain damage. I'm saying there *might* not be any long term damage. You can't assume there's permanent damage because she's lost her short term memory. Try not to panic until we know something definite."

"When'll she get her short term memory back?" Morrison asked.

"Depends on how serious the injury is," Kevin said. "Please know, I'm not saying there's no permanent damage, only that the response Gerry described doesn't mean she definitely has brain damage. They'll know how serious her injuries are when they complete the MRI."

"Has anyone called Tori's parents?" Dottie asked.

"Oh my God!" Gerry said. "I was so worried about Tori, I forgot about her parents."

Gerry turned to Kevin, "What can I tell them? They need to know Tori's been injured. Think I should tell them to fly down?"

Kevin said, "Tell them their daughter was injured, but is being looked after by the best doctors in the country. Her injuries are not life threatening. Tell them you'll keep them up to date with her progress and let them know when and if they should come to Gainesville. Right now, I don't think they can make the decision to come without more input from the doctors."

Gerry stepped outside to call his former in-laws. He was a strong man, but telling Tori's father she was gravely injured took more courage than facing murderers in the line of duty. When he'd seen Tori in the hospital bed he had been crushed. Now he was angry. After the call, he descended on the waiting room and demanded details about what had happened to Tori.

Kevin described the hit-and-run. Gerry's eyes were blazing, "Are you telling me someone tried to kill Tori?"

"Yes, he was waiting for her. I saw him pull a ski mask over his head and realized he was up to no good. By the time I got outside, Tori was walking to her car and he was driving toward her. Best I could do was shout a warning. Tori jumped between two cars, but wasn't fast enough."

"It's a good thing Kevin was there and spotted the driver, or Tori would have been hurt more seriously," Dottie said.

Gerry said, "Thank you, Kevin. Thank God you were there." He wiped his mouth with his hand.

Then Gerry turned to Morrison. "What's going on, Morrison? Tori's a psychologist for God's sake. Not a cop. Why did someone try to kill her?"

Morrison said, "It's a long story."

"Tell me." Gerry's voice was as hard as his eyes, but Morrison did not look away.

"A security surveillance camera caught a retired school teacher burglarizing a house. Had no motive. Swore she'd never been in the house. Couple days later a truck runs her down. It's suspicious. I asked Tori to do a psychological autopsy."

"Tori's done dozens of psychological autopsies. No one's ever tried to kill her before," Gerry said."

"I didn't think she was in danger this time. She must've found out something. Murderer thought she was getting close."

"It's your job to find the murderer, not Tori's."

The two men stood facing each other. Both big and powerful— a physical confrontation between them would not be pleasant.

"Come on, you two," Dottie said. She placed a hand on each man's upper arm. "We're all upset about Tori. Let's spend our energy finding who did this, not arguing with each other."

Morrison looked down. "I'd never ask Tori to do a psychological autopsy if I thought she'd be in danger."

After a moment Gerry patted Morrison's shoulder. "I know, Herb. I'm sorry. I'm hot after seeing Tori lying there."

# CHAPTER FORTY EIGHT

Gerry paced the waiting room, downing coffee as fast as Kevin could provide refills. He watched the door. Every couple of minutes he asked the nurse whether Tori was back from the MRI. Dottie still sat with her arm around Sean, whose eyes followed his father. Morrison squirmed in a chair. He wanted to pace, but there was not enough room for two to pace and he didn't want to get in Gerry's way. He stood up and stretched his arms in the air. He walked over and whispered to Dottie, "Need air. Back in a minute."

Kevin had been using his clinical skills to keep Tori's friends from going over the edge. He thought Morrison was overwrought. "Mind if I join you?" he asked.

Morrison preferred to be alone, but he could not refuse Kevin. He shrugged. They walked side by side down the corridor to the outside door. They continued out the driveway and down the hill toward the main campus of the university. They progressed in silence up the hill to the Reitz Union. When they reached the top, Morrison took a deep breath, stopped and turned back, facing the direction from which they had come. He put his hands in his back pockets and asked, "What do you think her chances are?"

Kevin looked over the quiet campus and shook his head. "I've no idea. That was some knock she got on the head. We'll know more when they get the results of the MRI."

"Could use a cigarette."

"I didn't know you smoked."

"Don't. Quit five years ago. I need something to do with my hands." He stretched his arms out with the fingers interlocked, cracking his knuckles.

Kevin nodded. "Know what you mean."

The two men stood for a couple of minutes looking in the direction of the hospital which they could not see from that distance. Without a word, they started back. When they arrived at the waiting room Dottie was alone with Sean.

"Where's Gerry?" Morrison asked.

"He's with Dr. Haney."

"Who's he?"

Dottie shrugged.

Kevin said, "Actually, it's a she. Dr. Lori Haney is the top neurologist at Shands."

"A nurse got Gerry after Tori came back from the MRI," Dottie said. "She said Dr. Haney wanted to go over the results with him."

Gerry sat on the edge of the chair, leaning toward the middle-aged woman in a white coat behind the desk. Gerry found her air of competence comforting. She was a no-nonsense woman who got right to the point. "Dr. Vincent does not appear to have permanent damage to her brain and should recover her short term memory. However, we need to watch her in the hospital until she's stabilized. She complains of pain in her ankle and her head."

"Have you given her something for pain?" Gerry asked.

Dr. Haney pushed a strand of graying hair behind her ear. "Mr. Arroyo, I understand your concern about your wife's pain. I would gladly give her an analgesic if it were best for her. We prefer to wait until she is more aware of her surroundings. We don't want to take a chance on doing more harm. There's a possibility she's had some other injury we haven't found."

"When will she get her memory back?"

"The time someone with head trauma takes to regain short term memory varies from patient to patient. I would guess hers will come back in a day or so. Meanwhile, we need to keep a close eye on her."

"Thank you, doctor."

Gerry nodded and went to relay the information to Morrison, Dottie, Sean, and Kevin. He told them he would stay with Tori for the night. "They moved her into ICU and no one else can see her."

Sean stood. "I want to see my mother!" Tears streamed down his face.

Gerry put his hands on Sean's upper arms. "Sean, I know this is tough, but you need to be strong for your Mom."

"Don't do that, Dad. I want to see her. NOW!"

Kevin said, "Sean, we'll get you in to see your mother."

Sean turned to Kevin.

The older man said, "Dry your tears. Go wash your face and your father will get you in to see her."

Gerry started to object, but Kevin shook his head. "It's his right to see her."

Sean raced into the Men's room and returned with a clean face. Gerry put his arm around Sean and headed to ICU.

Twenty minutes later a somber Sean returned to the waiting room with his father.

Dottie said, "Sean, you shouldn't be alone tonight."

"Sean can stay with us," Morrison said.

"Thanks, Morrison," Gerry said. "You need to go home and get some sleep. I'll let you know if there's any change."

Gerry returned to ICU and sat by Tori's bed. He had his hands full convincing her not to pull the IV out of her arm. She told him it hurt. "I understand, Babe, but it's good for you."

He kept consoling her. "It's okay, Babe, you'll be all right."

When a male nurse came in to check Tori's vital signs, she asked him, "Babe, would you take this out of my arm? I could sleep, if you did." She gave him a big smile.

The nurse grinned. Gerry did a double take. After the nurse left, Gerry asked Tori, "Do you know who that was?"

Tori responded promptly. "Babe," as if Gerry should have known.

When Tori started calling Gerry "Babe;" he became alarmed. He often called her "Baby" or "Babe," but she called him "Love" or "Honey."

"Do you know who I am?" he asked, trying to keep the concern out of his voice.

"You are Special Agent Geraldo Arroyo," said Tori, in a serious voice. Gerry patted her hand and said, "You can call me Gerry."

Gerry had faced tense and dangerous situations, but he had never been as frightened as he was now. He looked at Tori, her head wrapped in bandages and her arm attached to an IV. Gerry was worried the MRI had not caught her brain damage. He was as close to praying as he had been in many years. If there was a God, surely He wouldn't let Tori die or be brain-damaged. Gerry was . not sure which would be worse. He knew Tori would not want to live if she could no longer work as a psychologist. He chastised himself for his negative thinking and tried to concentrate on being calm for Tori.

A uniformed officer stood guard outside the ICU, a member of the round the clock protection team Morrison had set up for Tori. Later that night, when the hospital staff moved Tori to a private room, the police officer followed the stretcher and took up his watch outside her new room. Gerry thanked the officer and went to sit with Tori.

Shortly after they settled Tori in her new room, there was a knock on the door. A dark suited woman introduced herself as the weekend head of administration. "You're Agent Arroyo, are you not?"

"Yes. What may I do for you?"

"Detective Morrison asked us not to give out any information about Dr. Vincent's condition. Of course, we never provide information on any patient. However, because the police were involved, I thought I should let you know that 'a man' (she used her fingers to indicate the quotation marks) called to check on the condition of Dr. Tori Vincent. He would not leave his name."

"Thank you for letting me know."

Gerry called Morrison and relayed the information.

"Did they tell him anything?"

"No, they aren't allowed to give information about patients. The receptionist told him that."

"Did she get a name?"

"No, she asked but he hung up."

Morrison said, "It's the guy who hit Tori with the SUV.

"Don't jump to conclusions. Maybe one of her colleagues called."

"No one knows she was hit except you, Sean, Dottie, Kevin and me. I kept the hit-and-run out of the media. Everyone who knows that Tori is in the hospital also knows her current condition. They know you are with her. They'd call you for an update, not the main number."

"Good God! He's still after her."

# CHAPTER FORTY NINE

Shortly after arriving at the ER, Dottie called Bruce and told him about Tori's injuries. She kept him updated throughout the day. Late in the afternoon, she called and said, "Honey, I know how much you've been looking forward to the Tom Petty concert, but there's no way I can go tonight."

"We got the tickets months ago. You've been dying to hear him."

"I wouldn't be able to enjoy it with Tori in the hospital."

"I understand. I'll give the tickets to Don. He's got a new girl and the tickets might impress her."

"Don't do that," Dottie said. "Go without me. There's no sense in both of us missing it. I'm going to be busy anyway."

"I'm in no mood for a concert either with Tori in the hospital. I'll give the tickets to Don."

"Okay. Gerry's staying with Tori tonight. I'm going to go to her office and check out her computer.

"I'll go with you. That killer might be at her office."

"Bruce, I'm a cop. I can handle an intruder."

"Honey, I know you're a cop," Bruce said. "I also know you can take down any man who tries something, but I'd like to see you. Why don't you let me drive you to her office and we can get a pizza."

She hesitated. "Okay. But it was the pizza that convinced me."

"Thanks."

"Oh Bruce?"

"Yeah?"

"Bring me some clean clothes. I'm still in my running shorts."

Dottie was outside waiting when Bruce pulled up in his blue Prius. She leaned in the driver's side window to kiss him. He handed her the clean clothes. She hurried into the hospital to change and was soon in the passenger seat. "I'm famished. Piesanos?"

He grinned. "I missed you, too."

"Have to have priorities." She patted his arm.

While they waited for their pizza, Dottie told Bruce more about what happened to Tori.

"What's her prognosis?"

"Unclear, but somewhat positive. We'll know more tomorrow. The doctor needs to watch her tonight."

"What about the guy who ran her down?"

"Don't know anything yet. Morrison put an APB out on the car and the FBI is working on it, too."

The waitress placed the large pizza between the two and offered Bruce another beer. "No thanks, I'm driving."

"What about you, honey, another Coke?"

"Yeah, thanks."

Dottie was polishing off her third slice of pizza when Bruce asked, "Why're you going to Tori's office?"

"I'm convinced the perp tried to kill Tori because she was getting too close. She must have discovered something Friday evening or this morning."

"Like what?"

"I wish I knew. I've a feeling the perp knows Tori suspects him."

"Why didn't she tell you and Morrison about her discovery?"

"Who knows? Maybe she wasn't completely certain."

Bruce pointed to the last slice of pizza. "Want it?"

Dottie didn't hesitate. The pizza didn't even get to her plate before she took a huge bite.

Bruce asked, "Where was Tori on Friday?"

"She met us in the evening. Said nada."

"Where'd she go? Home?"

"No, she went to the university. Planned to grade papers all evening. She said hello to Kevin, but later he went to see if she'd like a snack and she was gone. I don't know who she planned to see this morning. I went through Tori's Smartphone but didn't find any appointments except clients."

Dottie wiped her mouth with a napkin.

The waitress picked up the empty pizza pan and looked at Dottie. "How do you eat like that and stay so slim?"

"High metabolism."

Dottie and Bruce walked down the dark corridor in the psychology department. "I'm glad you're here," said Bruce. "It's spooky. I wouldn't want to be alone."

"Don't worry, I'll protect you."

They turned into the next corridor. Dottie grasped Bruce's arm. She held her finger to her lips. "Sssh." She pointed to the third office on the left. Light slithered under the door into the hallway.

Dottie handed Bruce her phone. "Stay here," she whispered. "Push this button if there's trouble. It'll call for backup."

Dottie took out her gun. She crept to the door. She turned the doorknob and inched open the door. A man sat at Tori's desk, his back to the door. Tori's computer was on, her calendar on the screen. The man was riffling through a drawer.

"Police!" Dottie said. "Don't move."

"I...I..."

"Shut up. Slowly place your hands on the desk."

He put his hands on the desk.

Dottie slapped a handcuff on his left wrist and twisted his arm behind his back. "Bring your right arm behind your back."

"But..."

"Now!"

She fastened the handcuff on his other wrist. "Turn around slowly."

"Dottie, I..." he said.

"Kevin! What're you doing here?"

"I... I was looking at Tori's calendar."

"How'd you get in her office?"

"There's a spare set of keys—in the main office," Kevin said. "How about taking these handcuffs off?"

"Not 'til you answer some questions."

"Dottie!" Bruce called. "Is everything okay?"

Dottie stuck her head out the door. "Yeah. C'mon in."

Bruce joined the others. "Who's he?"

"I'm Kevin, Tori's counseling partner. I'd shake hands, but…"

"How'd you get into Tori's computer?" Dottie asked.

"We've got each other's passwords." Sweat beaded on Kevin's forehead. "In case one of us needs to… Dottie, you know me. I'd never hurt Tori."

"You're the only one who saw the SUV run Tori down," Dottie said. "How do we know you didn't do it?"

"Me? Why would I hurt Tori?"

"You tell me. Maybe she knows something about you."

Kevin's eyes were huge. "I've known Tori for years. We're partners. I want to find who tried to kill her."

"What did you find on her calendar?"

"No appointments except clients."

Dottie thought, *he could have erased something. I'll check the computer after he goes.* She unlocked the handcuffs. "Don't make me regret letting you go." She looked around the office. "Where could she have gone last night or early this morning?"

"Check the phone. She's got caller ID," Kevin said.

"Good idea." Dottie checked the caller ID from Tori's office phone. "There's a call from Seth Rothstein, but that's not unusual. I think they're seeing each other."

"I'm pretty sure she's dating him," Kevin said.

"There's a call from Annie Currie—she's Margaret O'Neal's sister." Dottie looked at her watch. "Too late to call tonight. I'll phone her first thing in the morning. She might have told Tori something important."

# CHAPTER FIFTY

Tori walked down the aisle on her father's arm in a Connecticut country church. She was wearing the gown she wore the day she married Gerry. She looked around and smiled at her friends. Herb Morrison was holding pruning shears and wearing gardening clothes covered in dirt. Tori wondered why Ruth, who was standing beside her husband, had not made him dress for the occasion. Dottie in a prim pants suit was standing with Bruce who was clean shaven. Kevin and Edie were each trying to contain a rambunctious twin. The boys had identical pea shooters and were taking pot shots at the other guests. Seth Rothstein with an arm around Lucille winked at Tori as she passed him. Tori looked ahead and saw Gerry standing at the foot of the altar. She felt ecstatic.

"Off with her head! Off with her head!" A fat little queen in a white dress with red hearts ran at Tori with a hatchet. "Off with her head!"

Tori tried to sit up. "Gerry!"

Gerry, standing at the side of Tori's bed, saw her face contorting and rang for the nurse. He took Tori's hand. "It's all right, honey."

When the plump nurse who had taken blood from Tori earlier came in with a needle, Tori screamed, "She's got a hatchet." Tori clasped Gerry's hand.

"Who does?"

"She does." She pointed at the nurse. "The Queen of Hearts."

"I'm right here," Gerry said. "No one can hurt you."

The nurse said, "Don't worry. I'm not going to stick you. I'm putting this in your IV." The nurse smiled and patted Tori's hand. Tori cringed.

"It's all right, Tori. She's giving you something for pain. You'll go back to sleep."

"But then we can't get married," Tori said. Her lips quivered and tears pooled in her eyes.

"We can get married in the morning, Babe," he said brushing a stray hair out of her eyes. She was still staring at him with desperation when sleep overcame her.

Gerry had spent the night talking with the FBI and police on his cell phone in Tori's hospital room. He would not have been able to sleep anyway; he was too worried. But in the event he could have slept, the hospital staff would have prevented him from doing so. Every 20 minutes some technician or nurse checked Tori's blood pressure, IV or pulse. Whenever Tori fell asleep, someone came in, switched on the light and examined some part of her anatomy.

Tori open her eyes. "What happened? I feel awful. Everything hurts." She tried to reach for the IV but Gerry held her hand still. Her hand was fastened to the bars on her bed so she could not undo the IV, but she got upset if she realized she was restrained. He explained for the hundredth time about the hit-and-run. She smiled wanly and went back to sleep.

Gerry had the FBI put a rush on the trace of the SUV. By early the next morning, he was able to phone Morrison.

"It was a rental car."

"A rental car?" Morrison asked. "Who wants to rent a beat-up old car?"

"I don't know who wants to rent them, but I know the place that does the renting—Rent-a-Wreck in Jacksonville. They specialize in renting old cars for low prices," Gerry said.

"I'll get someone up there to find out who rented it."

"No need, Morrison. An agent's on her way. I'm going to talk to Tori's doctor and then I'll go myself. I'll call you when I get something. Meanwhile, keep an eye on Tori."

"I've got two men there, now," Morrison said. "Epstein's staying with her today and she's worth any ten guys on the force."

The FBI agent called Gerry while he was driving to the airfield where he had left the plane he flew to Gainesville. He relayed the information to Morrison. "The car was rented by Giovanni Romero."

"Who?"

Gerry thought Morrison had misunderstood the name and repeated it slowly. "Giovanni Romero."

"I heard the name the first time. Who the hell is Giovanni Romero?"

"You've heard the name before?"

Morrison filled Gerry in on the other hit-and-runs. "We picked up a migrant worker driving an old red truck. ME confirmed it's the same truck that killed Margaret O'Neal. Poor sucker driving the truck said he bought it from 'Giovanni Romero.' He had the title and sure enough, it was in Giovanni Romero's name. The worker identified Carlos Sanchez as Giovanni Romero."

"Wait a minute! Wait a damn minute! I thought you said Carlos Sanchez was killed by that truck."

"He was."

"Then how could Sanchez have sold the truck?" Gerry asked.

"Sanchez sold the truck the night before he was killed. Said he'd leave it for the migrant worker in the morning."

"Who was driving the truck when Sanchez was killed?"

"Damned if I know."

"Good lord! This Giovanni Romero is one devious hombre."

"Yeah. Why I asked who the hell he is."

"I don't know, but I am going to find out," Gerry said.

"Tori must've got too close to whoever killed Margaret and Carlos," Morrison said. "The killer tried to get rid of her, too."

"Do you know where she was and who she spoke to on Friday evening and Saturday morning?"

"Epstein's working on it."

# CHAPTER FIFTY ONE

Dottie drummed her fingers on the arm of the chair, eyeing her watch as it crawled like an unmotivated snail toward 8:30 a.m., a time she thought acceptable to phone Annie Curry. Still asleep, Tori pulled at the sheets and moaned. Dottie's eyes darted to Tori and back to her watch—6:47. Had it only been 15 minutes since she'd taken Gerry's place by Tori's bed? She walked to the window, hugging herself to keep her hands still.

At exactly 8:30 Dottie phoned Annie Curry. Annie was in the mood to talk, but Dottie cut her off. She wanted facts, not chatter. With Annie's information Dottie was able to find Karen Baker's phone number. She called Karen.

"I told Ms. Vincent Margaret couldn't have robbed anyone. I'm glad to hear the police are going to find who really broke into the house."

"Yes, we will. Could you tell me what you told Dr. Vincent on Friday?"

"Dr. Vincent?" Karen asked. "I didn't know she was a doctor."

Dottie took a deep breath. "She's a psychologist. She's working with us on the case involving Margaret O'Neal."

"She's a psychologist, is she? I knew she was bright, but I'd no idea she was a doctor of psychology."

Dealing with retired women who liked to chat was not Dottie's forte. *Why can't she just answer the questions?* She took another deep breath and asked Karen again what she had told Tori.

"Why don't you ask her if she's working with you?" Karen asked. "How do I know you're who you say you are?"

*Oh damn!* Dottie thought. *Why can't I play along? I'm becoming as tactless and impatient as Morrison.*

She said, "Dr. Vincent was hit by a car yesterday. She's in the hospital and can't remember what happened on Friday or Saturday."

Dottie did not tell Karen Tori was run down on purpose, but Karen was nobody's fool. "Oh, my God! You think it's the same person who ran over Margaret? He tried to kill Dr. Vincent?"

"We have the name of a person of interest in Margaret's hit-and-run. We're trying to find out what Dr. Vincent did on Friday and Saturday. We think she might have gotten a clue about the murderer. It would help if you told me everything you told Dr. Vincent."

"I'd like to help, but I need to be certain you're a police officer," Karen said. "You could be the murderer trying to find out what Dr. Vincent knows."

Dottie could not fault Karen for being on guard. She gave Karen the number for the Gainesville Police Department. "Call Officer Carter and she'll confirm I'm working with Detective Morrison. Please ask her for the cell number of Detective Dottie Epstein—that's me. Then call me back."

In a matter of minutes Karen called. "What do you want to know?"

"Exactly what you told Dr. Vincent when you called her Friday."

"I didn't call her. She called me. I sent Annie Curry a note and she told Dr. Vincent about it."

"And what did Dr. Vincent talk to you about?"

"Dr. Vincent wondered how I knew Margaret and why I went to see Dr. Rothstein." Karen told Dottie about her problems with drinking and her DUIs in more detail than Dottie thought necessary. Dottie clenched her teeth, but said nothing. Karen explained how Dr. Rothstein spoke to her AA meeting, "and I decided to go see him about my problems.

"I used to see Margaret O'Neal in Dr. Rothstein's office after my appointment. I had to wait for my daughter, you see, so I was still there when Margaret got there."

Dottie closed her eyes and took several deep breaths, slowly. "What did Dr. Vincent want to know about Margaret?" Dottie said. She wondered, *is she rambling because she's lonely or has she started drinking again?*

"That's what I'm trying to tell you," she snapped.

"I'm sorry, please go ahead," Dottie said choking on the words.

"Dr. Vincent wanted to know about the day Margaret supposedly robbed the house. Margaret would no more take something that didn't belong to her than she would've run naked through downtown Gainesville. She didn't have a dishonest bone in her body."

"What about the day Margaret was supposed to be robbing the house?" Dottie asked. She could feel her normally low blood pressure rising. She would have a heart attack if Karen didn't get to the point.

"That's what I've been trying to tell you. Margaret couldn't have robbed the house. I saw her come in for her appointment that afternoon."

"You sure it was the afternoon of the burglary?" Dottie asked.

"Yes, I'm positive. But Dr. Vincent said something on the video might be wrong. She said she was going to look at the video again."

"Thank you, Mrs. Baker." Dottie hung up the cell phone, cutting Karen off as she started to ask another question. *What could be wrong with the video? The owners were out of town. Could the video have the wrong date?*

Dottie called Dr. Rothstein. He was not happy being disturbed on Sunday, his "only day off."

Dottie apologized profusely. She was determined not to annoy him the way she had Karen. She needed his cooperation.

"I'm trying to find out where Dr. Tori Vincent was on Friday afternoon and evening," said Dottie. "I wonder if you saw her."

"Why don't you ask her instead of bothering honest citizens on a Sunday?" Rothstein said, an edge to his voice.

Dottie thought, *Damn, I annoy people even when I'm trying not to. Losing my touch. I used to be good at gaining people's confidence. I've been around Morrison too long. His method of interrogating—rolling over interviewees, taking no prisoners—has rubbed off on me. No wonder no one gives me information.*

She took a breath and tried to sound apologetic. "I'm sorry for disturbing you on a Sunday."

Dottie decided to exaggerate Tori's condition. If Rothstein relayed the information to anyone who had anything to do with the hit-and-run, she did not want the perp to try again. She said, "Dr. Vincent was hit by a car yesterday and is in a coma. She's not expected to survive."

"Oh my God." Rothstein gasped. "I'm sorry to hear that."

"Again, I'm sorry for calling on your day off. We're trying to find where Dr. Vincent was on Friday evening and Saturday morning. I'm checking with everyone she's seen in the last couple of weeks, to determine if they know where she was." Dottie purposely did not mention Karen, no need to get Rothstein upset with his client.

Rothstein said, "I'm sorry I was impatient. I had no idea Tori was in an accident. Where is she? Can I see her?"

"She's at Shands. But, only her family's allowed to visit."

"I hope she'll be all right."

Dottie seized the opportunity. Her voice cracked. "Thank you for your concern. I think there's little hope for Tori. Do you have any idea where she was Friday evening or Saturday? Did she call or visit you?"

"Yes, she called Friday afternoon and left a message. I called her back at her office on Friday evening. She told me about those poor women who were virtual slaves. She asked if I'd counsel them. She knew I speak Spanish. Of course I said I'd help. She was going to call Saturday after she set up the appointments." He sighed. "No wonder she didn't call."

"Thank you." Dottie was about to hang up when another thought hit her. "Dr. Rothstein, do you know a Giovanni Romero?"

"Can't say that I do."

"What about Carlos Sanchez? Does that name mean anything to you?"

"Sounds familiar. Wasn't he in some kind of accident recently?"

"Thank you for your help, Doctor." Dottie hung up.

211

# CHAPTER FIFTY TWO

After spending the morning rehashing the case, Morrison and Gerry went to see Eduardo Delgado. Gerry looked at Delgado's house. "This smacks of Cuban Mafia money."

"Unfortunately, we can't pin anything on him," Morrison said. He knocked on Delgado's door.

Delgado opened the door while restraining a growling Doberman pinscher by the collar. "What do you want now? This is harassment." The dog surged at the visitors, his front legs off the ground. "My dog hates cops."

"You're not being friendly. Let me introduce my colleague from the FBI," Morrison said. "Agent Geraldo Arroyo."

Delgado blanched. "FBI?" The dog lurched. Delgado struggled to control the dog. "Stay, Satan."

"Nice name for your pooch," Morrison said. "Can we come in?"

"Not without my attorney present."

"No problem. I've invited Mr. Lavanderos to join us. Can we wait inside?"

Morrison turned at the sound of a car pulling into the circular drive. Lavanderos parked and got out of his car. "See, what'd I tell you? Here he is." Morrison smirked.

Lavanderos walked to the front door. "Detective Morrison," he said, shaking Morrison's hand. Morrison introduced Gerry. Lavanderos raised his eyebrows and shook Gerry's hand.

"Ed," Lavanderos said, taking his client by the shoulder, "let's go inside."

Gerry looked over the interior of Delgado's living room and thought, *No vice president of a small bank makes enough money to furnish a room like this.* The traditional furniture was excellent quality and the arrangement bespoke the hand of an interior designer. He sat in a Queen Anne chair. *This chair would cost a bank v.p. a month's salary.*

Delgado led his snarling dog through a doorway at one side of the room. "Stay, Satan. Good boy." He gave the dog a treat and closed the door. Delgado sat on the sofa next to his attorney and they held a whispered conversation.

Morrison interrupted the whispering. "Where were you last Sunday between 5:00 and 7:30 a.m.?"

Lavanderos asked, "Is that when Mrs. O'Neal was hit by a truck?"

Morrison nodded and turned to Delgado, "Well?"

"I already told your dark sidekick I was on a weekend hunting and camping trip at a cabin in Ocala," Delgado said.

Gerry thought, *he looks sure of himself, must have a good alibi.* "Can anyone vouch for your whereabouts Sunday morning?" Gerry asked.

"You might check with Mack Landry."

"The city councilman?" Morrison asked, glancing sideways at Gerry.

"The one and same," said Delgado. "Mack and Bob Cramer—our former mayor—and Randy Hansen—Mack's brother-in-law were all with me." He paused. Gerry thought, *He wants to be sure we understand who's providing his alibi. Smug lowlife.*

"We spent the weekend at Mack's cabin. Went to Ocala Friday afternoon, stayed until late Sunday. I can tell you nothing about the hit-and-run." He looked down his nose at the officers. "Any other questions, or may I get back to enjoying my Sunday?"

"Where were you between noon and 3:00 yesterday?" Gerry asked.

Delgado looked quickly at his attorney and back at Gerry, "Why?"

"Answer the question," Morrison said.

Delgado whispered to his attorney. Gerry noted Delgado's smug expression had vanished. His fists were clenched and his face was flushed.

He turned to Gerry, "I drove to Ocala to meet a friend."

"What time did you leave?"

"About noon."

"Can this person verify your presence in Ocala?" Gerry asked.

Delgado whispered with Lavanderos again. He lowered his eyes. "My friend did not make our meeting."

"Who was the friend you planned to meet?" Gerry asked.

After conferring with Lavanderos, Delgado said, "My attorney advises me not to respond to that question."

"Why didn't Giovanni make your meeting?" Gerry asked.

Delgado's opened his eyes wide and clutched his throat.

# CHAPTER FIFTY THREE

Dottie was nodding off on the lounge chair in Tori's hospital room, her arm dangling over the arm, cell phone in hand, when Morrison tapped on the door and edged it open. Dottie jumped up, dropped the phone and pulled out her gun.

"Sit down. Sit down. Don't shoot your colleague," Morrison said. "Wouldn't look good on your record. How's the patient?"

"Better. She knows who I am. Memory's coming back. But nothing that would indicate who hit her."

"Gerry and I went to see our friend Delgado." Morrison grinned. "Wasn't pleased about our visit."

"Learn anything?"

"Nah. Got an alibi for Margaret O'Neal's murder. At a hunting lodge from Friday to Sunday night. Get this—he was with Mack Landry, the city councilman, Bob Cramer and his brother-in-law."

"An alibi almost too good to be true," Dottie said.

"Yeah, that's what I thought. Who better to vouch for him?"

Morrison looked at Dottie. She wore baggie sweat pants and a tee-shirt. Her eyes were puffy and her face was haggard. "You look awful. I'll take over here until Gerry gets back. Go home. Rest."

"Thanks, I could use a night's sleep."

Hearing voices, Tori began to stir. Morrison walked to the side of her bed as Tori opened her eyes.

"Morrison?"

Dottie joined Morrison and Tori opened her eyes wider. "Where am I?"

Morrison took Tori's hand. "You're safe—in the hospital. You were hit by a car yesterday."

Tori tried to rub her head. She looked at the tape holding her arm and followed the tube up to the IV. "My head feels foggy."

"I bet it does," Dottie said. "You in pain?"

"Not really."

Morrison asked her where she had been Friday afternoon. "At Sean's soccer game," she replied. "Why do you ask?"

Morrison and Dottie exchanged looks. The worry Dottie had been feeling was now reflected in Morrison's face.

"Epstein's been here all morning. She's going home to sleep. I'll be here if you need anything."

Tori was asleep again before Morrison finished his sentence.

Dottie had been going for almost 32 hours. She was beyond exhausted. She drove north on 13th St. toward Bruce's house on autopilot. He had promised he would have soup ready. Bruce was a man of many talents; his major one in Dottie's eyes was his ability to make homemade soup. Soup as good as her granny's. She was salivating.

SCREEEECH!! Dottie jerked her head up. Her tires scraped the curb. She jolted awake. Her heart beat against the seat belt. Her palms were damp on the steering wheel. She rubbed her eyes, opened the window and tuned the radio to a country music station. She raised the volume. She hated country music and the twanging voices would irritate her enough to keep her eyes open for the drive to Bruce's house.

Bruce was watching for her and went to the car to open the door. "You poor baby, you look exhausted."

"I am."

"Soup's ready."

"How about a glass of red wine?" She asked.

"It's breathing, ready to pour."

Bruce put his arm around Dottie and guided her to the kitchen table. He had set out a big bowl of cream of chicken soup and crackers for her. There was an open bottle of Pinot Noir and two glasses on the table.

Dottie collapsed into a chair. She pulled the bowl of soup toward her and hunched over it. Bruce poured the wine and sat back. "How's Tori?"

Dottie swallowed a large spoonful of soup and picked up her glass. "She looks pale and fragile with a mess of bandages around her head."

"Has she told you where she was Friday night or Saturday?"

"Yes and no. She's told me nothing I didn't figure out myself. And she keeps getting things confused." She twirled the stem of the wineglass.

"Like what?"

"She asked me if Gerry knew about her accident within five minutes of his leaving. He was there yesterday afternoon until early this morning. She didn't remember seeing him."

"That doesn't sound good."

"Kevin said people with head injuries lose their short term memories for awhile, but this's been over 24 hours." Dottie buried her head in her hands. "If I hadn't interviewed Carlos Sanchez against Morrison's direct orders, none of this would have happened."

Bruce leaned across the table. He took her hands from her face. "Dottie, this isn't your fault. Tori's being hit might not have anything to do with your talking to Sanchez. Sanchez is dead. He couldn't have tried to kill Tori."

Dottie wiped a tear from her eye. "You're right, but I still feel guilty."

"Have another glass of wine and I'll fix you a big steak."

"Your answer to every problem is a big steak," Dottie said. "I'd love the wine, but soup was enough." She moaned. "All I want is sleep. I'm so tired, nothing makes sense."

"Go sit in a comfortable chair and let me take care of you."

Dottie groaned as she stood up. She walked into the living room. When Bruce got there with his dinner, a salad, she was lying on the couch with her arm draped across her eyes.

"Are you asleep?" Bruce asked in a hushed voice.

"No, just thinking." Dottie sat up to face him. She rested her elbows on her knees, sighed and reached for the glass of wine he had set out for her. She raised the glass to tap his and took a sip of the wine. "Thanks, Sugar."

Dottie told Bruce about her conversations with Karen Baker and Rothstein. "Do you think he's lying?"

"Why would he lie? The Baker woman had her days confused. She's a recovering alcoholic. Who knows whether she was drinking when she says she saw Margaret in the office?"

Dottie scratched her head. "Yeah, she couldn't stay on topic when I spoke to her."

"Why would Dr. Rothstein say Margaret didn't show for her appointment, if it weren't true? It's not like he's a suspect. He couldn't have burglarized the house. He was in his office seeing patients. He had nothing to gain by lying. The video is obviously Margaret O'Neal and he said she missed her appointment."

"Yeah, Tori said the same thing."

"You need to find out why Margaret broke into the house and how she got the alarm code."

"You're right. She must've gotten the alarm code and key from Sanchez. That's why he was so upset when I asked him about the burglaries."

"You need to find the connection between Sanchez and Margaret. Why did he give her the code?"

"No kidding!"

# CHAPTER FIFTY FOUR

Tori woke about 1:00 and saw Morrison snoozing in the chair by the window. *What's he doing here?* She wondered.

Dr. Haney entered the room accompanied by a nurse. "How're you doing?" she asked.

Tori turned to the doctor. "Who are you? I remember talking to you."

"I'm Dr. Haney. I'm your doctor." She smiled. "This is Holly. She's going to clean your stitches and remove the IV."

"Stitches? Stitches?"

Hearing their voices, Morrison rubbed his eyes and stretched. He got up, placed his hands on the small of his back and leaned back. He rotated his shoulders as he walked over to Tori's bed. "How're you feeling, Doc?"

"What're you doing here, Morrison? And what's this about stitches?"

"You cracked your head," Morrison said. "You were almost run over by a SUV."

"I don't remember being hit."

"It's not unusual to forget an incident like that," Haney said. "You're a psychologist, right?"

"Yes. I know our brains can protect us from bad memories."

"Good! You're functioning better."

Morrison asked, "Do you want me to leave?"

"Not unless you faint at the sight of blood," Haney said.

"Would be a major handicap in my line of work."

"I was joking." Haney unwound the bandages around Tori's head and Holly cleaned the stitches. "We can put a smaller bandage on your head, now."

"Thanks."

"Holly, get rid of that IV. Our patient doesn't need it anymore."

"What about my ankle?" Tori asked. "It hurts."

"You sprained your ankle. Dr. Doyle wrapped it for you. He'll be by in the morning."

"What time is it?" Tori asked.

"1:00," Haney said.

"I'm fine. I'm ready to go home. I need to be with my son."

"We'll see." Haney smiled.

Gerry tapped on the door and Morrison said, "Come in." Gerry pushed the door open. Sean looked around his father at his mother in bed. "Hi, Mom."

They walked over to where Tori was lying and stood looking down at her. Gerry took her hand. "How're you doing, Babe?"

She sat up. "When did you get here?'

"Yesterday afternoon."

"Why didn't you tell me you were here?" she asked.

"I did tell you," Gerry said. "You aren't remembering too well. I was here all last night."

"Last night? What day is it?"

"Sunday."

"How long have I been here?" she asked.

Haney said, "Since about 2:00 yesterday." She turned to Gerry. "I was telling your wife she needs to stay another night."

"Seems like a good idea," Gerry said.

"Wait a minute," Tori said. "He's not my husband. I'll decide when I'm ready to leave."

Hands on hips, Haney glared at Gerry. "You told me you were her husband. I'd never have discussed her condition with you if you weren't her closest relative."

"I apologize," Gerry said. "I'm Tori's ex-husband and her nearest relative is our son Sean." Gerry put his hand on Sean's shoulder. "He was staying with me for the weekend. He needed to know about his mother's condition."

Tori looked at Sean. "Where did you stay last night, Sean?" Tori asked.

"I went to the Morrisons' for the night," he said.

"Really?" Tori was not convinced.

"Are you all right, Mom?"

"I'm fine. And I'll be even better when I go home."

"I would not advise you to leave," Haney said. "We should watch you one more night."

"I'll stay with you," Morrison offered.

"Why?" Tori asked.

"Make sure no one tries to hurt you."

"Morrison, you're over-reacting," Tori said. "No one purposely hit me with a car."

"Tori, don't get upset," Morrison said. "Kevin saw the driver pull a stocking over his head before he ran you down."

"Why would someone try to kill me?"

"We think you found out something Friday night or Saturday morning. Whatever it was, the murderer thought you were getting too close," Morrison said.

"I didn't learn anything Friday. I told you everything I knew Friday evening."

"You don't remember what you did after you left us Friday evening and on Saturday morning."

"Don't tell me what I remember and what I don't remember. I remember everything I did Friday and Saturday."

"Calm down, Dr. Vincent," Haney said. "Detective, I'll have to ask you to leave if you upset my patient."

"I'm the one who's leaving," Tori said. "I'm fine and I need to be home for my son."

Gerry said, "I'll take Sean back to your house and stay with him until you go home."

"I'm doing just fine and I don't need you checking on me. How did you find out I was in the hospital?"

"Dottie called me."

"She had a hell of a nerve calling my ex-husband without my permission."

"You were unconscious," Morrison said. "Sean was with Gerry."

221

Dr. Haney said, "I'm going to ask all of you to leave. You're upsetting my patient. She needs to rest."

"I do not need more rest. I need to go home."

Gerry put his arm around Sean's shoulder. "Let's go, son."

"Look at that!" Tori said. "The perfect father. For 12 years you ignored Sean unless I coerced you into seeing him. I raised him without your help. Where were you when I needed you? When I needed a break from child-rearing?"

"Now, Tori," Morrison said.

"Don't, 'now, Tori,' me."

Sean's eyes were brimming. He wiped them with the sleeve of his shirt. Gerry guided him to the door. "Your mother is distraught. She doesn't mean what she said. Let her rest."

"I'm not distraught." Tori burst into tears.

# CHAPTER FIFTY FIVE

Morrison left the hospital early Monday morning, before Tori awoke. She remembered his bending over her bed and patting her hand before the sun peeked under the blinds and into her room. The previous night she had come to a compromise with Morrison about the police guarding her. He would remove the guards when Dottie picked her up. The plan was for Dottie to take Tori home and stay with her until Morrison was sure she was safe.

Tori was pale and had an Ace Elastic Bandage wrapped around her ankle, but she was dressed and ready, the large bandage on her head replaced by a smaller, less conspicuous one. Her doctor had signed her discharge papers. She was leafing through a *Time* magazine which Gerry had brought to read. But, as Gerry had done, she was turning pages without taking in the information. It was still early, 7:30, when Dottie knocked on Tori's door, looked around it and came in. Dottie kissed Tori on the cheek and said, "You look much better, like your old self."

Tori looked askance at her friend. "I have a mirror, you know."

Dottie chuckled. "At least you haven't lost your sense of humor."

"No, just a patch of hair in a noticeable location," she said, gingerly patting her head where she had combed her hair to cover the bare spot.

"It'll grow back."

Tori said, "Don't patronize me."

"Sorry."

"Enough self-pity. Notify the nurse that you're springing me."

Dottie left and returned in a few minutes, accompanied by a nurse's aide pushing a wheel chair.

"What's that for?" Tori asked.

"Hospital rules," the nurse's aide said. "Everyone is taken to the door in a wheelchair."

"I don't need that thing. My legs are fine."

The aide looked pointedly at Tori's bandaged ankle. "Really?"

Tori followed her gaze and said, "Okay, maybe this time."

When she stood to get in the wheelchair, Tori was woozy and thought the wheelchair was a good idea after all. The nurse's aide wheeled Tori out to the front entrance while Dottie fetched her car to pick up Tori. Tori got in the car with assistance from the aide and Dottie. She hated not being able to do things she was used to doing. She thanked the aide.

As they drove off Tori said, "Don't you share your boss' viewpoint that since your pay is so low, you can park wherever you want? He says it's one of the perks of the job."

"Morrison and I share few viewpoints about social issues. I'm a libertarian, he's a Nazi."

"Morrison's authoritarian, but hardly a Nazi."

"Your opinion," Dottie said. "Morrison and I never agree about things owed to people," Dottie said with more than a little venom.

"You and Herb have another falling out?"

"To use Morrison's hackneyed phrase, 'is the Pope Catholic?'"

"What's it about this time?"

"This case," she said as she turned into Tori's driveway. "Wait in the car while I check out the house."

"That's not necessary."

Dottie looked Tori in the eye with her hand held out palm up, "Give me the key. I'll tell you about Morrison and me when we get inside."

Tori sighed, but handed over the key. Dottie went into the house and came back saying, "Everything's fine."

Tori leaned on Dottie as they walked into the house. As they entered the foyer, Gerry came around the corner waving a large white pillowcase. "Truce?"

Tori could not help grinning. "You're such a clown."

He assisted her into the den where she sat on her favorite lounge chair and put up her feet. When she was settled, Dottie explained about her feud with Morrison, "He wants me to use the computer to check on Giovanni Romero and Giovanni El Grande. It's a waste of time."

Gerry interrupted. "You got that right. I'll check him out; the FBI has better sources." Gerry pointed to his laptop set up on the kitchen table. "I'll let you know what I find."

Dottie said, "Tori, you look exhausted. Why don't you rest and I'll be a good computer nerd."

Tori nodded. She closed her eyes for a full 45 minutes before she started to become antsy. She looked at Dottie, hunched over her computer. "I can't sit here doing nothing," she said.

"I feel like I'm doing nothing, too; at least nothing productive. Giovanni is not going by that name; he must have assumed another identity."

Gerry came in and said, "I tracked Giovanni Romero. He was known as 'Giovanni the Great,' a night club hypnotist in Miami eight or ten years ago."

"That's what Irma meant when she said he was 'Giovanni El Grande,'" Dottie said.

"He still in Miami?" Tori asked.

"No such luck. He left Miami five or six years ago. The nightclub where he worked is still there and owned by the same man. I'm going to fly down to Miami. I'll interview him and anyone else I can find who knew Giovanni."

Tori put the foot rest down on the lounge chair, "Not without me, you're not."

# CHAPTER FIFTY SIX

As hard as Gerry had tried to convince Tori she needed rest, she would have none of it. "I've spent enough time lying around doing nothing." He knew Tori well enough to realize that no amount of arguing would change her mind. She was "stubborn as a mule." Thus, Tori accompanied Gerry as he headed toward his plane at the Gainesville airport.

Tori wore a black tam to hide her head bandage. Her ankle was still wrapped but her slacks hid it. By leaning on Gerry's arm, she managed to walk reasonably well. Gerry said he enjoyed having her arm through his—"it's been too long since we walked like this."

Tori's stomach was in knots. She hated to fly in small planes. Although Tori had flown with Gerry and Sean on a couple of trips, she had never admitted her fear of small planes to Gerry. Now she sat next to him, but they spoke little. The engine noise made conversation difficult in the small plane, and Gerry needed to keep checking with air traffic control. Despite the uncomfortable seat and her stomach turning, Tori slept through much of the flight to Miami. Gerry landed at the Kendall-Tamiami Executive Airport, about 15 minutes from downtown Miami. It was much easier to fly into a small airport than the large ones airlines used. There was no long walk to the terminal, only a short walk from the landing field to the reception area in the terminal. When he checked at the desk, the receptionist gave Gerry keys to the rental car he had arranged and pointed to where it was parked in front of the airport.

Gerry had not been in Miami much in the last few years. However, he had spent lots of time there after he and Tori were divorced. His Cuban relatives lived in Miami and he stayed with them while he partied in the city. Miami was a great place to party—he'd had some wild times. He said, "I feel guilty—I haven't visited Tia Carmen since I moved to Jacksonville. I feel doubly guilty being in Miami and not going to see her."

"She's a sweet lady," Tori said. "I keep in touch with her and visit when I get to Miami."

"You make me feel like a cad."

"You can be inconsiderate."

"You mean self-centered and egotistical." He patted Tori's arm looped through his.

"I think 'inconsiderate' is strong enough." She looked up at him and smiled.

Gerry said, "I promise I'll visit her as soon as this case is finished." He squeezed Tori's arm. "Seeing you in the hospital made me realize how vulnerable people are. Tia Carmen is getting on in years and we could lose her at any moment."

"I'm surprised how well I remember how to get around in Miami," Gerry said as he drove into the city. His internal GPS directed him to the area where nightlife thrived—he'd spent enough time there. It was easy to locate the nightclub, El Gato Negro, where Giovanni had performed. Gerry remembered the huge black cat on the sign. He parked the car in the empty lot and he and Tori went to the front entrance. By putting their faces close to the dark glass door, they could see a crew cleaning the vacant club. Gerry tried the door—it was locked. He rapped on the door; but the cleaning crew ignored him. Gerry rapped harder and held up his FBI identification. The apparent supervisor came to the door. He reluctantly unlocked and opened it and explained the club was closed until 9:00 p.m. Gerry pointed to his FBI identification and the man said apologetically, "I see your ID, but, I'm sorry the club is closed."

"I can see it's closed. I still want in," Gerry said in an authoritative voice.

The cleaner stood back allowing Gerry and Tori to enter.

"Where's the owner?" asked Gerry. The cleaner was flustered. He bowed toward Gerry and hurried to the back of the club. Gerry and Tori walked past chairs turned seat down on table tops and people mopping the floor. A stage at the far end of the room had a small dance floor in front of it. Gerry remembered being in the club, but could not remember much about his visit. *Probably drinking too much*, he thought, with a flash of shame about his former life style.

A tall tanned man with heavy features appeared from the side of the stage where the cleaning man had disappeared. "Antonio DeVito," he said in a hardy voice, holding out his hand.

Gerry shook his hand and showed DeVito his identification. He introduced Tori as his colleague.

Antonio held up his hands as if to ward off evil. "I don't want any trouble with the Feds. Believe me, my workers are all legal. I check."

"Relax. You aren't in trouble with anyone. I'm looking for information about someone who worked here eight or ten years ago."

"Everyone who ever worked for me is legal. I'm careful about that."

"I'm not interested in illegal immigrants. I want to find out about one of your performers. Giovanni the Great."

"Giovanni! That scumbag! I hope he's in a heap of trouble." Antonio's face deepened into purple rage. He doubled his fists and Tori and Gerry had no doubt about the reception Giovanni would get from his former boss.

# CHAPTER FIFTY SEVEN

Dottie hunched over the computer at the police station, a Styrofoam cup of Starbuck's café latte on her desk. She leaned back, picked up the cup and took a gulp of coffee. She continued checking on John Rodriguez. Before she left for Miami with Gerry, Tori had asked her to check him out. It took a while but Dottie found a police file on him. John Rodriguez was the major suspect in a hit-and-run. His two brothers were run down by a red pick-up truck. John Rodriguez had been released from a New Jersey prison three weeks before he bought the truck.

Dottie rushed to tell Morrison about her discovery. She'd been avoiding her superior officer this morning because he looked, to use one of Morrison's granny's phrases, like "something the cat dragged in." Besides looking like he died last week, he was in a horrible mood even for Morrison. Still, this discovery might bring the old grouch out of his depression. Dottie knocked on his office door and opened it without waiting for his permission.

"Did I say come in?" He snarled.

"You'll want to hear this," Dottie said. "John Rodriguez used a truck to run down his two brothers in New Jersey."

"Who the hell is John Rodriguez?"

"I'm trying to tell you. He got out of prison in New Jersey before killing his brothers."

"When?"

"Nine years ago."

Morrison waved Dottie off and turned, picked up his Knicks mug and poured himself a cup of thick black coffee from the coffee maker on the credenza behind him. "Epstein, that's too long ago to have anything to do with this case. Besides, it's nowhere near here."

"Wait! Wait!" She said as he turned back to the work on his desk. "Hear me out."

Morrison looked at her over his half glasses—impatience on his face.

"Listen. It's the same red pick-up truck—it was sold to Giovanni Romero."

Morrison sat up, his bloodshot eyes attentive above dark circles.

"Two brothers were killed—Joseph and Marco Rodriguez. The main suspect is John Rodriguez, their younger brother. Rodriguez sold the truck to Giovanni Romero."

"Why did Rodriguez kill his brothers?"

"The report is pretty sketchy. Call the Chief in Belmar and get the details."

"Give me the info," he snapped. "Better not be one of your wild goose chases."

"It isn't. Put the phone on speaker so I can hear."

"How the hell you do that?"

Dottie refrained from rolling her eyes as she pushed the speaker button. "See this button." She pointed to the "SPKR" button. "It means speaker."

Morrison glared, but made the call.

Struggling through the Belmar, New Jersey Police Department bureaucracy made Morrison even grumpier. He waited while someone looked for an officer who knew something about the old case. He was about to hang up when Detective Delaware picked up the phone. Morrison asked about the murder of the Rodriguez brothers.

"A couple of rotten no-gooders, if I ever saw any. The world's a better place without them."

Morrison asked, "Can you tell me about John Rodriguez? My Sergeant tells me he's the main suspect."

"No doubt about it. He ran his brothers down all right. I'd bet my pension on it."

"Why kill his brothers?"

"The family was a bad lot. The father, Guillermo, was a mean bastard. Beat his wife and kids for the heck of it. He and his wife were small-time con artists. Used the kids—six of them—in their scams. Started when they were babies. Whenever the cops got close, the family moved. They racked up records in every county in Jersey."

"Ever catch them?" Morrison asked.

"We caught Guillermo a couple times. Never could put him away for more than a year or so. The older brothers, Joseph and Marco, were worse than the father. Had a Ponzi scheme. Made a truck load of dough. Kept one step ahead of the law for years. When the feds were breathing down their necks, they brought John into the scam."

"Why'd they bring John in?"

"Let him take the fall. Turned states evidence at his trial—said they knew nothing about the scheme. Swore John was the brains behind it. John went to the slammer. When John got out of prison he moved in with Marco.

"Joseph and Marco were deep into the rackets—drugs, prostitution, you name it. They raked in the dough. Had these big mansions—out on the shore. The brothers used to walk a trail on Joseph's estate every morning. Gave them privacy. John knew their routine. The day the brothers got killed, Marco's wife said John left in the morning for work in his red truck. Later we heard a red truck ran Marco and Joseph down."

"Nice family," Morrison said.

"Here's the kicker. Joseph bought the truck for John."

"Where's John Rodriguez now?"

"Walked off the face of the earth. Never seen after the day his brothers were killed. Got out of prison nine years ago. Never reported to his parole officer. No one's seen or heard from him since."

"Okay, Epstein, you got a hit," Morrison said in an excited voice. "Find out where this John Rodriguez is now."

"You heard the chief. He's disappeared off the face of the earth."

"Find him." Morrison said as he turned back to the papers on his desk.

Dottie cursed under her breath as she left the office.

# CHAPTER FIFTY EIGHT

"Come back to my office. I'll tell you everything you want to know about Giovanni. I'd love to get that snake in trouble. This way." Antonio signaled with his head.

Gerry and Tori followed the heavy-set man down the hallway beside the stage into his office. DeVito sat at a chair in front of the desk. He gestured to similar chairs for Gerry and Tori. "Have a seat."

"What do you want to know?" Antonio asked. "Has he been arrested?"

"No, he hasn't been arrested. We can't find him," Gerry said. "We think he was involved in some criminal activity, but no one knows where he is. We thought you might have some information that'd help us find him."

"Don't know where he is."

Tori asked, "What can you tell us about him?"

"The bastard took a vacation for two weeks in August six years ago. Never came back. Left me out on a limb. After I gave him his big break. Ungrateful swine."

"What was he like?" Tori asked.

Antonio leaned forward in his seat. "A con artist. Claimed he was a great hypnotist. That much was true. The act I had wasn't bringing in customers, so I gave him a chance. He was good. The audience loved him."

Gerry asked, "How long was he here?"

"Not long. Couple years. Got this beautiful young girl for his assistant. They were a big hit. Then he goes and beats her up. For no good reason—got drunk. I told her to go to the cops. She was afraid. I sent her to my doctor and gave her money to get out of Miami."

"Did he have any friends?" Gerry asked. "Anyone who might know where he is?"

"No. Everyone was as surprised as I was when he didn't come back. He had a good thing going here. He must've found a better con or else someone killed him."

"What about other people he hung out with? Anyone still around?"

"His biggest friend was another con artist, a real low life. He dressed like a big drug dealer—maybe he was." Antonio shrugged. "Who knows?

"Wore expensive clothes, flashy jewelry. Always had eye candy on his arm. Picked these beauties up in South America. Brought them to the U.S. Promised to marry them. He supplied the whore houses in Miami with prostitutes. I think that's where Giovanni got Angela, to tell the truth."

"So who's this friend and where can I find him, now?" Gerry asked.

"He left Miami a couple years ago. The INS was on to him. It was getting hot for him. He took a couple of girls with him and left."

"What's his name?"

"Some Hispanic name." He shook his head. "Sorry, don't remember."

"Was it Carlos?" Tori asked.

"Yeah! Carlos! That's it."

"What's Carlos' last name?" Gerry asked.

Antonio stroked his chin. "Carlos…Carlos…Gonzales? Perez? Hell, I can't think of it. It was some Spic name." He shrugged his shoulders.

Tori winched internally at the ethnic slur, but managed to keep her reaction off her face. She asked, "Sanchez, perhaps?"

"Yeah. Yeah. That's it—Sanchez."

"Any idea where Carlos went?" Gerry asked.

"Nah, he didn't want anyone following him."

"Do you by any chance have a photograph of Giovanni the Great?" Tori asked.

Antonio huffed. "You've come to the right place. I got a dozen posters and flyers. You can have them. Don't know why I kept them. Guess I thought he'd come back." Antonio got up and searched through a file cabinet. He found the flyers and gave a handful to Gerry who shared them with Tori.

Gerry and Tori examined the flyers. Giovanni was a good looking man, light complexion and dark eyes, heavy eyebrows that met over his nose, and curly black hair worn to his shoulders. He was dressed in a fitted tuxedo which displayed his powerful physique. A young woman stood with him. "Who's the beauty?" Gerry asked.

"That's Angela. The little girl he beat up."

"Do you know where I can find her?"

"Yeah, she's in Georgia. Must be doing all right. Sent me back the money I lent her. And a thank you note. She's real decent. Going to college in Savannah," he said with the pride of a parent.

"She's got family there. Working as a waitress, I think. I'll get her address." He walked behind the desk and opened the center drawer. After shuffling some papers, he said, "Here it is. I'll write the address for you. I want to keep the note."

"Thanks," said Gerry taking the slip of paper.

Tori took out a photograph of Eduardo Delgado and showed it to Antonio. "Do you recognize this man?"

Antonio examined the photograph, but shook his head. "Sorry, don't know him."

"Is there anything else you can tell us about Giovanni?" Gerry asked.

Antonio sat behind the desk and rubbed his chin, "He had illusions. Said he could make it in the legitimate world—as a doctor or a lawyer or something. Wanted to be a big man—respected—that kind of thing."

Antonio shook his head. "He could never make it in the honest world. Not with his temper. Least affront and he'd threaten to kill you."

"Do you think he'd kill someone?"

"He convinced Angela that he'd killed some people. Said they crossed him and no one got away with that. Told her he'd been in

235

prison up north. The killings might've been when he was in prison."

Gerry was famished—it was almost 4:00 and he hadn't eaten since breakfast. He asked Tori, "Hungry?"

"Better believe it."

"I remember a small Cuban restaurant near the El Gato Negro." Sure enough—he spotted it after driving fewer than two blocks. His mouth watered. It had been a long time since he had had Ropa Vieja the Cuban way, the way his mother used to prepare it.

The place was deserted this late on Monday afternoon, during siesta hours. They walked to the back and sat at a booth. While waiting for their food, Tori called home to check on Sean. "He doesn't answer." She was worried. She left a message on the answering machine.

"Maybe he's with Randy or he went to Morrison's. I'm going to call Morrison to exchange information, I'll ask him." Morrison told Gerry about John Rodriguez, and Gerry brought Morrison up to date on Giovanni. Gerry asked Morrison about Sean and shook his head at Tori. Tori tried to call Randy but got the answering machine. "Maybe Randy and Sean went someplace," she said with a hint of anxiety.

Gerry relayed the information about John Rodriguez to Tori. She rubbed her chin but said nothing. After a moment she said, "I told Dottie to check on John Rodriguez, but she got the wrong one. I wanted her to find John Rodriguez, a psychologist who was Seth Rothstein's former partner."

"It's a common name. Lucky Dottie found the one she did."

When the food came Gerry almost enjoyed it. It was tasty, but his stomach was tense thinking abut Tori's accident and he was more concerned about Sean than he had let on. Even worse, he could not have a beer with lunch since he had to fly back to Gainesville.

Gerry checked his watch. "We better get to the airport and return the car if we want to fly back before dark." He dropped some money on the table and they left. "Sorry, Tia Carmen," he said to the air.

The drive was quicker than he had anticipated, leaving time to spare. Gerry called his aunt. Gerry did not let on he was in Miami.

He would have a huge battle with Tia Carmen if he were in Miami and didn't go visit her.

Tia Carmen was thrilled to hear from her "favorite nephew." Gerry grinned. All her nephews were her favorite.

"How life treating you?" she asked, the remnants of her Cuban accent still obvious.

"It was going pretty well until last Saturday."

"What happen?"

Her voice was full of trepidation. Carmen Morales had received too many calls with depressing news for one lifetime. Her husband, Tio Alberto, a forklift operator, was killed in an accident at work. Less than a year later, their second oldest son was shot. Roberto lived, but his dreams of a career in soccer were destroyed with the injury to his knee. Tia Carmen seemed to wait for painful news.

"Tori was hit by a car on Saturday," he said.

"How bad?" In his heart Gerry knew Tia Carmen always saw the worst possible outcome for any incident—her defense for a life of bad outcomes.

"Tori's out of the hospital. No broken bones."

"Oh, Gerry, I so sorry. Please tell her I pray for her. I go see Sister Maria this afternoon and ask her to put Tori's name on prayer list."

"Thanks. I appreciate it."

Gerry knew Tia Carmen thought the divorce was a mistake on Gerry's part. Instinctively, she knew he was at fault. "You should no let that lovely lady go," she said.

"I couldn't agree more. I was a fool. I'm hoping to reconcile with Tori. We had lunch today."

"Good. Good. You should remarry that lady. I hope it no too late."

"I hope so, too," he said.

"That boy need mother and father," she said.

"Tia Carmen, I see Sean almost every weekend."

"He only 8 when I see him last."

"He's 12 now."

"It too long since you visit. You bring Tori and Sean down here."

Gerry checked his watch and said, "Tia Carmen, I've got to go. I'll call you and let you know how Tori is."

"You always running, running, running. You need slow down, enjoy life," she said. His mother's sister still thought of him as a boy who needed direction. Maybe she was right.

"Thanks, Tia Carmen, I'll try to do that."

"Yeah. Who you think you kidding? Take care, Gerry. Call your old Tia Carmen again soon."

"Bye, Tia Carmen."

"Bye, I love you."

"I love you, too."

Gerry was still smiling about Tia Carmen as he checked out the plane for the flight back to Gainesville. Tori told him she had called Sean again. Still no answer. He was glad he was flying himself. There was so much to think about while flying he could not ruminate over Tori being in danger or Sean not being at home. He would have plenty of time to do that when he should be sleeping tonight, he told himself as he taxied for takeoff.

# CHAPTER FIFTY NINE

Tori called home as soon as the plane's wheels touched the ground. "Sean isn't there," she said.

"I'm sure he's fine."

"Gerry, you don't know he's fine."

Gerry looked at his former wife, "You're right. Sorry. I feel helpless. I'm used to being able to handle things." He reached for her hand.

Tori took his hand. Her heart pounded.

Gerry parked the plane, got out and went to help Tori.

She said, "I can do it."

"Don't be stubborn. You'll hurt your ankle more if you put too much weight on it."

Tori said, "Let me try. She managed to get down herself, but grimaced when she stepped on her injured ankle. Gerry put his arm under hers without saying anything, and she allowed him to help her to the car. They were fraught with worry on the ride to Tori's house. When they pulled into the driveway, Tori clutched her heart. "There're no lights on."

Tori unlocked the door and switched on the lights. Tori spotted Sean's backpack in the den. "He's been home," she said. She looked at her watch: "8:00." She hugged herself. She riffled through her purse and found her cell phone. She dialed Randy's number.

Gerry pulled out his cell phone and called Morrison's office. There was no answer.

When Randy answered the phone, Tori asked, "Is Sean with you?"

"No," Randy said. "He went straight home. Why? What's happened?"

"We just got back from Miami and I've been calling him since 4:00."

"I'll call you if I hear from him."

Tori looked at Gerry. "What should we do?"

Lights moved across the room. A car was coming in the driveway. Gerry said, "Someone's here."

Tori wiped her eyes and went to the door just as Sean opened it. She pulled her son into a bear hug. Then she held him by the shoulders and asked, "Where have you been, young man? I've been worried out of my mind."

Sean pushed away from his mother. "I tried to call you, but there was no answer on your cell. You didn't tell me you were going to Miami with Dad."

"I left a note."

"I saw it. I left a note, too," Sean said. "Did you look on the fridge?"

Tori sighed. "I just got in. I haven't looked for a note."

"Don't blame Sean, Tori," Seth Rothstein said, walking in the door behind Sean. "I took him for a ride. I promised him a ride in my Jag when we went to dinner on Thursday." He extended his hand to Gerry, "Seth Rothstein. I assume you're the father of this fine young man."

"Gerry Arroyo," he said, ignoring the extended had. "Where did you take my son?"

Seth raised his eyebrows and turned to Tori. "I've been worried about you. That detective led me to believe you were at death's door."

Sean said, "Mom, Seth called to see how you were. I told him you were fine."

"Sean said you were gone for the afternoon, so I invited him for a ride," Seth said. "We called and when you weren't home we went for a hamburger. We left a message on your answering machine."

Tori turned and saw the red light blinking on the answering machine. *Idiot*, she thought.

240

"Dad, he's got the most wonderful wheels. A red Jaguar convertible. He let me drive it. It was brilliant."

Gerry looked at Seth Rothstein. "You should ask his mother's permission before you take our son for a ride." Venom shot from Gerry's eyes.

Seth said, "Sorry. Tori sort of gave me permission to take Sean. I'll ask her next time." He turned to Tori with a huge smile. "I need to go. I'll call when you aren't so busy."

Tori walked Seth to the door. "I'm sorry, Seth. It's a stressful time."

Seth took her hand. "I understand. I didn't mean to add to your worries." He kissed her on the cheek.

As Seth drove out of the driveway, Gerry asked, "Is that your new honey?"

"Seth is a psychologist. He's offered to help me counsel the women Sanchez held as slaves."

"You didn't answer my question." When Tori did not respond, Gerry said, "Still a sucker for dark Spanish eyes."

"What's that supposed to mean?" Tori asked.

"Your new el novio." When Tori frowned, he added, "Seth, your novio with the Spanish eyes."

"Seth is Jewish, not Spanish." She looked at Gerry. "You're jealous."

"Jealous of some gigolo who takes my son out in his hot car without telling me or his mother?"

When the phone rang, Tori sighed and thought *thank God*. "Hello."

"So you're alive, after all."

"Cindy?"

"You got it—the sister with the marrying obsession."

"Mom says you're getting a divorce."

"Right.

241

# CHAPTER SIXTY

The sun was peeping over the horizon when Gerry and Tori arrived at the Gainesville Airport to begin the hour's flight to Savannah. Glancing at the pink sky, Tori said, "Let's hope the adage about red skies isn't accurate. We don't need a storm."

"The internet weather forecast says clear skies," he said.

Tori's stomach was jumping around like a small child in a bounce house despite taking Dramamine. She did not want Gerry to know she got motion sickness in his small plane. He had encouraged her to eat before they left, but she said she wasn't hungry. She was starving, but did not dare have anything in her stomach for fear of vomiting in the plane. She had a barf bag in her purse. If she got ill she could attribute it to her head injury.

Quickly and efficiently Gerry checked the plane and they were in flight a few minutes before 7:00. The previous night he had called and arranged to interview Angela Gutiérrez before her 9:00 class. While far from eager, Angela could not refuse an FBI agent. Even honest people are intimidated and worried when a federal officer contacts them 'to talk.'

The flight to Savannah was uneventful and Gerry made it in record time with the help of a tail wind. But the flight felt interminable to Tori who was on the verge of nausea. She watched the GPS showing the remaining distance and willed the plane to get there. When it landed, she got out quickly and breathed in the outside air.

"Motion sickness?" Gerry asked, coming around to her side of the plane.

"Why do you ask?"

Gerry pointed the direction to the terminal and they headed toward it. "Tori, I'm not a psychologist, but I'm trained to evaluate people's behavior. When you white-knuckled the flight to and from Miami, I thought it was the aftereffects of your accident. But, when I thought about it last night, I realized every time you've been in a plane I flew, you sat in the back and Sean sat up front. I never saw your reaction to the flight."

"So I don't like small planes. So what!"

"Don't get defensive."

"Who's defensive?"

"Whatever. Let's go to Angela's house."

MapQuest led Gerry directly to the rundown section of Savannah where Angela lived with her cousin Orlando. The houses were old and in need of repair—the type of house advertised as a 'fixer-upper' in areas being restored. This dilapidated section of Savannah was not getting much needed refurbishment; even the lovely parks for which Savannah is noted were run down and in need of maintenance in this area.

Gerry parked his rental car in front of the house and scanned the area as he pushed the button on the key to lock it. Poverty was stamped on every house. Gerry and Tori walked to the front porch, avoiding sunken and tilted concrete slabs lying in wait for pedestrians. They climbed the steps watching for broken boards, reacting to the creaking with caution. The disrepair was too extensive for a coat of paint to cover. Gerry reached for the doorbell, but a young woman opened the door before he could ring it. Angela Gutiérrez had her finger over her lips. "Shh…I don't want to wake my cousin. He got home after 3:00 this morning."

Angela, on the Giovanni the Great flyers, wore a slinky red gown with a slit up the side revealing her shapely left leg. A slim young woman with long dark hair curling down to her waist, she appeared to be in her late teens. She wasn't exactly beautiful, but her youthful vitality made her appealing. With her huge black eyes and olive complexion she could be one of Gerry's cousins.

243

This Angela had the curly hair shown in the poster, but it was shoulder length and highlighted with a deep red hue. The poster had not exaggerated her big black eyes and clear, olive complexion. She had to be late twenties now, but looked no older than the teenage hypnotist assistant in the poster. Perhaps it was her size: slim and petite, about 5'2" Tori estimated.

Angela led Gerry and Tori into a tiny kitchen, a smaller version of the kitchen Gerry's Tia Carmen invited people into for a chat. Angela indicated some chairs and sat at the table across from her visitors. Gerry introduced himself and handed Angela his FBI identification, which she scrutinized closely.

She handed back his credentials and said, "Okay. Those look authentic." She pointed her chin at Tori and asked, "Who's she?"

"This is my colleague. She's a forensic psychologist."

"What do you want with me? Am I in trouble?"

"No, I'm not investigating you," Gerry said. "We want to know about someone you know. You've been in Savannah for six years. Is that correct?"

She said, "I'm a legal immigrant. Everyone knows I'm legal. I've a green card. Do you want to see it."

"Believe me I'm not with the immigration service. I'm investigating a murder. Please answer my question—how long have you been in Savannah?"

"A murder? Who's been murdered?" Angela stood. "Is my aunt all right?"

"Angela, no one you know has been hurt," Tori said. "Please sit down and let's start over, okay?"

"Sorry I upset you," Gerry said. "I tried to alleviate your concerns on the phone last evening. Not clear enough, apparently." Gerry looked at Angela. "Would you please sit down and let me explain."

When Angela sat again, he said, "I'm investigating a series of murders in Gainesville, Florida. None of the victims is anyone you know. Okay?"

Angela nodded and sighed.

"Someone you knew in Miami may've been involved in the murders; that's why I'm asking when you moved to Savannah. You've been in Savannah for about six years. Is that correct?"

He was trying to keep his voice soft and gentle, not an easy task for an experienced interrogator who tended toward authoritarianism.

"Yes." Angela took a deep breath and relaxed in her chair. No longer worried, her talkativeness surfaced. "My cousin and I work at a restaurant in the tourist area of Savannah—at night and weekends. We're taking college courses at Savannah State. It takes a long time to get a degree when you can only take two or three courses at a time. But I can see the end now. I've only got six more courses before I graduate.

Gerry, familiar with the talkativeness of female relatives, cut to the chase. "I'm interested in how you knew Giovanni the Great."

"Oh." Angela appeared to choke. "I should've guessed. He's the only criminal I know." She stared out the window for a moment, before reaching for a pack of cigarettes on the table behind a salt shaker.

"Mind if I smoke?"

Tori shook her head.

After lighting the cigarette and inhaling deeply, Angela exhaled and looked at Gerry. She spoke at a slower pace. "I lived in Venezuela, near the Columbian border. My aunt and uncle brought me to Miami when I was 16. I wanted an education. Wasn't there three weeks—my uncle was killed in a car wreck. My aunt was left with six kids and no income. I got a job after school."

"What kind of job?" Tori asked.

Angela watched the smoke from her cigarette curl toward the ceiling. "Waitress. I didn't mind working. I went to school. No drug lords kidnapping people or terrorizing us."

"You worked with Giovanni the Great for about three years? Is that correct?" Gerry asked.

"Yeah, that sounds right."

"How'd you get the job with Giovanni?" Tori asked.

Angela tapped the ashes off her cigarette into a green glass ashtray and watched the smoke while she spoke. "Giovanni came in the restaurant where I worked. Wanted me to be his assistant. I was 16. Too young to work around alcohol. He said he'd take care of it."

Angela stood up. "Like some coffee?"

"Yes, thanks," Tori said.

Angela filled the kettle with water. She took a drag on the cigarette. "Giovanni tried to charm my aunt—said she must be my sister. 'I look like her sister?' she said. 'You crazy.' My aunt is 4'11'' and weighs 200 lbs." Angela crinkled her face and shook her head. She leaned over the table and tapped the ash into the ashtray.

Gerry asked, "What happened?"

"She told me not to take the job. I wouldn't listen. Wanted money and knew everything when I was 16." She rested her cigarette in the ashtray. She took a French press coffee pot out of the cabinet and measured coffee into it.

"Giovanni gave me this slinky costume. I thought I looked beautiful, like a sexy movie star."

The kettle started singing and Angela poured the water into the French press. "Things were okay at first. Antonio, the nightclub owner, took me under his wing. My cousin Orlando hung around the nightclub. It went pretty well. Later, Antonio told me Giovanni'd been in prison."

She brought the French press to the table and sat. "Then my aunt moved to Savannah with Orlando and the other kids. Things got bad."

Gerry asked, "Why'd your aunt move?"

"Afraid of crime. Worried kids would get in with a bad crowd. Her brother lived in Savannah, so it was a natural choice."

"Who are these people?" an angry voice asked.

Tori saw a young Latino standing by the kitchen door. He was chunky, muscular but not very tall.

"Orlando, they're from the FBI," Angela said. "About Giovanni."

"El buscapleitos."

Gerry flashed his ID and introduced himself and Tori. "You don't like Giovanni?"

"He's a good-for-nothing weasel." Orlando looked at Angela. "Don't you have a 9:00 class?"

Angela looked at the clock. "Yikes! I got to go." She jumped up and ran out of the room. "Sorry," she said over her shoulder.

Orlando frowned and stamped out Angela's cigarette stub. "Maybe I can help you." He picked three mugs off a mug stand and put them on the table. He pressed the coffee and left it to settle.

246

"Why didn't Angela move to Savannah with you and your family?" Tori asked.

Orlando shook his head and looked out the window. "Mi madre didn't want her. Said six kids were enough."

"What happened to Angela?" Gerry asked.

"It was tough for her. Giovanni tried to get her to move in with him. She wouldn't. She lived with Antonio and Maria, his wife. Giovanni was furious, but didn't dare cross Antonio."

Orlando poured the coffee. "Cream? Sugar?"

Gerry shook his head. Tori said, "Sugar, please."

"Bye," Angela called from the other room. The front door slammed.

Orlando sat at the table and handed Tori the sugar bowl.

Tori put a spoonful in her coffee. "What happened to Angela after your family left? Why'd she move up here?"

"Angela doesn't like to talk about it. She dropped out of high school. Had a year to go. Maria helped her get into the GED program at Miami-Dade Community College. She did well. Maria's a teacher. She tutored her."

Orlando took a sip of coffee. "Giovanni didn't want her to go to school. Afraid she'd get independent. Wouldn't do what he said. He was right. She cut her hair. Giovanni was livid."

Orlando clenched his fists. "Giovanni beat her up. Did a job on her face."

"So she left?" Tori asked.

"Yeah," Orlando said. "Antonio flipped out. Angela thought he would kill Giovanni. Antonio gave her money. Helped her move up here. Mi madre wasn't happy. Money was tight."

"Do you have any idea where Giovanni is now?" Gerry asked.

"No." Orlando shook his head.

Tori smiled encouragingly at Orlando, and asked, "What did Giovanni tell Angela about his life before he went to Miami?"

"Giovanni grew up in the northeast—New York or New Jersey, or something. Had lots of sisters and brothers. His parents were crooks. His father was mean. Beat his wife and kids."

"That's helpful. What else?" Gerry asked.

Orlando frowned. "Giovanni hated his older brothers. They ganged up on him and beat him. He couldn't get back at them, so he took out his frustration on animals. He frightened Angela when he told her what he did to them." Orlando winced with the memory. "He dipped cat's tails in lighter fluid and set them on fire. He liked to see them run around and scream."

Tori cringed. *I can look forward to another nightmare*, she thought.

"Anything else you remember?" Gerry asked.

"Said his brothers got him sent to prison." Orlando said.

"How'd they do that?" Gerry asked.

"Got him involved in some scheme," Orlando said. "Said he got even. Killed them. We were terrified of him."

Tori asked, "Can you remember anything else?"

"He read books about hypnotism in prison. That's how he learned to be a hypnotist. He practiced on the guards and other inmates. Changed his name and became Giovanni the Great when he got out."

"Giovanni Romero isn't his real name?" Tori asked.

Orlando shook his head.

"Did he tell you what it was?"

"No."

# CHAPTER SIXTY ONE

Morrison was engrossed in a report from the New Jersey police department about John Rodriguez and his family, when Gerry tapped on the door and opened it.

"I thought I told you not to ..." Morrison stopped and softened his voice. "Oh, hey, Gerry. I thought it was Dottie again."

He waved for Gerry to come in. Gerry walked across the office with his hand extended. "Hello, Morrison."

Morrison stood to shake hands and remained standing as Gerry placed his briefcase on the desk. Morrison spotted Tori coming in behind Gerry. "Tori, how are you?" He walked around the desk and hugged Tori. Then he pulled up a chair. "Have a seat."

"Don't treat me like an invalid," Tori said. "I'm fine."

"Sean all right?"

"Yeah, he was out with a friend," Tori said.

Morrison leaned over his desk and watched as Gerry opened the briefcase, rifled through his papers and pulled out a flyer of Giovanni the Great. With a flourish Gerry handed it to Morrison.

"What's this?" asked Morrison.

"That's Giovanni the Great. Don't you recognize him?"

Morrison looked closer, but shook his head, "Never seen this man before."

"Damn!" Gerry was crestfallen. "I was positive Giovanni was one of the people you interviewed about the hit-and-runs."

Morrison's shoulders slumped. "I was, too."

"Where do we go from here?"

Morrison sat down, ran his hands over his face and took a deep breath. "Did you learn anything from your interview in Savannah with…with what's her name?" Morrison waved his finger in the air.

"Angela. Angela Gutiérrez." Gerry sighed. "She said Giovanni was violent and served time in prison."

"Anything else?"

"Angela confirmed Giovanni was friends with Carlos in Miami. Said no one crossed him. Her cousin told us Giovanni said he killed his brothers."

"Wait a minute! Wait a minute!" Morrison hit the intercom. "Dottie get in here. NOW." He grinned. "This might be the break we need."

As soon as Dottie came into the office, Morrison said to Gerry, "Tell Epstein what you told me about this Giovanni the Great killing his brothers."

Gerry reiterated what he had told Morrison. Dottie gave a celebratory fist punch into the air. She said, "Rodriguez got out of prison and ran over his two brothers with a truck. He sold the red pick-up truck to Giovanni Romero nine years ago—the same truck that killed Carlos."

Gerry said, "Let me guess. Rodriguez hated his brothers. They had a sweet scam going, but when the authorities got close, they brought John into it. Then they let him take the rap and he ended up in the slammer."

"You got it!"

"That's the story Giovanni told Angela and her cousin," Tori said. "He must've stolen Rodriquez's history to frighten Angela."

"So Giovanni and Rodriguez knew each other," Epstein said. "Maybe they met in prison."

"Yeah and Giovanni used Rodriguez's background to make himself look dangerous," said Morrison.

"Where's Rodriguez now?" asked Gerry.

"He vanished after he got out of prison. Never reported to his parole officer. Authorities can't find him." Morrison slammed his right fist on his desk.

"Maybe Rodriguez killed Giovanni and stole his identity," Tori said.

"There's no sign of Giovanni in the last seven years, either," Gerry said. "Dottie, what've you found?"

"According to the police report John Rodriguez stayed with his brother Marco after he got out of prison. The day his brothers were killed, Marco's wife said John left the house after Marco and she never saw him again. I can't find any sign of him after that."

Gerry crossed his arms and stared into space without speaking for awhile. He said, "We need to check out Giovanni Romero. Angela said he was from New York or New Jersey. He might have known Rodriguez before he went to prison or met him in prison. Maybe he helped Rodriguez get rid of his brothers."

Dottie said, "Perhaps Rodriguez gave Giovanni the truck for his help and Giovanni brought the truck to Florida."

"Or, as Tori said, Rodriguez killed Giovanni to get his identity," Gerry said.

"Yeah. Or maybe Rodriguez and Giovanni are working together again on the burglaries and murders," Morrison said.

Gerry pulled out his cell phone. "I'll get my office to trace John Rodriguez."

# CHAPTER SIXTY TWO

Raised voices resounded throughout the station.

"For God's sake! Are those two at it again?" complained the patrolman checking in at the desk.

The officer standing next to him rolled his eyes.

Behind Morrison's closed door, Dottie was arguing in a loud voice. "Jimmie Rafferty inherited $50,000 from Margaret O'Neal. He was in debt to Delgado. Delgado's tied in with the Cuban Mafia. He could've forced Rafferty to kill Margaret O'Neal."

"I told you to forget about Delgado. Don't you listen to anything I tell you? I don't care if he is a creep."

"Delgado was in Miami when Giovanni and Carlos were there. He was involved with the same thugs. Your friend said he was an enforcer." Dottie, hands on hips, leaned across the desk toward Morrison.

"The nightclub owner and Giovanni's assistant didn't recognize Delgado's photo. Besides, Delgado was a teenager when Giovanni was in Miami."

"Maybe he dealt with Giovanni through Rodriguez."

"No one's seen Rodriguez in years," Morrison said. "He's either dead or got a new identity."

"Delgado has no alibi for the time Carlos was killed."

"We have the truck used to kill Carlos and it belongs to Giovanni Romero." Morrison retorted, standing to face his partner.

"Maybe Delgado placed bets with Romero for Rafferty."

"Damn it, Epstein, get a grip. Remember Carlos is the one who gave O'Neal the key and the alarm code."

"Delgado is involved."

"He's got an alibi for Margaret's death. Now, drop it, Epstein," he said, pointing a huge finger at her nose as his face deepened in color, a blue vein pulsated on his forehead.

"He could have gotten Rafferty to do the killing."

"Epstein, drop it."

Dottie knew the signs—Morrison was about to explode. She typically would have backed down, but this time she was so convinced she was right, she continued the argument. She crossed her arms. "I've a gut feeling."

"I don't give a damn about your 'gut feeling,' I'm telling you to concentrate on finding Rodriguez and Giovanni," he said leaning toward her, hands on the desk. "Listen up, Epstein, I'm sick of this women's intuition shit." Morrison sat and pivoted his chair around so his back was to Dottie.

Dottie was not intimidated or put off easily, but she worried about Morrison having another attack. She softened her voice. "I don't want to upset you, Morrison, but remember it was my gut feeling that Carlos was involved. If I hadn't checked on him on my own, we'd be nowhere."

Morrison swung his chair around, his red face deepening in color, verging on purple. "And, Miss Go-It-Alone, Carlos would still be alive if you hadn't decided to scare him." His voice was not loud, but the anger was palpable and Dottie knew better than to keep pushing. Morrison was frightening when he was shouting, but when he lowered his voice, even Ruth knew to back off. Dottie took a deep breath.

"Morrison, I think Delgado is in this up to his neck," Dottie said. "He asked Rafferty about Margaret and where she walked. He was friends with Carlos. Tori says he's got an anti-social personality disorder."

Morrison pointed his finger at her one more time and commanded, "Go check on Rodriguez and Romero. Got it?"

Dottie thought, *shit, I've done it this time.*

"That's a direct order," said Morrison, speaking slowly and distinctly.

Dottie saluted, but knew he was wrong.

# CHAPTER SIXTY THREE

Dottie drove home clutching the steering wheel, her knuckles white and her breathing forced. She slammed on the brakes skidding into the driveway. She banged her fists on the steering wheel, took a deep breath and snatched her computer off the passenger seat. She slammed the car door summoning her nosy next door neighbor who pulled aside the curtains on her back door for a look. Dottie ignored her neighbor's watchful eye and climbed the back stairs two at a time. Bruce was sprawled out in front of the television watching the 6:00 news. Dottie stormed through the back door, dumped her computer on the kitchen table and stomped into the living room. She was so wound up she could not even sit down.

"Do you have any idea how difficult it is to work with that condescending bastard?" Dottie strode up and down the room.

"Good evening, nice to see you."

Dottie frowned at Bruce, "Sorry, sometimes he makes me so mad." She took a deep breath, leaned over and kissed Bruce.

"That's better. Now tell me what the condescending bastard did." Bruce tried to pull Dottie onto his lap.

She resisted. She pulled him to his feet. "Get your lazy ass up and come run with me," Dottie said. "I can't sit still."

Bruce groaned. "I was just relaxing."

"Get up." Dottie headed for the bedroom.

Bruce reached under the couch for his shoes. "Wait a sec while I put on my running shoes."

In a few minutes Dottie joined Bruce at the back door dressed in her running togs. Bruce was standing on one leg, bending the other knee back in a stretch. "Aah!"

Dottie led the way out the door, down the steps, and around to the front of the house. As he descended the steps, Bruce waved to the neighbor peeking around the curtain. The curtain dropped into place. He grinned.

"I assume you were talking about Morrison," Bruce said as they started off at an easy pace to warm up.

"Who else?"

"What's he done?"

"It's not what he's done; it's what he won't do, or won't let me do."

Loud barking startled the couple.

"That friggin' monster," Bruce said. "Good thing he's behind that fence."

"He's harmless," Dottie said.

The large black dog followed them along the other side of the fence as they ran. He growled.

"He got out the other day," Bruce said. "Growled at me. Would've taken a chunk out of my calf, if the kid hadn't stopped him."

"Bruce, you've got to learn to make friends with dogs."

"He doesn't want friends. He wants a tasty bite."

When they reached the corner, they jogged in place waiting for traffic to clear. The light changed. A truck careened around the corner. Dottie saw an opening in the traffic. "C'mon."

When they safely reached the other side of the street, Bruce said, "Tell me about Morrison."

"We know Tori must have done something Friday to alert the murderer she was close. I think she might have talked to Jimmie Rafferty."

"He's the guy with the big gambling debts, isn't he?"

"Yeah. And he inherited $50,000 from Margaret. I think he was in debt to Delgado and Delgado forced him to kill Margaret. But Morrison wants me to spend my time looking for John Rodriguez and Romero."

"Who's John Rodriguez?"

"Why don't you stop interrupting and I'll tell you," Dottie said. She picked up the pace as they turned into the neighborhood park.

Bruce caught up to Dottie. He pantomimed zipping his lips.

Dottie explained about John Rodriguez and his connection with Giovanni Romero. She said, "I've thought and thought about the case and gone over the list of suspects in my head. Delgado keeps popping up." She ran faster.

"Hey, slow down if you want me to listen."

Dottie laughed. "You need to run more if you want to keep in shape." She ran ahead and thumbed her nose at Bruce. Bruce stopped. "Do you want to talk or prove you run faster than I do?"

"Okay, you win. Let's go slower."

They proceeded at a moderate pace. "Tell me about Delgado," Bruce said.

"He asked about Margaret's walking habits, he knew Carlos Sanchez and didn't have an alibi for his murder, he worked with the Cuban Mafia in Miami, and Tori said he has an anti-social personality disorder. But, he has an ironclad alibi for Margaret's murder."

Bruce pantomimed zipping his mouth again.

"Okay, you can talk now."

Bruce slowed and ran behind Dottie as they passed a young woman pushing a baby in a stroller. He caught up to Dottie and asked, "Why don't you check out his alibi? I've seen more than one strong alibi vanish under closer scrutiny."

"I did. I called Mack Landry to check on Delgado's alibi for Margaret's murder."

"Mark Landry, our city counsel member?" Bruce asked.

Dottie snorted. "Landry said Delgado and Bob Cramer—our former mayor—and Randy Hansen—Landry's brother-in-law went camping and hunting at Landry's cabin. They went to Ocala Friday and stayed until late Sunday. Delgado was with them from Friday afternoon until Sunday evening."

"So much for the possibility of destroying his alibi," Bruce said. "Maybe he left during the weekend."

"Possibly, or he forced Rafferty to kill Margaret."

Bruce said, "Slow down a minute. I've got a stitch in my side." Bruce rubbed his side. He bent to one side then the other. He grimaced. "I thought Gerry said this Giovanni guy was friends with Carlos."

"He was. He was also friends with John Rodriguez." Dottie bent her right knee and stretched her left leg behind her. A group of teenage boys jogged toward them. The group opened up and went around Dottie and Bruce. One lone straggler huffed past them a moment later.

Bruce smiled at the straggler. "I know the feeling." He started jogging slowly. "Dottie, Carlos gave Margaret the key and alarm code. It seems to me you should pursue the link between Carlos and Giovanni. And the link between Giovanni and this Rodriguez guy."

"That's what Morrison said." She sighed.

"You obviously don't agree. Why not?"

"I don't know." Her frustration was building. Dottie jogged off the path and sat on the bench. She looked up at the live oak dripping Spanish moss. She ran her hands through her short Afro. "Who did Tori see on Friday? What did she discover that made her a threat to the killer?"

Bruce sat next to Dottie. He stretched his legs.

Dottie asked, "Did she see Rafferty? She could have seen Delgado. Delgado asked Rafferty a lot of questions about Margaret and where she walked."

"I thought Tori regained her memory. Did she say she saw either Rafferty or Delgado?"

"No. But she might not remember things as well as she thinks."

The teenage boys ran past going the other way. The straggler still straggled.

Bruce gave him a 'thumbs up.' "No one would just confess to Tori. If someone told her anything suspicious, she would have called you or Morrison. She wouldn't have gone to her office to see clients the next morning without contacting you."

Dottie looked around and shrugged. She stood up and headed back to the house.

Bruce jogged next to her. "I think Morrison might be right this time, you need to concentrate on Rodriguez and Giovanni."

Dottie was not convinced. "My gut tells me to check on Delgado and Rafferty."

"And my gut tells me we should get some Indian take-out."

# CHAPTER SIXTY FOUR

As Tuesday night crept into Wednesday morning, it was Dottie's turn for restless sleep and nightmares. The latest nightmare featured Dottie standing surveillance in the parking lot of Tori's office, watching an old SUV. The driver has his back to her, but he is somehow familiar. She watches him pull a stocking over his head. She walks up to the driver's window with her gun drawn. "Take off that stocking," she orders. She can see the driver's eyes watching her and knows she will recognize him. A powerful hand reaches up and jerks the stocking off. She's shocked. It couldn't be. He shouts at her, "Didn't I tell you to concentrate on Giovanni and Rodriguez? What are you doing watching this SUV?" Morrison yells. Dottie woke up with a start. *Damn,* she thought, *now the cantankerous old buzzard is watching me in my sleep.* She rolled on her side and looked at the clock— 2:43 a.m. She pulled a pillow over her head and went back to sleep.

Dottie dreamt she was hiking in the woods. The trees were just budding and the air was clear with the sound of birds and crickets. Then a new bird joined the chorus. This bird had a harsh, grating song that kept getting louder and louder. Dottie half awakened, still immersed in her dream, as the bird transformed into her bedside phone. She opened her eyes to see it was 5:15. She picked up the phone.

"Epstein, here," she said sitting up on the side of the bed.

"Sorry for the early call," said Gerry. "I'm at the airport. I'm taking the 5:30 flight to Newark. I need you to watch out for Tori. Stay with her. She won't let anyone else stay there."

"Of course. I'll go over right now."

"No need to rush. She's still asleep and Morrison has a man parked outside her house. You can go over after 7:30. I'll keep in touch. Don't go anywhere without calling me first. I need to go, my flight is boarding." He hung up.

If Gerry had to take a commercial flight, using the small Gainesville Airport was the least frustrating of his options. There were fewer flights, fewer people, shorter lines and less waiting around. He was flying up and back in one day, so he didn't have any hold luggage and the only carry-on was his attaché. He went through security quickly because of his FBI ID, even though TSA personnel questioned the gun in his attaché. He produced his authorization and continued to the gate.

The worst part of flying commercial was wasted time. While waiting to board, he bought a newspaper, but instead of reading it, he paced the area, scrutinizing the other passengers. He was even more paranoid than usual after what happened to Tori.

Finally the gate agent called his flight for boarding. There were only seven people on this early flight so everyone boarded at once. He had a front seat near the left window—the best place to observe what the pilot was doing. He watched as the pilot pulled from the gate and navigated the plane to the takeoff runway. After the plane lifted off, there was nothing to take his mind off his worries. When he piloted a plane he was so busy checking instruments, keeping at the right altitude and flying in the appropriate direction, he had no time for ruminating about personal concerns.

Gerry looked out the window of the plane. He would have seen nothing even if the plane were not flying through thick clouds. His eyes were focused inward.

"Important business meeting?" It took a moment for the voice to penetrate his thoughts before Gerry turned toward the source. He had been unaware of the woman in the seat next to him. Gerry disliked talking to people he didn't know. They inevitably wanted to know where he worked. He hated lying, but if he told the truth they became cautious and distrustful. If he gave an ambivalent answer, they considered him stand-offish. One more reason he didn't like flying commercially. He nodded. "Sorry, I don't mean to be unfriendly, but I need to review my presentation." He turned back to the window and his thoughts.

Gerry was grateful when the pilot announced their arrival at the Newark airport about an hour later. His seatmate smiled. "Good luck with that presentation." He looked at her blankly until he remembered their brief conversation, hesitating long enough before thanking her so she realized he had lied. Her smile reverted to a frown. She turned her back and walked off the flight. Gerry shrugged.

# CHAPTER SIXTY FIVE

Gerry went directly to the Hertz office to pick up the keys for his rental car. The pleasant woman at the desk handed him a map and pointed out the route to the turnpike. He hadn't been in New Jersey for a couple of years, but he easily followed the map.

After a short drive, he exited the turnpike toward Belmar on the Jersey shore where the families of John Rodriguez's two brothers lived. The azaleas had finished blooming in north Florida in February, but they were at the height of their beauty in New Jersey. It was early spring here and the scenery glowed with that unique green of new growth. He almost felt peaceful on the drive south, surrounded by budding trees and new grass.

Armed with his MapQuest directions, Gerry located Maria Rodriguez's house. Maria was Joseph's wife, the older brother of Marco and John Rodriguez. The plan was for Marco's wife Gemma to join them there. This arrangement had been made at Gemma's request. She told him, "I'm remarried. My second husband was Marco's attorney. He doesn't like to be reminded that the house we live in is the product of Marco's business."

Gerry thought, *Yeah, right, he doesn't want the feds after Marco's illegal gains. Besides, Marco's underworld dealings were probably an embarrassment for the new husband.*

Gerry drove some distance along the high black wrought iron fence delineating the Rodriguez property before he came to the entrance. Thick foliage blocked any view of the house from the road. He pulled up to the intercom at the gate, pushed the speaker button and gave his name. The heavy gate swung open and he drove slowly up the driveway. Gerry observed razor wire hidden in the foliage edging the wrought iron fence. The Rodriguezes did not want any uninvited guests. The driveway was nearly half a mile long, ending in a circle around a fountain at the front entrance. Gerry whistled when he spotted the Rodriguez home. It was gray with white trim, three stories high with a half dozen dormers. *Joseph did not leave his wife destitute*, thought Gerry, *there must be forty rooms in the place.* The house reminded him of estates in his home state of Connecticut, homes of the super-wealthy in Greenwich, Stamford, and New Canaan.

He parked his car in the drive and climbed the dozen steps. His first apartment with Tori and Sean was smaller than the porch. Gerry rang the bell and waited at the front door, thinking he was probably the first FBI agent welcomed into this house. An impeccable butler opened the door. The butler led him to a living room where the Rodriguez widows were waiting. Gerry knew the complete history of both women, thanks to Dottie and his office staff.

Meanwhile, back in Gainesville, Tori sat in the lounge chair with her feet up while she and Dottie tried to figure out what Tori had said or done late Friday or early Saturday that made Margaret's murderer thinks Tori knew too much. Dottie said, "We know you called Karen Baker."

"Yeah, then I went to visit her. But we knew that, too."

"What did you talk about with Karen?"

"She told me all about her problems with drinking and how she went to see Seth Rothstein. She told me about her therapy."

Dottie asked, "Didn't she tell you she saw Margaret in Rothstein's office when she was supposed to be burglarizing the house?"

"Yes, but Seth says she's mistaken. He checked his records. He says she's confused and suffers from alcoholic blackouts. I tend to agree with him. Her thinking was scattered. After all she's in her late 60s and drank a lot. We both saw the video. We know Margaret burglarized the house."

"So you talked to Dr. Rothstein."

"Yes, we had a long chat. He offered to help counsel the women Carlos held in that horrible house. We had a laugh over Karen telling me that punishment was the same as negative reinforcement."

"What about Delgado or Rafferty, did you see either of them?"

"I'm pretty sure I didn't. Why?"

"I'm convinced Delgado is involved with this. But he has an ironclad alibi for Margaret's death."

"Maybe there're holes in his alibi."

"That's what Bruce says. "Delgado was in Ocala with Mack Landry and the former mayor from Friday evening until Sunday night."

"Ocala's less than 30 minutes from here. Delgado could have come back, killed Margaret and gotten back to Ocala in a little over an hour—especially that early in the morning."

"I think I should re-interview our city councilman about that ironclad alibi," Dottie said.

"Yeah, that's a good idea. Maybe find out something about Delgado hiring someone to kill Margaret O'Neal."

"But, I can't do it until Gerry gets back."

"Why not?"

"I can't leave you alone."

"Who said anything about leaving me alone? I'm going with you."

"Morrison will have my hide. Not to mention Gerry."

"They'll never know," she said handing Dottie the phone. "Call Landry and tell him we're on the way."

Mack Landry lived in a rural area in southwest Gainesville. On the long drive to the Landry homestead, Dottie told Tori about the man they were going to interview. "Mack Landry might be a Gainesville City Councilman, but he's still a good ol' boy. He hunts, camps, fishes, everything a good ol' boy does. He grew up on a family-run farm on the outskirts of town and still lives on it and runs it—that's where we're going. Mack prides himself on being 'just a local farmer' and runs for office on that word picture. He says he loves the outdoors and wants to protect it. His voting record indicates he's done what he promised."

Dottie found the address easily with her GPS and spotted the sign 'Landry Farms' hanging on the split-log fence surrounding the property. Acres of fields were newly planted with a crop breaking the surface. Cows roamed another section of the farm. The expanse of land dwarfed the ranch house set far from the road. The gate was open. Dottie turned into the driveway and proceeded to the house surrounded by a minuscule lawn. The red ranch house, typical of the 1960s, looked tiny from the street, but there was a large addition in the back not visible from the road. Carol Landry answered the doorbell. She was a sweet-looking middle aged woman dressed in jeans and a denim shirt. "Come in, come in," she said. "I'm Carol. Mack is waiting for you in the den."

She led them into a wood-paneled room hung with stuffed wildlife—deer, boars, and a huge swordfish over the mantle. Mack Landry was sitting on a leather recliner, feet up, reading the *Gainesville Sun* and sipping a cup of coffee. He dropped the newspaper on the floor next to his chair, lowered the foot rest and stood to greet his guests. After the usual pleasantries, Tori drew attention to the photographs on the table next to his seat.

"Are those your children?" she asked.

"Sure are. Got three young 'uns—all girls." He smiled, picking up one of the photos. "They're girly girls. You know, all they do is shop and look pretty. Don't get me wrong, they are pretty. They're my porcelain dolls." He shook his head. "But a boy would've been nice. You know, someone to go fishing with, to teach how to shoot…"

"Oh, Mack," his wife said. "You love to talk about wanting boys, but you'd be heartbroken if you didn't have your girls to pamper you." She turned to Dottie, "He dotes on them and they worship their papa."

Dottie was determined to revert to her own manner of interviewing people and not use the Reid Technique she had picked up from Morrison. She had recently read about the false confessions the approach elicited. She looked at the photograph of Mack and his family on the table and then at Carol. "I see where they get their looks."

Mack said. "Sure were lucky they got their mother's looks and not their papa's."

Mack Landry was 60ish, 6'1" or 6'2," with the leathered skin of someone who spent a lot of time in the sun. He was portly, but not soft—an outdoors man, his bronze tan offset by a mass of white hair. He reminded Dottie of Matt Dillon. He said, "Please, sit down, sit down. What can I do for you?"

Dottie said, "We'd like some information about the weekend you went camping with Edward Delgado."

"Oh, yeah. You called about that. We went hunting at my camp outside Ocala. We've been hunting there going on four years. For a city guy, Ed's a good hunter. So's Seth."

"Seth?" Dottie asked.

"Seth Rothstein."

Tori said, "I didn't realize Seth Rothstein was with your group."

"Yep, he loves to hunt. When I first met him, I expected he'd be a tree-hugger, a PETA member, that sort of thing. No offense, Doctor, but my experience with shrinks is they're not into hunting, or that kinda stuff."

"Mack, you better stop while you're ahead," Carol said.

"Yeah, you can tell I go around putting my foot in my mouth. Ain't got no couth. What I think is what I say. Sorry. As Carol said, I better shut up." He gave them a huge smile and asked, "What do you want to know?"

"Tell us about the weekend," Dottie said. "When you got there, when you left, that sort of thing."

"Sure. I already told you, but I don't mind repeating myself to two good-looking gals." Tori and Dottie smiled politely.

"It wasn't such a hot weekend. Got to the camp Friday night. Played poker 'til late. Up at the crack of dawn to find deer. They come out first thing in the morning to a water hole. We saw deer, but they saw us, too." He laughed. "They took off. We didn't get a thing."

The conversation was interrupted by a ringing cell phone. Tori said, "I'm sorry, I should've turned my phone off." She noted the call was from Gerry. *I'll call him back later,* she thought.

Dottie pulled her phone out of her pocket and shut off the ringer. "Just in case." She smiled. "What did you do Saturday night and Sunday morning?"

"Even thinking about it hurts my head." Landry held his hands against the sides of his head as if in pain. "Never had such a hangover."

"Serves you right," said Carol.

"You said it, gal." He groaned. "Played poker late Saturday night—lost a bundle. So hung-over none of us could get up Sunday morning. Funny thing is, I tried not to drink much. I planned to get up early and get a deer."

"I've heard that before." Carol shook her head. "Men!"

"Even Randy couldn't get up. That's my brother-in-law, Randy Hansen. He don't even drink, but he said he thought he got the flu—head hurt so bad he couldn't lift it off the pillow.

Dottie asked, "No one was up and around on Sunday morning?"

"Only one functioning Sunday morning was Seth. He got up before the rest of us and went hunting. Tried to wake us but couldn't get us up. I don't know how he does it. He drank as much if not more than the rest of us. He sure can pack them away. But, he stayed away from the hooch, he just drank beer."

"Hooch?" asked Tori. "What's that?" She looked at Dottie and Carol but they seemed to understand.

"You're a northern gal. Southerners know about hooch. It's home made liquor. Strong enough to take the enamel off the kitchen sink. I don't know where Seth learned to make the stuff, but it's the strongest I've ever had. Tasted okay. Smelt awful, like rotten oranges. Yuck! I'll never eat another orange."

Carol stood up and walked toward the back of the house. "I'll get us a snack."

Mack chuckled. "Anyway, we were just getting up when Seth came back mid-morning."

"Was Seth alone?" Tori asked.

"Pretty sure Seth was alone," Mack said. "But you know, I was in bad shape."

"Was Ed Delgado with him?" Dottie asked.

Mack shrugged. "Anyway, Seth didn't have any luck. He hit a deer with the truck, but the dang deer kept going. Only thing he had to show for his efforts was a new dent on the truck and a little blood. Of course, with that old truck one more dent wouldn't make no difference."

"I didn't know Dr. Rothstein had a truck," Tori said.

"He don't drive it around town; keeps it at the camp. It's an old pick up. It ain't fit for anything 'cept driving on dirt trails around the camp."

"What does it look like?" Dottie asked casually, trying to keep the excitement out of her voice.

"It's real old. I guess at one time it was red, but it's rusted now—real beat up."

Tori asked who else was on the hunting trip and Dottie took down the names, including the former mayor.

"Why are you so interested in our hunting trip?" asked Mack.

"It's part of an on-going investigation," Dottie said. "I'm sorry I can't tell you more. I'm sure you understand."

Dottie was ready to leave, but Mrs. Landry came back with cookies and lemonade. Tori was grateful for the snack. She hadn't eaten since morning—half an English muffin and some tea at 6:30. When they finished their snack, the two women stood.

"Thank you for all your help." Tori said as she and Dottie shook hands with Mack and Carol bid them goodbye.

As soon as the car door closed Dottie said, "Seth Rothstein has an old beat up pick up."

"He was lying about Margaret O'Neal," Tori said. "He killed her."

"He drugged the hooch," Dottie said.

"Yeah he drugged everyone at the camp while he went to run over Margaret."

"That orange smell is interesting—that's the hooch guys make in prison," Dottie said. "But why did Seth kill Margaret?"

There was something nibbling at the edges of Tori's mind. She knew it was the reason Margaret was killed, but she could not bring it to her conscious mind. "Yes, why would Rothstein run over one of his patients? And what is his connection to the burglaries?" Tori asked.

"And who is Giovanni Romero and John Rodriguez?" Dottie asked.

Tori snapped her fingers. "That's it. I should have seen it."

# CHAPTER SIXTY SIX

Before boarding his 12:30 flight from New Jersey, Gerry called Morrison and brought him up to date on his interview with the Rodriguez widows. "They showed me photographs of John Rodriguez. I was stunned. It cleared everything up. It boils down to John Rodriguez and Giovanni Romero are one and the same person."

"Of course, makes sense. Romero didn't *steal* Rodriguez's identity, he changed his own identity." Morrison mulled that over for awhile, then his shoulders slumped. "Yeah, great. So what good does it do us? We can't find either of them."

"I've got some more information. I don't know how helpful it is, but maybe you could follow-up on it. The FBI found a John Rodriguez who was murdered in Baltimore six years ago. There's no evidence the murdered John Rodriguez ever existed prior to that time."

"Okay, I'm on it."

Gerry hung up and called Tori's house. No answer. He called her cell phone, but, again no answer. He called Dottie's cell phone. Once more—no answer. He left an irate message. "Where the hell are you? I told you not to leave the house without letting me know."

He checked his watch—12:15. *Maybe they went out for lunch.* He left a message on Tori's phone to call him and not leave the house unless she told him where she was going.

He called Morrison back to see if he had heard from the women, but Morrison was on a long distance call and Gerry could not stay on the line because he needed to board his flight.

Morrison had left word not to disturb him. He was calling the Chief of Detectives of the Baltimore PD. No one dared interrupt Morrison. His temper was legendary. When he got through to the Chief, he said, "I'm trying to find out about the death of John Rodriguez. Happened about six years ago."

Chief of Detectives Bill Clark told him, "Today's your lucky day. I investigated that case."

"First thing's gone right all week. What happened?"

"Worst murder scene I've ever investigated." He paused. "You don't sound like a southerner."

Morrison said. "Nah, I'm from Jersey. Moved to Florida for the weather."

"Ah, a northern guy, one of our own." Clark chuckled. "But kidding aside, it took me forever to get the image of the poor sucker out of my head. I still cringe thinking about it. He was beaten beyond recognition. Face was a bloody jumble of bones, skin... God it was awful."

"How'd you ID the victim with his face messed up?"

"That was the easy part. He was in his office and his partner ID'ed him."

"How'd his partner recognize him if his face was missing?"

"The way we identified him was by where the incident happened. Victim was murdered in his own office. Partner saw him go in with a patient."

"Anyone else ID him? Next of kin? Friend?"

"Nah, had no next of kin, no friends. Was alone in the world except for his partner. But, no need for another ID. The partner heard him calling for help. Had a loaded gun in the office. Rushed in and shot the murderer. The creep was still beating Dr. Rodriguez. But the partner wasn't fast enough to save his friend's life. He was distraught when he called 911."

Clark said, "I wondered why the partner had a loaded gun in his desk. You know, them kind of doctors are touchy-feely types, they don't have guns. Told me Rodriguez's patients were inmates from the work release center and the jail. Those guys were violent—had no conscience. He warned Rodriguez one of them would attack him. Couldn't get Rodriguez to protect himself, so he took matters into his own hands. Got a gun. We checked it out. He'd gotten the gun a couple weeks before. It was legal and all."

"Why wasn't there a police guard if Romero was seeing someone from work release?" Morrison asked.

"The guard brought prisoners to the office all the time. Nothing had ever happened. Dr. Rodriguez told him to wait outside so the clients wouldn't feel intimidated. Guard went to the kitchen to get coffee."

"Why'd the guy kill his doctor? In his office of all places? And with a witness in the building? Doesn't sound like he was firing on all cylinders. What did the perp say happened?"

"Nada. Stone cold dead. Partner killed him by the time we got there."

"You sure the patient killed Dr. Rodriguez?"

"No doubt. Still holding the book end he beat Rodriguez with. Covered in blood and gore from the vic."

"Know anything else about Dr. Rodriguez?"

"Not much. Hadn't been in Baltimore long. Had no friends except his partner. They lived and worked together. Partner sold the house and office building. Said he couldn't stand being where someone murdered his friend. Left the state after the funeral.

"The partner was a weird guy. Soon as we closed the case, he stopped returning my phone calls. I had a couple questions I needed answered to tie up the case. I went to the house, but no one answered. The neighbors said he'd moved. They said someone turned the partner's cats loose from the house. Were they mad. They insisted the doctor would never do that. Thought the new owners had done it. But the new owners didn't even know about the cats. Said they wouldn't buy a house that'd had cats in it."

"Thanks. That's helpful."

Morrison was about to hang up when he asked, "One more question."

When he got the answer, Morrison almost fell off his chair.

# CHAPTER SIXTY SEVEN

Driving back to her house, Tori said to Dottie, "When we get to my house, fire up your computer. I've got an idea."

"You're not going to tell me your idea now, are you?"

"I don't want to distract you from driving," Tori said, clinging to the passenger side door handle and bracing herself against the dashboard.

After a moment of silence, Dottie said, "I feel like the car is moving in slow motion."

"I assure you the car is going at maximum speed," Tori said. "Mind you, I didn't say it was a safe speed."

Dottie grinned, but didn't slow down. She was going fast and made a wide turn into Tori's driveway, skidding to a stop. "Sorry. Can't wait to see what you want to do on the computer."

Dottie raced up the front steps two at a time. She quickly checked out the house and was back on the front porch jumping from foot to foot. "It's clear, come on, come on."

Tori walked slowly up the front walk.

Dottie asked, "What's keeping you?"

"My ankle." Tori limped. Every time she stepped on her ankle a sharp pain shot up her leg.

Dottie jumped down from the porch and gave Tori her arm to climb the steps. "Sorry, I forgot about your injury."

"Thanks, I didn't bring the meds for my ankle and the pain slows me down."

Dottie opened the door and stepped aside so Tori could go in first. Dottie assisted Tori to her chair and asked, "Where are your meds?"

"On the end table."

Dottie got Tori a glass of water. "Can I get you anything else?"

"I'm fine. Set up the computer."

Dottie powered up the computer and was ready by the time Tori took her medicine.

"Pull up the photograph of Giovanni the Great," Tori said. She looked over Dottie's shoulder. "Can you make his hair gray?"

"Drat," Tori said, "I just remembered the call I got at the Landry's was from Gerry. I didn't want to interrupt the interview, so I turned off the ringer. I better return the call or he'll worry."

She rang his cell, but there was no answer. "He must be on the plane or still in the interview."

"Did he leave a message?"

Tori nodded.

"What'd he say? Anything new?" asked Dottie.

"Just 'where the hell are you?'" Tori said, "Sentimental isn't he?"

"Wait a minute. He left me a message, too." Dottie listened to the message and laughed. "He basically said the same thing to me only in stronger language. I'd better check in with Morrison or he'll be furious."

Dottie called Morrison's office, but he was on an important phone call and could not speak to her. She turned back to her computer and asked Tori, "What else do you want me to do to the photo?"

Tori looked at the adjusted photo and asked Dottie to give him short hair. When Dottie did that, Tori asked, "Can you straighten the hair and trim the eyebrows?"

Dottie made the changes. "Anything else?"

"Make him tan." Tori asked for one more change.

When Dottie saw the results, she said, "That's it!" She pumped her fist in the air.

The two women high-fived each other.

Tori said, "Why don't I call Karen and see if I can get more information from her."

"Good idea." Dottie stood next to Tori. "Put the phone on speaker so I can hear."

"Karen, This is Tori Vincent. How're you doing?"

"I'm fine, Dr. Vincent. It's you I'm worried about."

"I'm fine." Tori was grasping for any clues. "Was there anything different about the Thursday when Margaret was supposedly burglarizing the house?"

"What do you mean?"

"Did Margaret tell you anything about the appointment?

"She said she had a two-hour appointment, that's unusual."

"Have you ever had a two hour appointment?"

"No, but Jackie has."

"Wait a minute," Tori said. "Who's Jackie?"

"She's the woman who has the appointment before me. Sometimes I see Jackie when she comes out of her session with Dr. Rothstein."

"And?" Tori asked.

"A couple months ago she had a two hour appointment. I got there early and Jackie walked in about 20 minutes before her session is usually over. She had a bag in her hand and walked straight into Dr. Rothstein's office. She pretended she didn't see me. Ignored my hello."

"Was that unusual? Not speaking?"

"Yes," Karen said. "When she came out of Dr. Rothstein's office, she was friendly, but sort of unsteady or something."

"Was she carrying the bag?" Tori asked.

"No."

"You said Jackie was different when she went into Dr. Rothstein's office," Tori said. "How would you describe her?"

"I'm not sure. It was like she wasn't completely awake. You know what I mean?"

"I know exactly what you mean." Tori slapped her head. *I should have seen it. That's how he's connected to the burglaries and to Carlos,* she thought. *How could I have missed **that**?* she asked herself. Now she understood why Dr. Rothstein had lied about Margaret. Dottie was watching her friend. Tori realized Dottie saw the flash of insight cross her face.

"One other thing, Karen, did Dr. Rothstein ever explain how negative reinforcement is different from punishment?" Tori asked.

"Negative reinforcement is punishment," Karen said. "I told you that on Friday. Psychologists call punishment negative reinforcement, so it's not so frightening."

"Did Dr. Rothstein tell you that?"

"Yes, I asked him once what the difference was."

"Thank you, Karen. You've been a great help. I'll call back if I have any more questions."

Tori turned to Dottie. "That's it. That's what's been nibbling at my consciousness about Seth Rothstein."

"What?" asked Dottie. "I don't get it. What's the big discovery? What's wrong with what Karen told you?"

"Negative reinforcement is confused with punishment by undergraduates. A psychologist who uses behavior modification would never make that mistake."

"I still don't get it. What mistake?"

"Negative reinforcement is when a noxious stimulus is removed to create reinforcement."

"Tori, tell me in plain English."

"I'm sorry. Say there's an irritatingly load noise. Punishment would be starting the irritating noise after a behavior you wanted to stop, like drinking. Negative reinforcement would be having the noise on-going and stopping it after a behavior you wanted to continue or reinforce, like refusing a drink. No real psychologist would mistake those two concepts, certainly not one who claimed to be an expert in behavior modification."

"So you talked to Karen on Friday and called Rothstein."

"Yes, but I thought Karen had it wrong and told Rothstein what she said. She didn't tell me he had explained it to her. I also told him I was going to review the video of Margaret burglarizing the house."

"He realized that if you checked back with Karen, you'd know he was a phony, so he tried to run you down with the SUV."

"Right. I didn't call you or Morrison because I thought Karen had misunderstood, not that Rothstein didn't know the difference between punishment and negative reinforcement." Tori said, "There's something else. It happened on Thursday when Seth and I were at dinner. I told him I'd seen a photo of him and John

Rodriguez, and they had reversed the names. He's John Rodriguez."

Dottie jumped up. "You better call Karen. Tell her not to see Rothstein until we arrest him. She might be in danger.

"Oh my God, you're right." Tori hit redial on her phone. "Hello, Karen?"

"Karen isn't here now. This is her daughter. May I take a message?"

"This is Dr. Vincent. Would you please tell your mother not to see Dr. Rothstein until I speak to her?"

"Okay, but she left a couple of minutes ago for her appointment with him. She won't be back until after 3:00."

"I thought she saw Dr. Rothstein on Thursdays?"

"She does. But he called and asked her to come in today."

"Does your mother have a cell phone?"

"No. Is there something the matter?"

"I hope not."

Tori hung up the phone and told Dottie about Karen's visit to Rothstein.

"I'd better call Morrison and have him intercept her," Dottie said. She dialed his number. "Fuck, he's still on a long distance call. I can't wait on this. I've got to go to Rothstein's. Tori, you stay here."

"Oh, no you don't. Morrison and Gerry told you to stay with me. If you go, I go too. Besides, I've figured out how the whole operation worked."

"You have? How?"

"I'll tell you in the car," Tori said as she picked up her purse and headed for the door.

"Morrison's going to kill me," said Dottie. "If I'm lucky, that is." She redialed Morrison's phone and left him a message.

# CHAPTER SIXTY EIGHT

As the plane taxied from the runway to the airport terminal, Gerry called Tori on his cell phone. There was no answer at her house and her cell phone was turned off. By then the plane was at the gate and Gerry called Dottie as he walked the short distance through the airport and out to his car. There was no answer anywhere. He leaned against his car and called Morrison. Before Morrison could fill him in on the murder in Baltimore, Gerry asked, "Where are Tori and Dottie?"

Morrison said, "I just called Tori's house. There's no answer. They must've gone out."

Gerry clenched his teeth. "I called, too. Where did they go? I told them not to leave the house without telling you or me where they were going. They didn't call you?"

Morrison said, "Wait. My phone's blinking, got a message. Got to hang up to get it."

"Call me right back." Gerry said closing his eyes and taking a deep breath. He had no patience for Morrison's lack of technological savvy, but this was not the time to berate him. He rested his forehead against the roof of the car, trying not to panic while waiting for the call back.

His phone rang almost instantly. Morrison said, "They're going to Rothstein's office. Damn! The Baltimore cops said John Rodriguez, the guy that was killed, was a psychologist. His partner was Seth Rothstone, or something."

"Those damn idiots. Get over to his office. I'll meet you there."

Dottie parked her car in the lot in front of Rothstein's office. She looked around the deserted parking lot and said, "It doesn't look like Karen is here. There're no cars."

"Karen doesn't drive. She takes the bus to her visits."

Tori pointed to the red Jaguar convertible parked at the side of the office. "Those are Rothstein's wheels."

"He does pretty well for himself."

"You would, too if you had his outside source of income."

They rushed into the office. When Tori saw Karen sitting in the waiting room reading a magazine she exhaled in relief. At that moment, Seth Rothstein came out of his office. His eyes flashed open wide at the sight of Tori and Dottie, but he quickly resumed a natural expression and walked up to Tori taking her hand in both of his.

"Tori. I'm so glad to see you looking so well."

"She was close to death," Dottie said. "We're lucky to have her with us."

*Damn,* thought Tori. *What were we thinking? I thought we'd get to Rothstein's office in time to get Karen out without his knowing we were here. Then, Morrison would send in the troops to arrest him.*

Dottie walked over to where Karen was sitting and smiled down at her. "Mrs. Baker? I'm Detective Dottie Epstein. I spoke to you on the phone about Dr. Vincent. Would you please go outside and wait until we are finished talking with Dr. Rothstein?"

Karen Baker frowned, she turned toward her psychologist, confusion on her face.

"What do you think you're doing with my patient?" Rothstein said in an ugly voice.

"I think it would be best if she waited outside while we spoke to you," Tori said, calmly.

Rothstein strode to Karen's chair and grabbed her arm.

Karen looked from Tori to Dottie to Rothstein with wild eyes. "What...?"

The door to the office slammed open and Gerry Arroyo plowed in. He sized up the situation, turned to Tori, and said in an agitated voice. "Tori, what are you doing here? The doctor said you weren't to leave the house." He walked across the lobby positioning himself between Tori and Rothstein, his back to Rothstein. "You need to go home right now." He winked at Tori.

Gerry turned around to face Seth Rothstein and said. "Please excuse my bad manners, Dr. Rothstein." He extended his hand. "Nice to see you, again. Remember me? I'm Tori's ex-husband, Gerry Arroyo." He shook his head. "You can imagine how worried I was when I found she wasn't home."

Rothstein looked from Tori's face with her mouth hanging open back to Gerry and slowly took the extended hand, releasing Karen from his grip. Gerry grasped Rothstein's hand tightly, seized his shoulder and twisted his arm behind his back. "That's FBI Special Agent Geraldo Arroyo," he said. "Dottie, give me your handcuffs and read John Rodriguez his Miranda rights."

Rodriguez/Romero/Rothstein was cursing malevolently when Morrison arrived with the other officers who took him to jail.

# CHAPTER SIXTY NINE

Gerry spent the afternoon alternating between hugging Tori while telling her he loved her and reaming her out for going to Rothstein's office. Gerry held her by the shoulders and said in a harsh voice, "Were you out of your mind going to Rothstein's office? He'd already killed his two brothers and two people here in Gainesville. He tried to kill you once."

Tori looked into his eyes. "Don't you understand?" she said. "Karen Baker was in terrible danger. I couldn't leave her at Rothstein's office. It would be like a lamb going into a wolf's den. She had no idea he was a killer."

"But you did. You should have let the police do their job." He tightened his grip on her shoulders.

"Gerry, I told you we called Morrison, they wouldn't let us through to talk to him." She pushed his hands away from her shoulders and turned her back, crossing her arms.

"He's not the only cop in the department."

Tori turned to face Gerry. "If we called someone else we would have wasted time trying to explain the situation. As it was we barely got there in time. Karen was about to go into see Rothstein. God only knows what he had in mind for her." She looked at him, "Gerry, you know I couldn't let anything happen to Karen."

Gerry hugged his ex-wife. "How can such an intelligent woman do something so dumb?"

That evening Gerry and Tori joined their friends at the Pomodoro Cafe to rehash the case and celebrate its successful conclusion. Herb Morrison had arrived early and ordered a pitcher of beer, a large portion of which remained. Morrison was sipping beer, not gulping it. Dottie sat across from Morrison. Morrison stood up and hugged Tori when she arrived, "Glad to see you in one piece, little lady."

"'Little lady?'" Echoed Dottie with a sneer.

"What's wrong with 'little lady'?" asked Morrison, looking at Gerry for support.

Dottie said, "Nothing, if it were 1960."

"I don't get it." Morrison said. "What's that mean? It's not 1960."

"God! You don't even understand sarcasm," Dottie said, smacking her head.

Bruce walked in and hugged Tori, kissing her on the cheek. "Thank God everything worked out all right."

"Thanks, Bruce."

"Yeah, no thanks to your girlfriend," Gerry said.

Bruce walked over, kissed Dottie and sat next to her. He draped his arm over the back of her chair and asked, "What did Dottie do?"

Dottie was staring into space.

Gerry was not sure whether he was angrier with Dottie or with Tori. He turned to Dottie, "You were supposed to be protecting Tori, not taking her into the office of the man who tried to kill her."

"Back off, Gerry," Dottie said. "I'm a cop. That's my job."

"Dottie tried to keep me from going; but you know how stubborn I am," Tori said. "Besides, we couldn't let a defenseless old woman like Karen Baker walk into his office unprotected. She didn't know he was a murderer."

Morrison had bawled Dottie out all afternoon for taking Tori with her to Rothstein's office. He joined in, saying, "Epstein should've known better."

"Maybe, if you figured out how to use call waiting you might've gotten our message and sent some officers over there," Dottie said. "We couldn't take the chance he'd harm Karen."

"Hey, you guys, I thought I was coming to a celebration, not a fight," Bruce said. "Why don't you be grateful everything turned out well and tell me, an ignorant outsider, what happened."

Gerry took a deep breath and put his arm around Tori. "You're right, Bruce. I'm angry because I almost lost Tori." He hesitated, "Twice."

The waitress interrupted to take their order. The group ordered a couple of large pizzas and more beer and wine, except Tori, who was still on medication and ordered club soda.

"So who's this Dr. Rothstein and why was he killing all those people?" asked Bruce.

Gerry began the story. "Seth Rothstein is really John Rodriguez. He's the youngest brother in a family of con artists. His older brothers ran a Ponzi scheme and when the authorities got too close the brothers set John up to take the fall. They let him in the loop just long enough for him to be arrested. Then they turned state's evidence so John went to prison. Rodriguez spent his time in prison learning how to hypnotize people. When he got out of prison he killed his brothers, changed his identity and moved to Miami where he became Giovanni the Great."

"Giovanni the Great! What a magnificent name," said Bruce.

"Giovanni was a night club hypnotist and had quite an act going until he beat up his assistant and she took off for Savannah," Tori said. "While in Miami, Giovanni met Carlos Gonzalez. Carlos was a slick character who illegally imported immigrant women from Columbia to supply the local brothels. When the authorities began watching him he moved to Gainesville and started Heavenly Maids. He used the illegal immigrant women as his workers. A few years later he saw an article about 'Dr. Rothstein' in the Gainesville Sun and recognized his old friend Giovanni the Great."

"How did he recognize Rothstein as Giovanni the Great when none of us did?" asked Morrison.

"Carlos probably saw Rothstein before he left for Baltimore. He would have already cut his hair and grown a beard," said Tori

"Wait a minute," Bruce said. "How did Giovanni become Dr. Rothstein and how did he get to Gainesville?"

Tori said, "Giovanni went to a meeting of the American Psychological Association in Miami. I guess, he thought he might pick up some ideas about hypnosis. He met the real Dr. Rothstein there."

Morrison said, "Tori, you checked Rodriguez's background and you're the psychologist. Why'd Rothstein, a real psychologist, hook up with Giovanni the Great, a night club hypnotist?"

"John Rodriguez's parents were con artists," Tori said. "they were constantly on the run, moving from place to place. John envied the other boys whose parents had made it in the world. His fantasy was to become a well-respected member of the community.

"He went to APA and saw psychologists and thought he could be one, too. He was particularly interested in hypnotherapy. He probably went to a session presented by the real Seth Rothstein on the practice of hypnotherapy and thought he could do that as well as Rothstein. He introduced himself to Rothstein using the name Dr. John Rodriguez. He discovered the real Seth Rothstein's wife had died a short time before and Rothstein was all alone. He was looking for a partner. Rodriguez could be quite charming. He convinced Rothstein to take him on as a partner in his Baltimore practice."

"Wouldn't the real Dr. Rothstein have questions about a character with long hair?" Morrison asked.

Gerry laughed. "You've never been to a psychology conference. Half the guys have long hair."

Dottie said, "I'm guessing the real Rothstein began to have suspicions about Rodriguez and Rodriguez decided to get rid of him. I don't know how he got the client to kill the real Rothstein."

"The client was in prison for violent crimes," Tori said. "Rodriguez hypnotized the client. He had some trigger that set the client off so when Rothstein said it, the client beat Rothstein to death."

"What's a trigger?" asked Dottie.

"Have you ever seen a hypnotist on the stage?" Tori asked. Everyone nodded.

"Okay. The hypnotist tells the people he hypnotizes that whenever someone says a particular word, like "dog," they'll bark and act like a dog—or something to that effect. The word 'dog' is the trigger. Rodriguez hypnotized the violent client and had the real Rothstein talk to him. When Rothstein said a particular word, one Rodriguez knew he would say; the client beat him to death."

Morrison said, "After Rodriguez had Rothstein killed. He stole Seth Rothstein's identity and moved to Gainesville."

"He set up a practice in hypnotherapy," Tori said. "He hypnotized his clients to help them quit smoking or lose weight, or whatever. That is, until he was approached by Carlos Sanchez. Together Rodriguez and Sanchez set up what they thought was a perfect scam. Carlos scouted out the homes and found ones keeping large amounts of cash and easily hocked jewelry. Carlos provided Rothstein with the key, alarm code and times the home owners would be out of town. Then Rothstein hypnotized people like Margaret O'Neal to burglarize the houses and bring the loot back to him."

"Wait a minute," Bruce said. "I've seen hypnotists at night clubs. They always say no one will do anything under hypnosis that he wouldn't ordinarily do. Nothing that violates his morals."

"Yeah," said Dottie. "I can understand hypnotizing a violent offender to kill someone, but I thought Margaret was a saint on earth. Did she have hidden desires to rob and steal?"

Tori said, "Hypnotists say hypnotized people won't violate their moral codes, but it's a myth. It's never been proven scientifically."

"Why do hypnotists say it then?" asked Bruce.

"Obviously to get people to take part in the show," Gerry said. "I remember when we went on a cruise and the hypnotist had one of the women steal everyone's shoes and stick them in her shirt. The audience laughed hysterically, but I thought how did he get her to do that? When I asked Tori she explained it was not documented that people will not violate their morals."

"But would Rothstein know that?" asked Bruce.

"He had enough experience hypnotizing people to know what they'd do," Tori said. "Remember how Margaret said she never took anything that didn't belong to her? He probably hypnotized her to believe the things she took were hers."

"But Karen said Margaret was in Rothstein's office and could not have burglarized the house," Dottie said.

"Margaret was in Rothstein's office," Tori said. "She went for her appointment. He hypnotized her and sent her out to burglarize the house. Then she came back and gave him the watches and bracelets."

Morrison said, "So Rothstein hypnotized different clients to burglarize houses. No wonder we couldn't identify the burglars."

"The homeowners told Carlos when they'd be out of town. Rothstein sent the burglars to the homes," Dottie said. "The hypnotized patients would use the keys and alarm codes provided by Rothstein to get into the houses. They took the money and jewelry and set off the alarm when they left."

Tori added, "Rothstein would collect the jewelry, tell them to forget what they'd done and bring them out of the hypnotic trance."

Morrison shook his head. "Have to hand it to them—an ingenious scam."

"Yeah," said Dottie. "The scam worked for three years."

Bruce said, "The burglars were all middle class, middle-aged people who looked like they belonged in the neighborhood. No one would be suspicious of their walking into a house."

"Most of them were honest people who'd never think of burglarizing a house, they were beyond suspicion." Dottie said, "Besides they didn't remember stealing anything."

"The scheme would've worked if the Phillips didn't have a closed circuit TV system that taped Margaret O'Neal," Morrison said.

"Why didn't Carlos know about the closed circuit monitor?" asked Bruce.

"They probably were using it on the Heavenly Maids and didn't tell him they had it." Gerry said.

"When we identified Margaret as the burglar we got too close and Rothstein—Rodriguez or whoever he was—decided to get rid of her," Morrison said.

"Why didn't he hypnotize one of his clients to run her down?" asked Bruce. "Then he wouldn't have been anywhere near her."

"He had an anti-social personality disorder and enjoyed hurting people," Tori said. "He wanted to see her die. Besides he was a night club hypnotist, not a trained psychologist. He wasn't sure how accurate his spiel was that no one would do anything to violate their moral standards. He didn't want to take a chance. And that would've been the end of it if Herb hadn't been convinced Margaret wouldn't burglarize someone's house."

"That led you to the phony Dr. Rothstein," said Gerry.

"But we wouldn't have known he lied about Margaret missing her appointment if Karen hadn't told Tori she saw Margaret at his office the day she was supposedly burglarizing the house," Dottie said.

"Tori, why did Rothstein think you knew he wasn't a real psychologist?" Morrison asked.

"The night I went to dinner with the phony Seth Rothstein, I told him about the photograph I saw in the FPA journal of the real Rothstein with Rodriguez. I told the phony Seth Rothstein that the names under the photograph were switched. He didn't say anything for awhile. His reaction was delayed. There was something wrong. I couldn't figure out why he was upset. It didn't make sense.

"I began to think there was something in the tape of Margaret burglarizing the house. I told Seth I wanted to see the tape again. He knew I'd realize she was hypnotized."

"I told him earlier that Karen said negative reinforcement and punishment were the same thing. If I spoke to her again and she told me Rothstein had told her that, I'd know he was a phony. I knew something was wrong, but didn't know what. I don't know why he thought I suspected him."

Gerry laughed. "Honey, I always tell you not to play poker. Every feeling and reaction is plain on your face."

Linda A. Foley is a psychologist who taught psychology and the law at the University of North Florida for many years. She interviewed inmates, conducted psychological autopsies for the police, consulted with attorneys on jury selection, and testified as an expert witness. She has written a psychology and law textbook, two books on offenders, and over 30 articles about legal, psychological, and criminal issues. She lives in Jacksonville, Florida with Roger Sharp. She now writes cozy mysteries.